MURDER IN TRAFALGAR SQUARE

A FAIRBANKS AND FLYNN MYSTERY

MICHELLE SALTER

Boldwood

First published in Great Britain in 2025 by Boldwood Books Ltd.

Copyright © Michelle Salter, 2025

Cover Design by Rachel Lawston

Cover Images: Rachel Lawston

The moral right of Michelle Salter to be identified as the author of this work has been asserted in accordance with the Copyright, Designs and Patents Act 1988.

Every effort has been made to obtain the necessary permissions with reference to copyright material, both illustrative and quoted. We apologise for any omissions in this respect and will be pleased to make the appropriate acknowledgements in any future edition.

A CIP catalogue record for this book is available from the British Library.

Paperback ISBN 978-1-83561-308-5

Large Print ISBN 978-1-83561-307-8

Hardback ISBN 978-1-83561-306-1

Trade Paperback ISBN 978-1-80635-254-8

Ebook ISBN 978-1-83561-309-2

Kindle ISBN 978-1-83561-310-8

Audio CD ISBN 978-1-83561-301-6

MP3 CD ISBN 978-1-83561-302-3

Digital audio download ISBN 978-1-83561-304-7

This book is printed on certified sustainable paper. Boldwood Books is dedicated to putting sustainability at the heart of our business. For more information please visit https://www.boldwoodbooks.com/about-us/sustainability/

Boldwood Books Ltd, 23 Bowerdean Street, London, SW6 3TN

www.boldwoodbooks.com

CHARACTER LIST

The Suffragettes

Mrs Coral Fairbanks – 36, receptionist at the Stanmore Gallery, actress, artist's model, widow.

Countess Minerva Stanmore – 50, owner of the Stanmore Gallery of Fine Art. Partner of Harriet Walker.

Miss Harriet Walker – 38, business partner and girlfriend of Countess Stanmore.

Miss Lavender Lacey – 27, actress, singer, lodges with Coral at 5 Adelphi Terrace.

Mrs Emmeline Pankhurst – 52, founder of the Women's Social and Political Union (WSPU). Members known as the suffragettes.

Miss Christabel Pankhurst – 30, co-founder of the WSPU, daughter of Emmeline Pankhurst.

Miss Penelope Bright – 30, daughter of mill workers, moved from Manchester to London to work for the WSPU.

Miss Irene Grayson – 21, artist, estranged from prominent London family, lives in basement flat in Camden.

Miss Marian Dean – 20, daughter of a mill owner, moved from family home in Bradford to live with her grandmother in London.

The Police

Detective Inspector Guy Flynn – 40, artist, widower. Has a sixteen-year-old daughter, Teresa.

Detective Sergeant Evan Goodspeed – 30, Flynn's sergeant, boxer with legendary right hook.

Detective Constable Jack Hall – 26, constable to Flynn and Goodspeed at Scotland Yard.

Chief Superintendent Ballantyne-Smythe (Bally) – 53, Flynn's commanding officer at Scotland Yard.

The Politicians

Mr Herbert Asquith – 58, Prime Minister.

Mr Winston Churchill – 36, Home Secretary.

Mr David Lloyd George – 47, Chancellor of the Exchequer.

Lord Ronald Carstairs – 50, Secretary of State for the Colonies, married to Lady Violet Carstairs.

Mr Nathan Jennings – 35, Member of Parliament.

Mr Charles Dean – 25, Private Secretary to Nathan Jennings, MP.

The Press

Sidney Watson – 41, reporter for the *Daily Mirror*.

Luke Chaplin – 28, photographer for the *Daily Mirror*.

1

FRIDAY 18TH NOVEMBER 1910

'Coral, run!' Marian screamed.

Coral ran. But not far. She found herself lifted off her feet. Dangling in the air, she desperately tried to jerk her elbow into the ribs of the policeman who'd caught hold of her.

She saw another policeman throw Marian into a group of jeering male bystanders. The young woman's hat was trampled on the ground, and her blonde hair had come unpinned and was falling around her shoulders.

Coral struggled to get free, her flailing hand smacking the face of the officer who clasped her by the waist. His jaw tightened, and he began to drag her towards the line of police carriages.

'Coral!' Marian called again as one of the men took her by the hand and tried to pull her away from the crowds. She was shouting, but her words were drowned out by the sounds of women screaming, horses whinnying, and the clatter of their hooves on the paving. All around was chaos.

Coral couldn't understand what was happening. The suffragettes were used to being heckled by onlookers who'd come along to marches and rallies to enjoy the spectacle. While some supported a woman's right to vote, most were indifferent to the cause. Coral would generally exchange friendly banter with them, no matter what their views.

Today, the mood had been different from the outset.

The procession, led by Mrs Emmeline Pankhurst of the Women's Social and

Political Union; Dr Elizabeth Garrett Anderson, the first woman in Britain to qualify as a physician and surgeon; and Princess Sophia Duleep Singh, the Indian goddaughter of Queen Victoria, had started peacefully enough from nearby Caxton Hall.

Three hundred women had arrived at the Houses of Parliament just after one o'clock, carrying banners in the suffragette colours of green, white and purple. Four hours later, their banners were as tattered as their dresses. They'd walked into a full-scale attack, and Parliament Square had turned into a battlefield.

Mrs Pankhurst was still attempting to deliver a petition to the prime minister via the St Stephen's entrance to parliament, despite being repeatedly forced back. Coral saw Dr Garrett Anderson swing her handbag into the midriff of the policeman who had hold of Mrs Pankhurst, showing surprising strength for a woman of seventy-four. It was enough for the officer who was dragging Coral to release his grip and rush over to help his fallen colleague.

'Let her go,' Coral yelled, running towards the group who were trying to pull Marian away through a gap in the crowd.

But what had started as a light drizzle had grown heavier, and the paving was slick with rain. Coral's feet went from under her, and she landed on her backside, provoking shouts of laughter from onlookers.

Winded, she was grateful for the thickness of her long skirts and petticoats for cushioning the fall a little. With ragged breaths, she tried to push herself up, wary of her hands being crushed underfoot, or hoof. An earthy smell warned her of the potential danger of running into one of the steaming piles of horse dung that now decorated Parliament Square.

Coral managed to scramble towards Marian but was stopped by a man, who deliberately held out his hands and placed them on her breasts. She staggered backwards, repulsed by his touch.

'Your husband's a lucky fella. He shouldn't let you out with tits like that.'

Fury rising, Coral wanted to punch the smirk from his thin lips. To her surprise, a large fist loomed into view and did it for her.

She turned to see the familiar and welcome face of *Daily Mirror* reporter, Sid Watson. Beside him was Luke Chaplin, a tall, skinny lad rarely seen without his camera, who was happy to accompany Sid into whatever trouble they could find. Luke appeared to be in a world of his own as he photographed the violent scenes surrounding him, shielded from attack by Sid's bulky frame.

'Coral,' Sid yelled. 'Get out of here.'

She did as she was told and ran back towards Parliament Square, looking for Marian, but bowled straight into the arms of a young police constable.

Instead of struggling, she turned to him. 'Why are you doing this?'

He blinked at her, seeming dazed by what was unfolding. 'Orders. I don't have a choice.'

'You always have a choice,' she replied. 'I haven't done anything wrong. Nor have any of these women.'

He nodded slowly, his frightened eyes taking in the mayhem all around them.

'I know,' he whispered and loosened his hold.

Coral didn't hesitate. She sprinted away, seeing Marian being dragged by three young men past the bronze statue of Benjamin Disraeli and into a side road. She pushed through the throngs of people, pulling away from outstretched hands trying to grab at her.

Seeing a discarded bamboo pole that had long since lost its pennant, she picked it up and ran across to Little George Street, where she'd seen the men taking Marian.

When she reached them, a young man was attempting to rip open Marian's blouse while another was lifting her skirt.

Coral took a deep breath and charged at them with the pole. 'Let her go. Or I'll batter each one of you to within an inch of your life.' Even if they did release Marian, she was tempted to thrash them anyway.

The men hesitated, seeming unsure whether to take the threat seriously. Coral drew close enough to smell their sweat, then swung the pole inches from the head of one. The look on her face must have convinced them she wasn't bluffing as they exchanged panicked glances before darting off in the opposite direction.

Coral lowered the pole and grabbed Marian by the hand, urging her to run. She led her out of Little George Street, and they sprinted down Victoria Street and Caxton Street until they were safely inside Caxton Hall.

The room where the suffragettes had gathered that morning now resembled a field hospital. Doctors and nurses were dealing with black eyes and bloody noses while some women had been taken by ambulance to St Thomas's Hospital with broken bones. Most were just covered in cuts and bruises.

A nurse took one look at Marian's ripped blouse and bleeding face and led her to an area that had been screened from view by a blanket hanging from string tied between two busts.

Someone handed Coral a cup of tea, and she flopped onto one of the wooden benches that lined the hall. A short time later, Sid appeared and sank down next to her, breathing heavily.

'It's calming down out there now,' he panted, gesturing for Luke to ask one of the wounded women if he could photograph her.

Coral had first met Sid at the start of his career when he was writing theatre reviews, and she was an up-and-coming actress. Fifteen years later, he was the *Daily Mirror*'s top reporter – famous on Fleet Street for throwing his hefty frame into the midst of any hostile situation and walking out unscathed. Today's events were bread and butter to him.

In recent years, he'd commandeered Luke Chaplin as his dedicated photographer, and the pair were well known on Fleet Street, as much for their contrasting body shapes as for their fearless approach.

'I don't understand.' Coral's heart was still racing. 'How could they do that? It was supposed to be a peaceful protest. Those policemen – how could they act like that?'

'Because they were ordered to,' Sid growled.

'Ordered to? By whom?'

Sid moved closer and said in an undertone. 'The home secretary.'

'Winston Churchill?' Coral whispered. 'That can't be true.'

'It's what I've heard. Some of those police officers were from Whitechapel. They're not used to dealing with suffragette protests but were drafted in on purpose. With orders to use their fists.'

'There were so many of them. And it wasn't just the police. The men in the crowd, the bystanders, they joined in.'

'Some were plain-clothes police officers. I recognised a few faces. They were there to stir up trouble; try to incite the rabble-rousers to get rough.'

'The police kept throwing us into the mob. Marian was nearly...' Coral trailed off. 'They grabbed our breasts, lifted our skirts.'

'I know. Luke's got pictures, though I'm not sure our editor will print them.' Even Sid, who'd witnessed every type of violence London's backstreets had to offer, seemed staggered by the Metropolitan Police's response.

'I don't understand why the government would do this. It's madness.' Coral's hands shook as she lifted the mug of tea to her lips.

'To scare you. Churchill was afraid of the suffragettes' reaction to the prime minister scrapping the Conciliation Bill.'

Earlier that year, Prime Minister Herbert Asquith had pledged to introduce a bill that would give around a million women, mostly wealthy property owners, the right to vote. It was hardly adequate, yet it had been enough for Mrs Pankhurst to suspend militant action. But she'd been betrayed.

Despite Members of Parliament backing the bill, the prime minister had reneged on his promises and dissolved parliament before it could be passed into law.

'Churchill knew you'd march on Westminster. And he knows Mrs Pankhurst will give orders to resume militant action. It was his idea to get in first – kick you hard enough to give you second thoughts about retaliating.'

'Then he's a fool.' Coral's eyes travelled around the hall, seeing the camaraderie of the injured women. 'This will escalate into war.'

2

'One hundred and fifteen women arrested. Only four men,' Marian whispered.

'One of those was Hugh Franklin.' Coral shifted her weight, feeling damp rising from the ground and into her aching bones. Hugh was a 'suffragent', one of a growing number of men who supported their cause. 'And they only arrested him for obstruction because he was trying to shield some of the women from attack.'

She shivered as a drop of water fell from the leaves above and trickled down her neck. The sycamore tree didn't offer much protection from the rain, but it allowed them to spy on the nearby clubhouse without being seen. As nearly half an hour had passed since the last light had gone out, Coral decided it was safe to get to work.

'May Billinghurst got thrown out of her wheelchair.' Marian picked up her metal stake and began to drag it towards the polo field. Wearily, Coral grabbed her own stake and trailed after her.

In the week since Black Friday, as it had been dubbed by the press, talk had been of little else but the atrocities of that day. Stories circulated of indecent assaults by the police and bystanders – of skirts being ripped apart and pieces of fabric distributed amongst the crowd as some kind of trophy.

The following morning, the front page of the *Daily Mirror* had shown a photograph of fifty-year-old Ada Wright, sprawled face down on the pavement outside the Houses of Parliament, surrounded by the men who'd beaten her to the ground. The headline shouted: *119 arrested after violent scenes at West-minster.*

Yet the charges against all those arrested were dropped the following day on home secretary Winston Churchill's orders. The government was playing a strange game.

Whatever that game was, it had led to a surge of civil disobedience by the suffragettes, involving protests that were becoming more deadly by the day. Coral drew the line at doing anything that might hurt someone, but she wasn't above leaving her mark on the grounds of the Hurlingham Club in an act of petty vandalism. Churchill loved to play polo, and the country club was a favourite of his and other Liberal MPs, including the Chancellor of the Exchequer, Lloyd George, and Secretary of State for the Colonies, Lord Carstairs. Of course, the club excluded ladies from becoming members or setting foot in the gentlemen-only clubhouse.

'This is a bloody big space just to knock a small ball around.' Coral had never visited this part of Fulham before and was amazed at the size of the private sports fields. She was beginning to wonder just how much damage they could do to such a vast expanse of green. It seemed sensible to concentrate on a section of the grounds that could be seen from the windows of the clubhouse.

'Have you never been to a polo match?' Marian panted as she dragged her metal stake through the neatly mown grass. She came from a well-off family in Yorkshire and was more accustomed to attending society events than Coral. 'It's an exciting game.'

'I have no desire to watch grown men riding around on horses trying to hit a small ball with a big hammer,' Coral retorted, digging her metal stake into the earth.

'They're called mallets.' Marian paused. 'What are you doing? I thought we were supposed to write Deeds Not Words, so they know it's us?'

Coral laughed. 'They'll know it's us.'

As it was ten o'clock on a cold November night, and she was reliant on the light of a small electric torch, she'd opted to carve the more succinct BALLS in five-foot-high letters into the hallowed turf of the Hurlingham Club.

Despite the cold wind, she was sweating by the time she completed the last curve of the letter S with a drag of sharp metal through soft mud.

'Shall I add an exclamation mark?' Marian was already stabbing the soil with vigour.

'If you've got the strength.' Coral was bent double with exertion, leaning on her stake for support.

'I've never felt stronger.' Marian's ordeal on Black Friday had only intensified her enthusiasm for their criminal activities, and she radiated defiant energy as she drove the jagged metal into the field and ploughed it through the grass. With a flourish, she dug the final dot into the green.

Coral smirked with satisfaction. 'Enjoy playing with your balls now, Mr Churchill.'

Marian was about to respond when the sound of horses' hooves and the wheels of a carriage silenced her. There was a road running alongside the polo field, and the noise was getting louder.

'Time to go.' Coral tried to pick up the torch, but the heavy gardening gloves she wore made it impossible to grip. Cursing, she pulled off the gloves and shoved them into her overcoat pocket.

Marian grabbed the torch and began to run. 'We need to get over to those trees before the carriage comes around the bend. After that, we'll be under cover all the way back to the meeting point.'

Coral swung the metal stake over her shoulder and ran after Marian, envying the younger woman her lithe, compact frame. Coral was built on more curvaceous lines with a figure much admired by artists. It was a body better suited to modelling than running, and every bit of her seemed to be moving in a different direction. The metal stake jolted against her shoulder, and her bosom heaved inside her corset. She was tempted to throw the stake away, but they were under strict instructions not to leave any evidence behind. Instead, she moved it from her shoulder to clutch against her chest, attempting to keep it, and her breasts, from bobbing up and down.

At any moment, Coral expected to hear a shout from the passing carriage, but to her relief, it drove on without stopping. When they reached the cover of the trees, she flopped to the ground, hoping the damp-smelling mass beneath her was nothing more than rotting leaves. She was a city girl, born and bred, and the country was a mystery to her, though she supposed not everyone would consider a sporting club in Fulham 'the country'.

'Shouldn't we keep moving?' Marian stood over her, still bouncing with energy.

As fond as Coral was of the girl, her enthusiasm could be tiring. But she was right. They needed to return to town to establish their alibis. She reached up for Marian's outstretched hand and got to her feet.

Drops of rain cooled their faces as they trudged through the woods, making their way back to the lay-by where Mrs Pankhurst's Vauxhall landaulette motor car was parked. Marian opened the boot, and with aching shoulders, Coral relinquished her heavy metal stake, reeling at the stench of petrol. The can was empty, so she supposed they'd had to refill the tank.

As usual, Penny Bright was in the driver's seat while Irene Grayson was consigned to the front passenger seat. She and Marian hopped in the back, and without a word, Penny started the engine and sped off. As she did, the rain began to fall in earnest, heavy drops pelting the mud-stained windscreen.

Penny had driven them to Fulham, dropping Coral and Marian off at the edges of the sports fields while she and Irene had gone to a nearby villa owned by Lord and Lady Carstairs. Riverside Lodge overlooked the Thames and had recently been built by the couple to host social events during the sporting season. When Penny heard the property was unoccupied, she decided it was practically an invitation for them to deliver some *Votes for Women* pamphlets – wrapped around bricks and hurled through the newly glazed windows.

'Can't you go any faster?' Irene hissed through gritted teeth.

Coral knew Irene would have preferred to drive, but because Penny was in charge of the secret garage where the car was kept, she had a claim on the driver's seat that was hard to challenge. Neither Coral nor Marian could drive and didn't care who was at the wheel.

'I don't want to draw attention to the car,' Penny replied as she drove sedately through Fulham.

'Were you seen?' Coral asked.

Irene shook her head. 'I don't think so, but as we drove away, we could see a police wagon heading towards the villa.'

'Perhaps they were looking for Lord Carstairs.' Marian gazed out of the back window. 'I met him once. I thought he was quite sweet.'

Penny's disgusted glance into the rear-view mirror showed exactly what she thought of describing a politician as sweet.

Ronald Carstairs MP hadn't been seen since the disaster of Black Friday, and newspapers were speculating he'd flitted to the continent to escape the backlash. The prime minister had yet to comment, either on Black Friday or Carstairs' disappearance, but was said to be furious at the repercussions of both. He'd scrapped the Conciliation Bill and dissolved parliament to try to achieve a majority by holding the second general election of that year. However, the actions of his cabinet ministers were not helping to instil public confidence in his government.

Once they'd left Fulham behind and were back on the road into Central London, Irene lit one of her long French cigarettes, seeming to decide they were far enough away from the crime scene to relax.

'Do you think we'll make tomorrow's newspapers?' Coral yawned. 'I'd like to see a photograph of my handiwork on the front pages.'

'Isn't balls a bit rude to appear in a newspaper?' Marian asked in her earnest schoolgirl voice. 'It's not a word one uses in polite society.'

Irene snorted with laughter.

'It is where I come from,' Penny retorted, making her Manchester accent thicker than usual.

Penny came from a family of paper mill workers, whereas Marian's father was the owner of several cotton mills in Bradford. It was a running joke between them. Sometimes it was northern lasses versus soft southerners when Penny and Marian would pit themselves against the Londoners, Coral and Irene. Other times, it was the working-class women, Penny and Coral, versus the posh girls, Marian and Irene.

'I hope Mrs Pankhurst won't be cross at what we wrote.' Marian was the baby of the group and the newest recruit, having only joined them six months ago. She was keen to come to the notice of the Pankhursts, and Coral suspected she was more than a little in love with Emmeline's daughter, Christabel.

Penny flicked her auburn hair over her shoulder and peered at them through the rear-view mirror. 'I think she'll have bigger things on her mind than your balls.'

Penny was the longest-serving member of the group, having been recruited seven years ago at the age of twenty-three when the Pankhursts founded the WSPU in Manchester.

'Mrs Pankhurst is going to make an announcement, claiming responsibility for the damage. That will be the headline.' Irene, known as the practical member of their little gang, turned to look at Coral and Marian. 'Have you got your alibis sorted?'

At twenty-one, Irene was barely a year older than Marian but far wiser. Her father was a prominent barrister, and she'd been raised in the sophisticated circles of London's high society. She was a talented yet unconventional artist, and, like Marian, had rebelled by joining the suffragettes against her parents' wishes.

Marian nodded. 'I'm going back to my grandmother's. She'll say I was at home all evening.'

After Black Friday, Mrs Pankhurst had decided she didn't want individuals offering themselves up for arrest as they'd done in the past. She wanted the union to take collective responsibility for any criminal damage. Coral wasn't about to argue. She'd already spent six days in Holloway Prison after smashing the windows of 10 Downing Street. She had no desire to pay a return visit.

At thirty-six, she was the oldest member of the gang. She'd joined the WSPU four years earlier, shortly after the death of her husband, Ernest. At that time, she'd needed a reason to get out of bed in the morning, and the camaraderie of her fellow suffragettes had pulled her through some dark days.

'I'll slip into Lavender's after-show drinks at Teddy's Bar. I can pretend I was there for hours.' Coral's lodger, Lavender Lacey, was starring as Nadina in the musical *The Chocolate Soldier* at the Lyric Theatre. The cast would be partying at Teddy's until the early hours of the morning, and Coral hoped that by the time she got there, most of them would be too drunk to remember when she'd arrived.

As it was, it had gone midnight by the time Penny turned into the forecourt of the garage on Long Acre. When Marian jumped out of the car to open the double doors so Penny could drive in, Coral scrambled out of the back, glad to leave the nauseating smell of petrol behind.

Penny's garage, as it was known, was an Aladdin's cave of practical and mysterious objects. As well as housing the car, it contained racks of tools – mostly hammers for smashing windows – a rail of clothes for disguises, an assortment of banners, and even a perambulator with a false bottom.

Coral went over to the clothes rail and slipped out of the heavy man's overcoat she'd borrowed, replacing it with the navy woollen coat she'd worn to the garage earlier that evening. It wasn't until she began to do up the buttons that she realised something was wrong. She stared in horror at the fingers of her left hand.

'My ring.' Coral turned to the others. 'I've lost my wedding ring.'

She dashed over to the landaulette and bent down to search the back seat and footwells.

'It could have come off when we put the stakes into the boot,' Marian suggested.

Penny, the tallest of the gang, lit an oil lamp and stood a foot away from the car, holding the light over them, while Irene opened the boot and started to remove the metal stakes, their torches, gardening gloves and the empty petrol can.

Marian began to poke around inside. 'I can't see it.'

Coral gave up her search of the back seat and pushed Marian to one side. In desperation, she ran her fingers over every nook and cranny of the boot space, but there was nothing.

She turned to Penny. 'We have to go back.'

'We can't, it's too risky.' Penny shone the lamp at Coral. 'Does the ring have anything on it that could identify you?'

Coral shook her head. 'It's a silver band engraved with Celtic love knots. It must have come off on the polo field when I removed my gloves. I have to find it.' She looked pleadingly at Penny. 'If we go now, we can search the grounds before anyone notices what we've done.'

Penny exchanged a glance with Irene, then reached out and put a hand on Coral's shoulder.

'I'm sorry, Coral, but we can't. The police will be everywhere. We set fire to Riverside Lodge.'

3

'How did they know?' Detective Inspector Guy Flynn peered into the smoke-filled hallway, holding a handkerchief over his mouth.

'Know what, sir?' Detective Sergeant Evan Goodspeed pulled up the collar of his thick black woollen coat, his dark curls swirling in the biting wind. He brought to mind an illustration of a pirate in one of Flynn's favourite childhood books, Robert Louis Stevenson's *Treasure Island*.

'About this place.' Flynn stood aside to let a fireman pass, the acrid smell of burnt wood filling his nostrils. 'Building work only finished last Friday. Lady Carstairs was due to inspect the property on Monday to organise décor and furnishings. How did the suffragettes know it was empty this week?'

Riverside Lodge had been aptly named, as behind them, lights flickered on barges moving slowly along the black waters of the Thames. In front of them, the villa crackled as a rubber hose doused the smouldering rooms.

It was a charming property – or would be if it weren't for the thick black smoke billowing through the broken windows. But the fire hadn't caught hold, and the brickwork and tiled roof looked unscathed.

The rain eased, and Flynn and Goodspeed made a circuit of the villa by torchlight, walking through landscaped gardens encircled by woodland. Lord and Lady Carstairs had obviously spent a considerable sum on making River-side Lodge the perfect venue for entertaining guests on summer days.

'If it was the suffragettes, I think our government spy has been at work again,' Goodspeed commented.

'It's got to be them.' Flynn was convinced someone high up in government was leaking information to the suffragettes. Too many times, they'd known exactly where and when to strike. 'Did anyone see anything?'

'Not here. This is a private road with no other houses. A police constable saw a car leaving the area at around half past ten. And a hackney carriage driver is sure there were two figures in the grounds of the Hurlingham Club at about ten o'clock.'

'The Hurlingham Club?'

'A sporting club nearby for posh people. Aristocracy and politicians. Lloyd George and Churchill are both members. As is the elusive Ronald Carstairs. Do you think there could be a link between this...' Goodspeed nodded at the smouldering villa '...and him going missing?'

Flynn grunted. 'I'm not sure. Bally's getting twitchy. He doesn't know whether to take Carstairs' disappearance seriously or not. If he pokes his nose in and it turns out his lordship is living it up on the continent, he's going to have to smooth over any embarrassment. However, that might be preferable to finding out the suffragettes have decided to take revenge for Black Friday and are holding him hostage somewhere.'

Known as Bally by everyone at Scotland Yard, although not to his face, Chief Superintendent Ballantyne-Smythe had the unenviable job of presiding over the Metropolitan Police and keeping on the right side of the government. This was a particular challenge when it came to the present home secretary.

'Kidnapping a politician? Bit of a stretch for them. Does Bally think the prime minister is going to get a ransom note? Give us the vote or Carstairs gets it. Asquith would probably tell the Pankhursts to keep him.'

Flynn chuckled. 'I agree, but we can't ignore the possibility.'

Lord Carstairs had a habit of speaking his mind; something Flynn admired and Ronald Carstairs' cabinet colleagues feared. He was the loosest of cannons, and it was reported that the prime minister held his breath whenever Carstairs got up to speak in the House of Commons.

'What do you reckon has happened to him?' Goodspeed asked.

'It's only been a week. I think we'll find he's run away. Pressure from the prime minister, pressure from his wife. He's packed a bag and gone abroad until all the fuss over Black Friday dies down.'

'Maybe pressure from the suffragettes?' Goodspeed suggested. 'Perhaps he did receive threats from them after last Friday's fiasco and decided to scarper?'

'It's possible.' Flynn rubbed his chin. 'Their level of violence has escalated. Hardly surprising, given what happened.'

Goodspeed sucked air through his teeth. 'Disgusting.'

Flynn nodded. He'd been as sickened as Goodspeed by the tactics used by the police officers at Parliament Square. When he raised the matter with Bally, the chief superintendent had defended the home secretary's instructions, saying 'a forceful approach had been necessary'. But the look on Bally's face told Flynn he didn't really believe it. He knew as well as Flynn that resorting to that sort of behaviour would sully the reputation of every member of the Metropolitan Police.

In Flynn's experience, violence bred more violence, and the government were setting themselves up for disaster. Emmeline Pankhurst's daughter, Christabel, had described politicians as 'wily serpents', and she had a point. The prime minister had repeatedly made promises to the suffragettes that he'd failed to keep. He couldn't be surprised by this escalation, not after they'd suspended their campaign of civil disobedience based on his assurances the Conciliation Bill would be passed.

'They're going to come back with a vengeance.' Goodspeed gazed at the billowing smoke. 'This is only the start.'

Flynn nodded. 'More women are joining the fight every day. Members of the peaceful suffrage organisations are turning militant and switching to the WSPU. And women who once would never have dreamed of getting involved are refilling the ranks of the passive groups. It's a never-ending tide.'

'You worried about your daughter, sir? She supports the cause, doesn't she?'

Flynn smiled at Goodspeed's ability to read his mind, which was either helpful or unnerving, depending on his thoughts. At first glance, his sergeant had the appearance of a Whitechapel thug, albeit a handsome one. His broken nose and lethal right hook were the result of his years of training as a boxer. But appearances could be deceptive, and Goodspeed was a compassionate and insightful man – skills that made him an excellent detective. People underestimated his intelligence at their peril.

'I'm not unsympathetic myself.' If Flynn were honest, he believed women should have the vote – he just didn't approve of the methods used by the suffragettes to get it. The law was the law, and if you broke it, you went to prison. However, this wasn't a view shared by his sixteen-year-old daughter.

Flynn was becoming increasingly concerned by Teresa's political views. Heaven forbid, she should get involved with the Women's Social and Political Union, as she'd once proposed. As usual at these times, he longed for the wisdom of his late wife, Julia, to help him deal with the problem.

To avoid conflict, he generally stayed silent on the matter, rarely voicing his opinion in front of Teresa – or his officers. The job was difficult enough without creating divisions within the team. Then there was Bally. The chief superintendent was under pressure from the prime minister to 'make the suffragette problem go away'.

And what was Bally's problem was Flynn's problem. As a detective inspector charged with investigating suffragette activity, it had been made clear to him that if the situation escalated, resignations would be called for.

'Sir.' Goodspeed pointed towards the gates of Riverside Lodge. The flash of camera bulbs spotlighted the reporters hoping to catch a glimpse of this latest 'suffragette outrage', as the newspapers were sure to call it, which is exactly what the WSPU wanted.

It had been a *Daily Mail* reporter who'd coined the term suffragette, using a feminised adaptation of the word suffrage to belittle the members of the WSPU. But they'd simply taken the word and started using it themselves.

News of the fire would be all over tomorrow's front pages, giving Flynn the opening he needed to talk to Teresa during their visit to the galleries on Trafalgar Square. Glancing down at his watch, he realised it was already the next day, and he'd have to get moving if he was to enjoy any sleep before taking Teresa out.

Flynn called to Sergeant Donaldson, a local policeman who'd been first at the scene and was now talking to the fire chief.

'Do they know how the blaze was started?'

Donaldson hurried over. 'The chief fire officer thinks windows were smashed and a couple of bottles filled with petrol and stuffed with lit rags were thrown inside. He reckons it happened at around ten o'clock. The fire brigade got here quickly and managed to stop the flames from spreading. The wet weather helped. Rain blew in through the windows.'

Flynn looked across at the firemen who were still dousing the embers.

'There's nothing we can do here. Let's see if they've done any damage to the Hurlingham Club.'

The three men got into the police carriage and made the short journey to the private sports venue, where the clubhouse was aglow with lights. They were greeted by an irate steward who'd been dragged from his bed by a local bobby.

The steward seemed more aggrieved by the fact that ladies may have dared to enter a gentlemen-only establishment than by any vandalism they might have done. After inspection, it appeared doubtful that anyone had entered the clubhouse, so they went outside to check the grounds.

To the obvious annoyance of the steward, Goodspeed roared with laughter when he saw what had been scrawled into the grass of the polo field.

Flynn asked Sergeant Donaldson to take the steward back to the clubhouse while he and Goodspeed spent a numbingly cold half hour inspecting the sports pitches. Flynn had a particular aversion to gentlemen's sporting clubs for reasons he couldn't quite fathom. Perhaps it was the smugness of those who took part in these pursuits, or perhaps it was just the outlandish clothes they wore when doing it.

Flynn pulled his heavy overcoat tighter against the cold November wind. 'My guess is that a couple of them were dropped off here while another two or three went on to Riverside Lodge. I'd say four, five were involved at the most.'

'Looks like they used some sort of stake.' Goodspeed shone his torch up and down the long cuts gouged into the earth.

Something glistening in the churned-up mud caught Flynn's eye, and he bent down to pick it up.

'What's that, sir?' Goodspeed pointed the torch at him.

'A ring.' Flynn held it up. 'Looks like a wedding ring. A ladies' wedding ring.'

'But this is a gentlemen-only club, sir,' Goodspeed said with a snigger.

'Balls to that,' Flynn replied.

4

'Is this what you were doing last night? I'm sorry, darling, but fire? It's too much.'

Lavender, dressed in a midnight blue silk dressing gown, her long dark hair swinging behind her back, thrust that morning's newspaper at Coral.

Suffragettes set fire to Carstairs home

Coral groaned at the headline and grabbed the newspaper. She sunk into a chair at the kitchen table and began to read.

A modern villa recently built for Lord and Lady Carstairs was damaged by fire last night. Riverside Lodge is situated close to the exclusive Hurlingham Club, frequented by politicians and royalty. It's suspected members of the Women's Social and Political Union were behind the arson attack.

Lavender placed a mug of tea in front of Coral and then went to the stove and returned with a coffee pot and her favourite delicate china cup.

Usually, Coral was up hours before Lavender, who would sometimes not emerge from her room until the afternoon. But this morning, Lavender was up early, smelling of shampoo and soap, while Coral had slept late, burying her head in the pillows when the events of the previous night had come rushing back. It was already nine o'clock, and she was due at work at ten.

'Well?' Lavender demanded. 'What happened? Wasn't the drinks party supposed to be your alibi? You didn't come to Teddy's, and when I got home, I peeked into your room, and you were asleep.'

Coral gave a brief account of her activities at the Hurlingham Club. 'When we got to Penny's garage, I realised I'd lost my wedding ring and wanted to go back to look for it. That's when Penny told me what they'd done. Marian and I thought they were just smashing a few windows and throwing some *Votes for Women* pamphlets inside.'

Coral had been so angry, she'd ignored Irene's instruction to mingle at Teddy's Bar. In fury, she'd marched out of the garage and barely drawn breath during the ten-minute walk from Long Acre to her home on Adelphi Terrace. Once inside, she'd gone straight to the drawing room and poured herself a large brandy. After sitting for a while in what had been Ernest's favourite armchair, she'd gone upstairs to wash and change, taking a second glass with her to drink in bed.

She'd fallen asleep thinking of Ernest, and when she woke, just for the briefest moment, she believed he was lying by her side. And then she remembered. Ernest was gone, and so was her wedding ring.

For a long time now, Coral had considered not wearing the ring any more and keeping it in her jewellery box. It seemed sensible to put it in a safe place and cherish it as a reminder of those eleven happy years of marriage rather than displaying it on her hand. But it was such a huge step. Now, that decision had been made for her. The ring was probably lying somewhere on the polo field of the Hurlingham Club.

'I'm sorry, darling.' Lavender reached over to squeeze her hand. 'I have to get to an audition, otherwise, I'd cook you one of your disgusting greasy breakfasts to cheer you up.'

Coral waved her away. 'I'm not hungry, but thanks for the tea.'

'Oh, and Harry, our director, said there's the possibility of a part for you in his next production,' Lavender called over her shoulder.

Harry had no doubt said that to keep his young and beautiful leading lady happy. Coral didn't hold out much hope of the part materialising. As an older and wiser actress had once told her, there were only three types of roles for women on the stage – the ingénue, the tart and the harridan. Coral had enjoyed a short run of playing the ingénue, a longer run of playing the tart, and was now in that dry spell before the harridan roles would start coming her way.

If it wasn't for her job at the Stanmore Gallery and Lavender's rent money, she'd be struggling to pay her bills. There was the occasional job sitting for artists – she was a favourite of Algie Posner's – but those were few and far between.

She drained her tea and poured another, carrying it up the narrow staircase to drink while she got ready for work. The house stretched upwards with a drawing room, dining room, kitchen and toilet on the ground floor; Coral's bedroom, spare bedrooms and bathroom were on the first floor, while Lavender's private quarters – a bedroom, living room and bathroom – were on the second floor. There were also the attic rooms, which she could always rent out at a push, though she'd resisted so far. She and Lavender were comfortable together, and neither would welcome the presence of someone else in their home.

Ernest had purchased 5 Adelphi Terrace at the height of his fame, hoping they would soon hear the patter of tiny feet on the polished wooden floors. But then he became sick, and when they slowly came to realise the seriousness of his condition, he got a solicitor to draw up a will ensuring the house and everything he owned would pass to Coral on his death. For an actor, he'd been surprisingly good with money, and she knew she was fortunate to have such an asset to support her.

As well as the house, he'd left a little to tide her over, but it hadn't lasted long. If Coral were to pay the bills, she had to work; she was damned if she'd lose her home as well as her wedding ring.

As she faced the cold, grey November morning and hurried along the Strand, pain shot up her legs, and she felt a dull ache in her upper arms. Once upon a time, in her twenties, she'd been able to perform six nights a week plus two matinees and suffer no ill effects. At thirty-six, it seemed that dragging a heavy metal stake through the grass and then running with it for a few hundred yards was enough to make her feel like an old lady.

She turned onto Pall Mall, and as she neared the Stanmore Gallery, saw a large gentleman and a slim, pretty young lady standing outside. The girl looked perplexed, and as she got closer, Coral saw why. The blind was down behind the ornate gold-painted window grilles.

'Good morning. I'm sorry I'm late opening up.' Coral took a set of keys from her bag and unlocked the door. 'Do come in.'

The girl hesitated. 'I particularly wanted to show my father the window display.'

'Of course.' Coral inserted a key in the central lock that held the pair of iron grilles in place and swung each one back to rest against the wall. Before she went inside, she glanced up at the windows of the apartment above. The curtains there were drawn too, but that wasn't unusual. Countess Minerva Stanmore often didn't emerge until after midday.

What was unusual was the black blind that had been pulled down to obscure the gallery's window display from view. The blind stopped anyone from being able to see into the gallery and blocked the light from showing when secret meetings were taking place inside. Coral suspected they were down because either Penny or Irene had paid a late-night visit to the countess.

There was a rear entrance to the Stanmore Gallery that could be reached via an alley running off St James's Square. If any of the gang needed to see Countess Stanmore, they'd use this entrance, and the blind would be pulled down to ensure no one saw them inside.

Coral went into the gallery and pulled at the cord to raise the blind to the ceiling, then went back out to the couple. The countess had recently taken on the work of a new artist, and Coral had placed three of his London scenes on easels in the window. She'd been rather pleased with the effect of grouping them together and was glad they were being appreciated.

'I told you they looked wonderful.' The young lady beamed at her father and then said to Coral, 'I came by the other day when you were closed and peeked at them through the grilles. You didn't have the blind down then.'

'We had a private viewing last night for some special guests,' Coral improvised. 'I forgot to roll the blind back up.'

'Private viewing?' The girl turned to stare across the road at the elegant exterior of the Reform Club. 'Do members of the club come here?'

When he created the Reform Club, Sir Charles Barry had been inspired by Italian Renaissance architecture, and its classical frontage dominated Pall Mall. The club's famous clientele included politicians, writers, actors, artists and even members of the aristocracy.

'They do, and these pictures have caused quite a stir. Whenever his royal highness requests a visit, Countess Stanmore ensures complete discretion.' Coral gestured towards the window. 'No prying eyes.'

The girl clapped her hands together. 'How exciting. The king has seen your paintings.'

With horror, Coral realised what she'd done. She'd just told a cock-and-bull story to the artist himself and would now be forced to brazen it out. 'Please come in and take a look at how we've displayed your work inside.'

Countess Stanmore had high hopes for this artist as she'd devoted an entire section of the gallery to his paintings. She'd even had them mounted in specially crafted frames to ensure they were shown to full advantage against the dove-grey silk-papered walls.

The couple followed as Coral ushered them over to where the collection was on show.

The man removed his hat and then pointed to the initials GF on one of the paintings. 'I should have introduced myself. I'm Guy Flynn, and this is my daughter, Teresa.'

'I'm pleased to meet you both. I'm Mrs Fairbanks. I'm a great admirer of your work, Mr Flynn.'

'And so is the king by the sound of it,' his daughter said proudly.

Coral was kicking herself for having taken her story too far. Would Guy Flynn now boast that he could count royalty amongst his admirers? If he was anything like the painters she knew, that was exactly what he'd do.

However, he didn't look like any of the other artists she'd met. For a start, he was well nourished and well dressed. Most painters of her acquaintance tended to be thin and red-eyed – a result of poor diet and alcohol consumption. They also either dressed like tramps in threadbare jackets and stained linen shirts or in flamboyant scarves that told the world they were artists.

Guy Flynn was a large man, both broad and tall, well over six foot, and had arresting eyes that his daughter had inherited – a rich hazel colour flecked with gold. He was dressed in a three-piece suit and round-collared white shirt, and in his hand was a derby hat. With his neatly trimmed beard and moustache, he looked more like a man of business than a painter.

Coral fixed a smile on her face. 'I'm afraid all private viewings are held in strict confidence. However, I can assure you that your work has generated a great deal of interest.'

This at least was true. Coral knew the countess already had several buyers lined up, although none of them were members of the royal family. Coral herself longed to hang one of Guy Flynn's pictures in her home, but that was an extravagance she couldn't afford at present.

She was drawn to his paintings because they depicted the London she knew and loved, rather than the postcard images the tourists were so fond of. He was adept at conveying the life of the city through the movement of people and vehicles – and his brushwork wasn't as obvious as some impressionist painters. It was more subtle, with colours and light blended to produce a slightly hazy quality.

'They're so captivating.' Teresa gripped her father's arm in a display of affection that Coral found touching. It was clear Mr Flynn was enjoying his daughter's pride, and it made her wonder why his wife hadn't accompanied them.

'I'm indebted to you, Mrs Fairbanks. You've made my paintings look extremely appealing. I'm embarrassed to be caught admiring my own work, but it's the first time my pictures have ever been shown in a gallery, and it's quite a thrill to see them on display.'

Given his talent, Coral was surprised by his modesty. Most artists were precious about their work and acted as if they were doing you a favour by allowing you to sell their paintings for them.

'I'm sure you're going to be a resounding success, Mr Flynn. If these sell as well as I predict, I hope you'll be honouring us with more of your work.'

'Let's see how these go first.' He took his daughter's arm. 'We're off to the national galleries now to admire some much finer works.'

'Yours are fine,' Teresa protested. 'Even royalty thinks so.'

Mr Flynn smiled at her but didn't offer a reply. Coral opened the door for them, and as he ushered his daughter out, his eyes locked with hers. From the brief, quizzical look he gave her, Coral knew he hadn't been fooled by her lie about a royal admirer.

She stood by the door, watching them walk arm in arm along Pall Mall, fervently hoping that Guy Flynn wasn't the type of man who would enquire too deeply into the circumstances of the private viewing.

5

Flynn glanced back at the gallery to see Mrs Fairbanks standing by the door watching them. With her glorious gold-blonde hair and violet-blue eyes, she looked like she should be in a painting rather than selling them.

Her curls glinted in the morning sunshine – as did the raised lettering of the words on the fascia above her head. Stanmore Gallery had been picked out in gold, matching the ornate window grilles below. The intricately shaped iron of the gold-painted grilles was a piece of work in itself.

Was it true what she'd said about a royal visit? He knew Countess Stanmore was well connected... but the king? He thought it more likely that having supposed them to be customers, Mrs Fairbanks was playing up the exclusivity of the gallery in order to bump up their prices.

'Didn't I say you'd someday become a renowned artist? Do you think the new king will buy one of your paintings to hang in Buckingham Palace?' Teresa squeezed his arm with hers. 'Perhaps you'll get invited to the coronation. I could be your guest.'

After the death of his father in May, George V was making elaborate preparations for his coronation in June the following year. Flynn very much doubted he and Teresa would be amongst the guests filling the aisles of Westminster Abbey. He was more likely to be patrolling the route of the royal procession along with Goodspeed. And that suited him fine. He had no desire for recognition.

'Wasn't Mrs Fairbanks lovely? I could see you looking at her. What's Countess Stanmore like? Is she beautiful too?'

Flynn smiled at Teresa's stream of questions. He'd had misgivings about selling his paintings through the gallery, but it had been worth it just to see his daughter's pride in him. Not something he experienced too often when he talked about his job at Scotland Yard. However, art was a passion they shared, whether it was browsing galleries or working on their own paintings.

And, although he'd felt self-conscious at admiring the display, he had to admit he'd enjoyed seeing his pictures framed and hung in such a high-class establishment. Mrs Fairbanks had a good eye. She'd arranged them in a way he would never have thought of, complementing each other, yet retaining their individuality.

'The countess is an intriguing woman,' he told Teresa. 'Striking but quite the opposite of Mrs Fairbanks.'

She gazed up at him. 'In what way?'

'She's regal and haughty-looking. At first, she seems icy and intimidating, though she thaws a little when you get to know her.' He was actually thinking that Minerva Stanmore's thin, angular body, with its jutting hips and high cheekbones, was in complete contrast to Mrs Fairbanks' full figure and soft curves.

'I'd love to meet her.' Teresa wrinkled her nose as the stink of manure competed with petrol fumes from the busy roads surrounding Trafalgar Square. 'National Gallery or Portrait Gallery?'

'I thought we were going to both?' he replied.

'We were. But as you didn't come home until three o'clock this morning, I think we should just visit one, have lunch at Simpson's, and then go home so you can rest.'

Although 'going home to rest' made him feel ancient, he couldn't deny her suggestion was appealing.

'There was an incident last night, in Fulham,' he began.

'I know. I do read the newspapers,' she said in an exasperated tone. 'I guessed that's where you were.'

He wished she didn't feel the need to be so well informed. She was a curious mix of naivety and sophistication. Was she too well informed for a sixteen-year-old, he wondered? He'd have to ask his sister.

'The suffragettes set fire to Lord and Lady Carstairs' new villa. People could have been killed.'

'The newspapers said the villa was empty. The suffragettes just did it to make a point.'

'It's dangerous and illegal.' He could have said more, but she had that stubborn expression that always made Flynn wary. He didn't want their precious day together to be spoiled by a quarrel.

'I thought you supported equal franchise?'

'I do. I don't support breaking the law.'

'The suffragettes have been forced into taking militant action by the government. Why are politicians so determined to stop women having any say over their own lives?'

'Not all politicians are. But big changes can take time.' It was an argument he knew he would lose.

'They've been given enough time. All they do is lie.' Teresa shot him a sidelong glance. 'Countess Stanmore supports the suffrage movement, you know.'

He did know. The countess had publicly voiced her opinion that women should have the vote but avoided association with any suffrage organisation. Many prominent society ladies had voiced similar opinions, so this hadn't deterred him from signing a contract with her.

His old university pal, Oscar Lambourne, a theatre impresario with an extensive art collection, had introduced him to Minerva Stanmore at one of his 'bohemian parties' as Teresa called them. Oscar knew everyone in the theatre and art world and had been friends with the countess for some years.

Hanging on the drawing room wall of Oscar's townhouse was a night scene of Shaftesbury Avenue depicting streams of people beneath glowing theatre lights. Flynn had painted it especially for his friend, and when Countess Stanmore had seen the picture, she'd asked to be introduced to the artist. The countess had insisted on seeing more of Flynn's work, and somehow, had persuaded him to let her exhibit his pictures in the Stanmore Gallery.

Flynn had never considered selling his paintings before. Once he finished them, he lost interest and became absorbed in his current work. The canvases were beginning to clutter up his attic studio and selling them had seemed like a good idea. The extra money would come in handy for Teresa's tuition fees.

But although it had seemed harmless enough at the time, he wasn't entirely sure Bally would approve if it became known one of his senior officers was also a professional artist. However, Countess Stanmore had promised discretion with regard to his position within the Metropolitan Police, and Oscar had assured him she was a woman of her word.

It was clear Mrs Fairbanks knew nothing of his occupation – he doubted she would have spun that yarn about private viewings for royalty if she had – so Flynn pushed any concerns regarding Countess Stanmore from his mind. For once, he would enjoy wallowing in his daughter's, probably short-lived, approval.

6

Countess Minerva Stanmore swept into the lounge wearing an uncorseted silver-grey satin dress that hung down in a straight line, trailing on the floor behind her. Around her neck was a diamond pendant, and a diamond-encrusted clip held her thick dark hair in an elaborate roll.

That afternoon, the countess's live-in companion, Harriet Walker, had asked Coral to join them for supper in the apartment they shared above the gallery.

Coral had taken the opportunity to ask Harriet if she'd drive her to the Hurlingham Club to look for her wedding ring. As well as the Vauxhall landaulette the countess had purchased for Mrs Pankhurst and the WSPU to use, she also owned a Rolls-Royce Silver Ghost landaulette, which was kept in a garage on Pall Mall. Admittedly, it wasn't the most inconspicuous car to use under the circumstances, but Coral was desperate.

She knew that neither Penny nor Irene would be willing to return to Fulham, and Harriet was the only other person she knew who could drive.

But Harriet had shaken her head. 'I can't. Penny and Irene called in last night to tell us what happened. If I took the Rolls, we'd attract too much attention – and I don't want Minerva dragged into this.'

Coral knew she was right, though that didn't stop her from sighing with exasperation. 'Did you know that's what they had planned? The Carstairs' fire?'

Harriet shook her head. 'Like you, Minerva and I found out after the event.

And we're not happy about it. But Minerva still wants to go ahead with her latest scheme. Come upstairs for supper after you lock up so she can explain. The others are coming.'

After she'd closed the gallery, Coral had climbed the curved staircase with its gleaming mahogany banister and knocked on the door of the apartment. Beryl, the countess's maid, had taken Coral's hat, coat and gloves, placing them in a discreet closet in the hallway. When you visited the countess, you could never tell if any other visitors were present by the coats hanging on the hatstand.

Coral had entered the cavernous lounge to find Penny, Irene and Marian already sprawled in the luxurious velvet armchairs. With its high, ornate ceiling and classical paintings adorning the walls, the room had the appearance of a private members' study in an exclusive gentlemen's club. That is, until you looked at the chairs. Rather than high-backed armchairs and sofas in green or red leather, the countess favoured rich velvet coverings with matching cushions in shades of plum and claret.

The countess had gently kissed Coral on the cheek, leaving behind the scent of Guerlain perfume. 'I'm so sorry you lost your wedding ring. I know how much it meant to you.'

Coral nodded, feeling tears well in her eyes. The countess was the only one in the room who'd known Ernest. She'd first met him after sending flowers to his dressing room with a note declaring his performance in a comedy Coral had long since forgotten the name of was the funniest she'd ever seen. That had been early on in Ernest's acting career, and he and the countess had gone on to become close friends.

Minerva settled herself in the corner of her favourite claret-coloured chaise longue and reached for her silver cigarette box before passing it to Irene, the only other member of the group who smoked.

Harriet expertly uncorked a bottle of the chilled Riesling the countess favoured and handed around glasses of wine before taking her usual place, perched on the end of Minerva's chaise longue. Publicly, Harriet was the countess's business partner and companion, but Coral was a close enough friend to know that their separate bedrooms were just for show. Although the others may have suspected the true nature of the relationship, it was never mentioned.

Penny and Irene eyed her warily as she sat in one of the silky armchairs.

Each of them would have arrived separately, via the alley off St James's Square, so no one would see which building they entered. They were sworn to secrecy regarding the countess's involvement with the suffragettes – and their loyalty to her was absolute. Minerva Stanmore was that kind of woman.

Coral's loyalty stemmed from the care that the countess had shown Ernest when he'd fallen ill. Minerva had paid for the most expensive doctors to treat him, then, after his death, had offered Coral a part-time job as a receptionist at the Stanmore Gallery. At first, Coral resisted, believing she would return to acting. But when no roles came her way, despite countless auditions, she gratefully accepted the offer.

The countess blew out a stream of smoke before turning to Penny and Irene. 'I think apologies are in order.' Her imperious, cut-glass tones were enough to make them squirm. 'Mainly to Coral and Marian, though it would also have been polite to have told Harriet and me what was going on.'

'I'm sorry,' Penny said, though she didn't look it. 'When we received information that the villa was empty, we had to act fast. It was decided only Irene and I should know.'

Coral wasn't pacified by this. 'The place was being renovated. Builders could have come back at any time. You could have hurt or even killed someone.'

Penny shook her head. 'The builders had finished work on the Friday before. Lady Carstairs wasn't due to inspect the property for another few days.'

'How do you know that?' It was something Coral had speculated about since reading this information in the newspapers. She was sure Lord and Lady Carstairs wouldn't have publicised their plans.

'I got a tip-off about the place and went to Fulham to check the details.' Penny was defensive now, clearly feeling they'd done nothing wrong.

'Who gave you the tip-off?' Coral suspected Mrs Pankhurst had found a sympathiser within the government and was receiving inside information.

'I can't tell you.' Penny folded her arms, her mouth set in a firm line. Her attitude didn't surprise Coral. Penny's loyalty was first and foremost to the Pankhursts.

'What about Lord Carstairs? He's been missing for over a week now, and the press are insinuating suffragettes kidnapped him. Or worse…' Coral picked up one of the evening newspapers lying on the glass table. 'The fire makes us look guilty.'

'That's all nonsense.' Penny waved a dismissive hand. 'He's fled the country because he's a coward.'

Marian appeared pensive. 'I don't think he would do that. I think something has happened to him.'

'How would you know? You only met him once,' Penny retorted.

'Yes, but—' Marian began.

Irene intervened before the quarrel could escalate. 'I'm sorry about your ring, Coral.' She looked genuinely apologetic as she took a long drag of her cigarette and exhaled heavily. 'At least if the police find it, they won't know who it belongs to.'

Coral gave a grim smile. 'They will if I tell them. I want my wedding ring back, even if it means going to prison.' She took a few moments to enjoy the expressions on their faces before relenting. 'I won't give them anyone else's name. I'll just admit to damaging the polo field and dropping my ring in the process.'

'But they might charge you with arson if they know you were there.' Marian was almost tearful.

'Even though I knew nothing about it,' Coral commented bitterly.

The countess held up an elegant hand. 'Why don't you give it a little more time to see what happens next? We don't know the police have your ring. Let's watch and wait, and if we find out where it is, we can make a plan to get it back.'

Coral knew Minerva would be true to her word, so she nodded, having no real desire to end up back in Holloway Prison. 'But I won't be involved in anything like that again.'

'Are you going to leave the group?' Marian sniffed. She was the newest member of the gang yet seemed the most upset by Coral's declaration 'We work well together. I don't want us to split up.'

'I'll continue to campaign, but I won't put lives in danger.'

The countess nodded her agreement, quelling any further argument from Penny. 'Quite right. Let's go and eat, then we can discuss a protest that will bring some much-needed humour to what's been a dreadful couple of weeks.'

Coral knew the countess was acting as peacemaker because she wanted to keep her little gang together. Not that they were exclusively hers, as the previous night's escapade had proved.

Harriet, dressed in the same tailored black jacket and matching long skirt she'd been wearing earlier, took Minerva's arm and like a courtly old gentleman escorted her into the dining room, where Beryl was already setting out aromatic dishes.

As the food appeared, so did Minerva and Harriet's beloved Persian cats, Sultan and Seraphine. One jumped onto the countess's lap while the other entwined itself around Harriet's legs. Possibly the ugliest cats Coral had ever seen, they were allowed to roam freely, and their silver hairs clung to the otherwise pristine soft furnishings.

The six women sat around the oval mahogany table to enjoy dishes of chicken lyonnaise, chateau potatoes, green beans and asparagus. Coral savoured every mouthful and allowed her glass to be refilled, fully aware the countess was trying to lull her into good humour before announcing her latest plan.

Minerva must have decided she looked either sufficiently compliant or drunk because once the table was cleared of dishes, she announced she had something to show them before dessert was served.

She turned to Coral. 'I want to talk to you about a protest we've been mulling over for a few months. After Black Friday, now seems the perfect time to put it into action. Irene, could you bring in your masterpiece?'

Coral watched with misgivings as Irene went out into the hallway. She was in no mood to take part in another protest so soon after the last. However, she was curious to hear what the countess had been working on.

Irene returned with what looked like a board covered in a turquoise cloth and placed it on the table.

'Ladies, I hope what you're about to see won't spoil your appetite for dessert.' She removed the cloth with a flourish to reveal a painting. 'I present Mr Winston Churchill, as I hope you've never had the misfortune to see him before. Au naturel.'

Coral gasped and then gave a gurgle of laughter. A director had once described her laugh as like a bubbling brook. However, she suspected on this occasion, she sounded more like a blocked drain.

'Excellent.' The countess smiled. 'That is the desired response.'

Marian wrinkled her nose. 'It's horrible. Grotesque.'

'That is also an acceptable response.' Minerva smiled wickedly. 'Irene has excelled herself.'

Irene gave a mock bow.

Coral got up to examine the painting more closely, noting the skilled brushwork and eye for facial detail that made it unmistakably Churchill. 'But what are we going to do with it?'

'Hang it in the National Portrait Gallery,' the countess replied.

This made Coral laugh even harder. She had to hand it to Minerva: she had style. Like her, the countess had no time for protests that could harm or endanger anyone. Instead, she used her wickedly inventive mind to devise stunts that embarrassed the government and got people talking. And she'd brought Coral, Penny, Irene and Marian together after deciding they had the right combination of skills to carry out her audacious schemes.

Harriet produced a map and rolled it out on the table. 'This is a floor plan of the galleries and offices on the ground floor. We want to hang it here, in the Westminster Gallery. It's tucked away behind the Royal Gallery and Contemporary Gallery. This is the least visited section, and it's close to the rear entrance where the trustees' offices are.'

'Monday is always the quietest day of the week, and at this time of year, people are more interested in Christmas shopping than visiting art galleries.' The countess was now standing, the draped sleeves of her silver dress swaying as she addressed her troops. 'At 8.55 on Monday the fifth of December, Irene, dressed as a deliveryman, will drive to the tradesman's entrance on Orange Street. The painting will be on a trolley and covered so no one can get a glimpse of it. Coral will meet her there and, after Irene has gone in, she'll walk around to the main entrance, where Penny and Marian will be waiting. When they see Coral, they'll know Irene has been let into the building. As soon as the gallery opens at nine o'clock, Penny and Marian will enter and make their way to the Westminster Gallery. Coral will follow a short distance behind.'

'What will Irene do once she gets in?' Marian had picked up one of the cats and was ruffling its ears. She glowed with either excitement or wine, Coral wasn't sure which. She knew Marian relished the thrill of being part of the countess's secret world.

'She'll tell the doorman she has instructions to take the painting to the basement for storage. It's a common occurrence. There are a large number of pictures kept down there, and I can produce an authentic-looking docket. Once inside, Irene will wait in the corridor or hide in the trustees' cloakroom for a few minutes. When she sees Coral leaving the Westminster Gallery with the attendant, she'll wheel the portrait in.'

'How do we hang it on the wall?' Penny asked.

'Marian will have a shoulder bag containing a heavy hammer and mason nails.' The countess picked up the portrait. 'The frame is lightweight, and there's string attached to the back. It will be a crude job, but sadly this masterpiece is unlikely to be on display for long.'

'That's a shame.' Coral was still laughing. 'I wish more people could see it.'

Minerva chuckled. 'They will, although sadly not in the flesh, if you pardon the expression.'

This made Coral laugh even more.

'I want you to go and see your suffragent friends, Sid Watson and Luke Chaplin,' the countess instructed. 'Tell Sid, if he wants an exclusive story, he needs to be at Trafalgar Square that morning and at ten minutes past nine go straight to the Westminster Gallery. I want Luke to get a photograph of the painting while it's hanging on the wall. He won't have long.'

'I'm not sure the *Daily Mirror* will print it.' Irene seemed resigned to the fact that her masterpiece would only be seen by a limited audience.

'They might if a black box is used to redact any areas that might be deemed upsetting to delicate females, or males come to that.' The countess's dark eyes twinkled with glee. 'Coral, mention that to Sid when you go and see him.'

Coral noted that her involvement in this seemed to be taken for granted, but after staring at the painting, she decided not to argue. This was going to be hilarious.

'You should all leave separately,' the countess continued. 'It will be difficult to follow all four of you. Marian is to leave first via the front entrance, taking the bag containing the hammer and nails with her. Penny will follow while Irene wheels the trolley out to the car the way she came in, via the tradesman's entrance. Penny then walks around to Orange Street and drives the car back to the garage. Irene will go home via the underground.'

'We have to act fast as the gallery will be expecting visitors later that morning,' Harriet explained. 'At eleven o'clock, a statue of the actor, Henry Irving, is going to be unveiled not far from the entrance. Minerva and I have been invited to breakfast in Irving's restaurant on Charing Cross Road ahead of the unveiling ceremony. We'll make sure we're seated by the window so we can keep an eye out for anything that might disrupt events. You can get a discreet message to us there if you need help. Any questions?'

'Just one. You said I'd leave the Westminster Gallery with an attendant?' Coral queried.

Harriet nodded. 'There's usually only one attendant who patrols the West-minster, Royal and Contemporary galleries.' She pointed to the floor plan. 'You're going to make sure he's in the Contemporary Gallery while the others hang the painting.'

'How?' Coral asked.

'By luring him away with your womanly charms, of course,' the countess replied with a wink.

7

Coral checked her watch as Irene pulled up outside the tiny Orange Street chapel. It was 8.55 a.m., and all was quiet. A short distance up the road was the tradesman's entrance to the National Portrait Gallery.

She went over to the car and helped Irene lift out a railway porter's upright trolley that was laid across the back seats. They placed it on the ground and then took out the painting, which had been resting against the front seats. It was wrapped in thick brown paper, tied with hessian string, and around that was a length of old carpet to protect it from being damaged in transit. The layers made it look like any other artwork delivery as well as shielding the contents from prying eyes.

Coral hurried to the end of Orange Street and watched Irene adjust the hat of her navy deliveryman's outfit before rapping on the tradesmen's door. With her short hair and narrow figure, Irene made a pleasant-looking youth, and when the door was answered, the man took the docket, barely glancing in her direction.

A second later, he opened the door wider and waved her in. The upright trolley was a method often used to deliver paintings, and the doorman showed no surprise as she wheeled it past him. He was probably more wary of objects being taken out than being brought in.

Coral hurried around to where Penny and Marian were waiting on Trafalgar Square. When the gallery opened at nine o'clock, they were the first visitors through the doors. Coral was about to follow when she noticed two well-dressed gentlemen crossing the road to her left. Both were wearing three-piece suits and carrying briefcases. They looked vaguely familiar, and she held back, watching them stride purposefully towards the gallery. When they drew closer, she realised with a start who they were.

The politician, Nathan Jennings, had a peculiar quiff to his blond hair that made him instantly recognisable. To her dismay, alongside him was his private secretary, Charles Dean – Marian's elder brother.

Coral cursed as they headed up the steps of the National Portrait Gallery and disappeared inside. She glanced across the road to Irving's restaurant, where the countess and Harriet were seated by the window. The countess gave a slight nod.

Coral took this to mean they should carry on, so she waited for a few moments before making her way up the steps and hesitantly pushing open the gallery doors. In the foyer, an attendant in a black serge uniform was emerging from behind the reception desk, gesturing for the two gentlemen to follow him down the corridor to Coral's right. Annoyingly, this was the direction of the Westminster Gallery; however, judging by their attire, it was likely they were heading to the trustees' offices for a meeting.

What business could have brought them to the gallery today of all days? Was it possible Charles had learned what was going on from Marian?

Coral trailed after them at a distance, relieved to see no other people on this side of the building. The larger, more popular galleries were on the left-hand side of the entrance hall and upstairs on the first and second floors.

Coral watched Nathan Jennings and Charles Dean pass by the doors of the Contemporary, Royal and finally, Westminster galleries without seeming to look inside. If Charles spotted Marian, they'd have to abandon their plan and try to get Irene and the painting out of the building.

A tall, grey-haired man in a tweed suit came out of the trustees' boardroom at the end of the corridor and shook hands with Nathan Jennings and Charles Dean before ushering them inside. As the attendant with them turned to walk back to his post at the front desk, Coral slipped into the Westminster Gallery.

As expected, only one attendant was patrolling the three galleries on this side of the ground floor. He was watching Penny and Marian, who were at the far end of the room, standing in front of a painting of Ronald Carstairs, the most recent politician to be honoured with a portrait in the gallery.

Coral smiled at Penny's choice of gown, a traditional dark green full-skirted dress with bustle that screamed respectability. While Irene and Marian preferred the new style for simple, long straight lines, favoured by the countess, Coral and Penny still clung to their corsets. Coral had a feeling it stemmed from their working-class upbringings – they'd had it drummed into them that it wasn't respectable for a lady to leave the house unless she was covered in layers of bodices and petticoats.

Coral made her way over to them, seeing surprise in their eyes. The plan had been for her to go straight to the attendant and lure him away, making no contact with Marian or Penny.

'He's a dish, isn't he?' She pointed to the portrait of Ronald Carstairs, before adding in an undertone to Marian, 'Your brother is here with Nathan Jennings. They've just gone into the trustees' boardroom.'

As Coral turned and headed towards the uniformed attendant, she caught the alarm in Marian's eyes. Penny kept her cool and looked at Coral with distaste, taking Marian's arm as if to protect her from the vulgar woman.

Coral approached the attendant with what she hoped was a winsome smile. He was a small man with chestnut-coloured hair and moustache that had been styled with a musky-smelling pomade.

'I do beg your pardon, Mr...' she squinted at the badge pinned to his black serge uniform '...Mr Norris. But I wonder if you could help me. I'm looking for a particular portrait, and I hope you might be able to tell me where it is.'

'Of course, madam. What's the name of the picture?'

'Ah, I'm afraid I don't know.'

'I see. And do you know who painted it?'

'Oh yes, it was Algie.'

Mr Norris smiled patiently. 'Algie?'

'Algernon Posner.' Coral feigned surprise. 'Haven't you heard of him?'

'Yes, of course.' Mr Norris now looked affronted. 'An interesting artist. Some of his paintings have caused quite a stir.'

'That's Algie for you. I am rather underdressed in this one.' Coral giggled, glancing at him from under her lashes in a show of modesty.

'You?' Mr Norris' eyes seemed to slide down her body.

'I'm the lady in the picture. I posed for Algie. He only told me recently that it's on display here. I should love to see it.' The painting had, in fact, been on display at the gallery for the last two years, and Coral had seen it many times.

'I think I know the one you mean.' Mr Norris took her arm, seeming delighted by the distraction. 'And where we can find it. It's called *Dawn Beauty*. Come with me.'

He ushered her out of the Westminster Gallery and into the corridor where she spotted Irene hovering with the trolley outside the trustees' cloak-room. Coral gave her a quick nod before turning her attention back to Mr Norris.

He led her along the corridor and into the Contemporary Gallery, as she'd known he would. This gallery contained modern portraits celebrated because of the talent of the artist rather than the celebrity of the sitter. Hence, the inclusion of *Dawn Beauty*.

Mr Norris scurried across to the picture, his eyes swivelling between the painting and Coral.

'Oh, my goodness.' Coral clapped a gloved hand over her mouth as if seeing the picture for the first time. 'What will you think of me!'

'It's a charming portrait.' Mr Norris smiled at her. 'I've always thought so.'

His eyes flicked between the pink and white curves of Coral's flesh in the picture and the woman dressed in formal burgundy silk standing beside him. A gleam of sweat appeared on his forehead, and he took a handkerchief from his pocket, first wiping his round metal spectacles and then dabbing his glowing face.

Coral exclaimed over the painting, wondering how long she'd be able to hold Mr Norris' attention.

'*Dawn Beauty*,' she read the plaque by the side of the frame. 'A study of morning light. That's a lie. I spent many an afternoon in that freezing cold studio.'

'The skill of the artist is in creating an illusion,' Mr Norris said pompously, showing no signs of wanting to hurry back to his post.

'You're so right,' she replied and began to point out the tricks Algie had used to create the feeling of first light.

It amused her that *Dawn Beauty* should be playing its part in the suffrage movement. When they'd heard that Coral was an artist's model, many of her fellow suffragettes had made disparaging remarks about the type of woman who allowed men to gaze upon their naked form. In truth, Coral wasn't entirely nude. In *Dawn Beauty*, she was wearing a pale blue silk robe. Well, half wearing it. Algie had captured a side profile of her body, the robe slipping from one shoulder to expose the mound of her left breast, the dip of her waist and the curve of her left buttock. Nothing more intimate was revealed.

'Thank you so much for showing me,' she gushed to Mr Norris.

'It's a pleasure, Miss...?'

Coral wasn't about to give him her name, though she knew the police would probably be able to find out if they were to track down Algernon Posner. She was sure Algie would have a frightful lapse of memory if she asked him to. But what did it matter if he did tell them? All she'd done was to ask to see a painting of herself – that wasn't a crime.

Before she could respond to Mr Norris, they were interrupted by raised voices coming from the foyer. Coral hoped it heralded the arrival of Sid and Luke rather than any other surprise visitors.

'Excuse me for one moment.' Mr Norris hurried off in the direction of the entrance hall, and Coral followed.

In the foyer, the harassed desk attendant turned to Mr Norris. 'I've told these gentlemen that cameras aren't allowed in the gallery. What's this about a new portrait of Winston Churchill going on display?'

'It's in the Westminster Gallery,' Sid declared. 'Come on, Luke, let's take a look.'

Luke obediently followed, as did Mr Norris and the front desk attendant. Coral trailed behind, relieved to see there was no sign of Irene, Penny or Marian.

In the Westminster Gallery, Mr Norris rushed over to the Churchill painting, his mouth dropping open in disbelief. 'What the hell?'

The picture was dangling precariously from a large nail, wonkily hammered into the wall. The way it hung lopsidedly on its hook somehow made it even funnier.

Sid's laughter echoed around the gallery as he stared at it with delight. Luke, who'd been warned he'd have only moments to get a shot of the painting before it was removed, barely glanced at it. He set to work unpacking and positioning his camera.

As Coral moved into the archway leading to the Royal Gallery, she spotted a lady in a purple dress she hadn't noticed before. She was standing in the corner as if she didn't want to be seen. Coral assumed she was a visitor who'd heard the commotion and come to see what was going on.

When Nathan Jennings and Charles Dean appeared with the grey-haired man they'd met earlier, Coral moved further through the archway into the next room. She guessed the man was the director of the gallery as he took one look at the Churchill portrait and started shouting orders to the attendants to either get it down or cover it up.

She noticed Nathan Jennings seemed more gleeful than appalled. Obviously not a fan of his fellow Liberal MP, Mr Churchill, then. Charles Dean was gazing at the painting in horror. When his eyes began to dart around the room, Coral knew it was time to make her escape.

She walked through the Royal Gallery and out into the corridor, then strolled out of the main doors, hoping Charles Dean hadn't spotted her. Or Marian.

On Charing Cross Road, she looked over to Irving's restaurant where the countess and Harriet were watching through the window. She smiled at them, and the countess raised her teacup in a toast.

8

'I think we'd better get over to the National Portrait Gallery.' Goodspeed sauntered into his office in a manner that didn't suggest it was a matter of life or death.

Flynn put down his pen, observing the smirk on his sergeant's face. 'From your casual manner, I assume it's not another fire.'

'No. But I suspect the suffragettes are behind this too.'

Mrs Emmeline Pankhurst had personally accepted responsibility for the arson attack on Riverside Lodge, though it was impossible for her to have carried out the act herself. She'd been speaking to a packed hall in Cardiff at the time. Even so, Bally was arranging for her to be arrested. Flynn pitied the officer who got that job.

He leaned back in his chair and looked up at the clock. A quarter to ten on a Monday morning, and they'd started already. It didn't bode well. Since the arson attack just over a week ago, there had been a spate of suffragette vandalism, mainly window smashing and setting fire to the contents of pillar boxes.

'What have they done now? Damaged a picture or stolen one?'

'We received a message to say they've added a painting to the collection, sir.' Goodspeed seemed to be struggling to keep a straight face. 'I've sent Detective Constable Hall to stop anyone from entering the gallery and said we'd be along shortly.'

'What sort of painting?' Flynn was reluctant to leave his desk for the sake of a prank.

'It's a nude. Done in oils.'

'A naked woman?' This sounded very un-suffragette-like to Flynn.

'It would appear to be Winston Churchill.'

A grin spread across Flynn's face. 'A portrait of Winston Churchill in the nude?'

'Precisely, sir.'

Flynn got to his feet and picked up his hat. 'I should very much like to see this.'

Outside Scotland Yard, a police carriage was waiting on Victoria Embankment. The road was congested with motor vehicles, and Flynn found it preposterous that there were now ten times more motorised hackney carriages in London than there were horse-drawn carriages, yet the Metropolitan Police were still reliant on animals or bicycles. Motor cars were reserved for chief superintendents like Bally to carry out their public duties. Coppers on the street didn't stand a chance.

They jumped out of the carriage at Trafalgar Square and dodged cars and horses to cross the road to the National Portrait Gallery.

'This should be right up your street, sir,' Goodspeed said as they strode towards the entrance.

His sergeant was the only colleague Flynn trusted enough to confide in about his paintings. Not that he'd mentioned their presence in the Stanmore Gallery.

At thirty years old, Goodspeed was ten years his junior, and they came from very different backgrounds. Despite or perhaps because of this, their working relationship over the last five years had turned into friendship. Goodspeed was one of the few people who knew of his hobby as an artist, although Flynn supposed it was more than a hobby as some of his paintings had actually been sold. He wondered where they were hanging now. Probably not in Buckingham Palace, as his daughter hoped.

'I was only at the gallery about a week ago with Teresa.' He winced. 'I'm glad this wasn't on display then.'

A flustered Detective Constable Jack Hall was waiting for them on the steps to the entrance. The young detective was smartly turned out as usual, but his dark blond hair was ruffled and his tie askew.

'The director is in a bit of a state, sir. No one's sure what to do with it.'

By *it*, Flynn presumed Jack meant the naked Winston Churchill. He had some sympathy for the lad. This wasn't a situation any amount of training could prepare you for. He swept past him and up the steps into the foyer of the gallery.

Detective Constable Hall followed and introduced him to a tall gentleman in a tweed suit waiting by the front desk.

'This is Mr Scott, sir. He's the director of the gallery.'

'Good morning, Mr Scott. Perhaps you can show me this painting. Detective Constable Hall, can you check the building to see if anyone or anything is still here that shouldn't be?'

'It's down there.' Mr Scott pointed along the corridor. 'But I don't care about that now. Something else has happened—'

'One thing at a time, Mr Scott. First, where is this painting of Mr Churchill?'

'Very well.' Mr Scott led the way into the Westminster Gallery, which was now clear of visitors.

Flynn didn't have to look hard to spot the rogue portrait. It was larger than he'd expected and much brighter than the others on display. His eyes were immediately drawn to the acres of pink-white flesh on show.

Sergeant Goodspeed let out a low chuckle while Flynn tried to suppress a smile. The politician was depicted lying on his side, head propped on one elbow, gazing adoringly at himself in a mirror.

Winston Churchill must have known he'd make an enemy of the suffragettes and would expect reprisals. But Flynn doubted he would have anticipated anything like this. With gloved hands, he lifted the portrait from the wall.

'Crudely done,' he commented, meaning the way it had been hung rather than the painting itself. A length of string attached to the back of the frame had been hooked over a large masonry nail hammered into the brickwork.

Mr Scott tutted when he saw the wonky nail. 'Look at the damage to my wall.'

Flynn examined the marks. The hole could easily be filled; however, replacing the red silk wall covering would be more expensive.

'Mr Scott, do you have anything we can use to wrap the picture? Detective Constable Hall will need to convey it to Scotland Yard, and I'd like to preserve what's left of Mr Churchill's dignity.'

'I don't care about that.' Mr Scott waved his hand dismissively. 'It was a trick. A stunt to draw everyone's attention away from the real crime.'

Flynn exchanged a glance with Goodspeed. 'What crime?'

'One of our paintings is missing. Come.'

Flynn thrust the picture into Goodspeed's hands. 'Cover it up and give it to Detective Constable Hall to take back to my office once he's finished searching the building.'

He then hurried out of the gallery and into the corridor, following Mr Scott to the Contemporary Gallery.

'Look.' Mr Scott gestured to a blank space on the wall.

Flynn read the label, '*Self-Portrait* by Sylvie Blanchet.' He recalled a picture of a striking young woman with long dark hair and a defiant expression. 'Kindly donated by Lord Ronald Carstairs.'

That bloody man again. What was going on?

'They wrenched it from the wall.' Mr Scott motioned to the twisted pieces of metal left in the brickwork.

The damage here was far worse than the single nail used to hang the Churchill portrait. Judging by the dents in the plaster, someone had taken a chisel and used it to lever the painting from the wall.

Mr Scott pointed to a discarded gilt frame lying on the floor. 'The canvas was stretched over a wooden mount. They've had the sense not to remove it from that, at least.'

'It happened this morning?' Flynn was aware he was stating the obvious but had to ask.

'Mr Norris, one of our attendants, assures me that nothing was out of place when he started work at nine o'clock. He was manning the three galleries on this side of the ground floor. It must have been taken when he was dealing with the incident in the Westminster Gallery.'

Flynn nodded. Obviously, someone had come prepared. You didn't just walk into a gallery with a chisel and hope the attendant would be distracted. Had that been the real purpose of the Churchill portrait – to distract the staff?

'Has anyone shown a particular interest in this painting recently?' he asked.

'Not that I'm aware of. I'll check with my staff.' Mr Scott sniffed. 'I was warned this was going to happen.'

Flynn turned to stare at him. 'Warned? By whom?'

'I had a visit this morning from an MP – Nathan Jennings. His office deals with national security. He came to warn me he'd heard a rumour the suffragettes were planning to target my gallery.'

'His warning came a little late.' Flynn observed the proprietary way he'd called it *my gallery* when the collection actually belonged to the government on behalf of the British public, including suffragettes, and was free for all to visit.

'Mr Jennings had no idea what was going to happen or when. Who could have predicted this?' Mr Scott ran a frantic hand through thick grey hair that was now standing on end.

But Nathan Jennings had believed something would happen. And Flynn wanted to know where his information had come from.

'Was Mr Jennings here when the Churchill portrait was put on display?'

'He and his private secretary, Mr Dean, were with me in the trustees' board-room. It's just along the corridor from the Westminster Gallery. One of my attendants, Mr Norris, came to tell me what was going on. The front desk attendant was trying to stop someone from taking a photograph of the portrait. We discovered later that the two gentlemen were from the press. The *Daily Mirror*.' By the disgust in Mr Scott's voice, this wasn't a newspaper he favoured.

Flynn scanned the Contemporary Gallery. 'Is this the only picture that's missing?'

'My staff have inspected all the rooms, and everything else appears to be in order. Apart from the monstrosity those women left behind.'

From the brief look he'd had of the Churchill portrait, Flynn didn't think it was a monstrosity. It was an accomplished painting that appeared to be the work of an experienced artist. He didn't say this to Mr Scott.

'Do you have a floor plan of the building?' Flynn asked.

Mr Scott nodded. 'In my office.'

Flynn and Mr Scott went into the corridor where Goodspeed was handing the Churchill portrait to an attendant to wrap in brown paper. Flynn indicated for his sergeant to join him, and they followed Mr Scott through a door labelled 'Director's Office'.

Mr Scott pointed to the wall, where a large, framed floor plan of the National Portrait Gallery showed the layouts of the ground, first and second floors.

Flynn focused on the ground floor. 'While all attention is on the Westminster Gallery here.' He pointed for Goodspeed's benefit. 'A painting is stolen from the Contemporary Gallery here.'

'Clever,' Goodspeed commented.

Mr Scott didn't seem to appreciate this remark.

'I want to interview every member of staff here today. I also need to compile a list of any known visitors—'

Flynn was interrupted by Detective Constable Hall stumbling into the office, his face ashen.

'The... there's something you need to see,' he stammered to Flynn.

'What's happened now?' Mr Scott groaned with the air of someone who knew their day was not going to get any better.

'There's a lady,' Detective Constable Hall muttered. 'In the cloakroom. I think she's dead.'

'Good God.' Mr Scott's hand clutched his forehead.

They all rushed out of the office and crossed the corridor, where Detective Constable Hall pushed open the door to the trustees' cloakroom. 'In there. On the floor.'

This statement was hardly necessary as Flynn could see the body from outside.

Mr Scott made a strange gasping sound as he gaped in horror at the figure lying across the porcelain tiles.

'Stay out here.' Flynn pushed Hall aside, indicating that only Goodspeed should join him.

They entered, and Goodspeed closed the door firmly behind them, enclosing them in a small room where the metallic smell of fresh blood mingled with the odour of disinfectant.

The young woman's head rested by a row of sinks while one foot touched the door of a toilet cubicle. She was lying on her side, her dislodged blue hat partially covering her face. The front of her blue coat was stained with dark blood that had seeped onto the floor.

Goodspeed knelt over her and felt for a pulse. He stared up at Flynn and shook his head. 'I'd say she's been stabbed.' He gently opened her coat and examined her body. 'No sign of a weapon.'

Close to her right hand was a brown leather bag that looked like it had slipped from her shoulder as she'd fallen. Flynn knelt down and lifted the flap to peer inside. Its only contents were a large hammer and an assortment of nails.

Flynn reached into the pockets of the bloodstained blue coat and pulled out an envelope. 'A letter addressed to a Miss Marian Dean.'

9

For the second time, the newspaper headlines were not what Coral had been expecting following one of their escapades. On this occasion, the consequences were far more devastating than the fire at Riverside Lodge.

She'd anticipated roaring with laughter at a front-page photograph of the Churchill portrait, complete with strategically placed black boxes. Instead, tears streamed down her cheeks as she read the words: *Suffragette murdered.*

The article went on to report that Mr Charles Dean had confirmed the body found in a cloakroom at the National Portrait Gallery was that of his sister, Miss Marian Dean.

'I don't understand. What the hell happened?' Coral was angry, although she wasn't sure who with. All she could think of was Marian. Who could have done that to the girl?

The others just stared back at her, grief and confusion rendering them silent. Once again, they were seated on plush velvet armchairs in the countess's lounge. Only this time, one of their number was missing.

The countess and Harriet had been first to realise something was wrong when they'd left Irving's restaurant the previous morning. Rumours were flying that a body had been found in the gallery, and by that evening, with the help of Sid Watson, they knew it was Marian.

'She left the Westminster Gallery and was supposed to go out via the main entrance.' Penny's eyes were red, and her usually glossy auburn hair looked damp and dishevelled. 'How did she end up in the cloakroom? It's in the opposite direction.'

'Perhaps she was hiding from her brother and Nathan Jennings,' Coral suggested. She'd been thinking about this since the previous day, anxious to discuss events with the others. But the countess had told them to wait until after six o'clock, when it would be dark and the Stanmore Gallery closed, before sneaking in via the alley off St James's Square.

'What were they doing there?' the countess asked.

'They had a meeting with someone in the boardroom,' Coral replied.

Irene picked up one of the newspapers. 'This painting that's been stolen. A self-portrait by Sylvie Blanchet. Could Marian have seen the thief? And they...?' She choked on the words.

The same thought had occurred to Coral. 'The newspapers say it was wrenched from the wall, which means the thief came prepared. Who else knew what we had planned?'

'Only the Pankhursts and the people in this room,' the countess replied. 'And you told Sid Watson, who told Luke Chaplin.'

Coral resolved to go and see Sid. She'd sworn him to secrecy, though he might have let something slip. She guessed the police would be paying him a visit too, and he might be cursing her for having involved him. But this was murder, and her only concern was finding out what happened to Marian.

'We need to go to the police.' Coral wasn't surprised by the silence that followed and understood their reluctance to trust the authorities. 'I'll take responsibility for the Churchill portrait. You don't have to be involved if you don't want to. They're going to find out who I am anyway when the attendant tells them I'm the woman in Algie's painting.'

'Algernon is in Greece, so they'll have to find him first,' the countess replied. 'But I agree. We should make contact with the police. Before we do, we need to try to make sense of what happened. I want each of you to tell me what you did at the gallery and when you left. And when you last saw Marian.'

'After Coral went out with the attendant, Irene wheeled the painting in,' Penny began. 'Marian unwrapped it, while Irene and I bashed the nail into the wall, trying to get it in far enough to hold the weight of the picture. Then we put the hammer and nails in Marian's bag and told her to go. She was supposed to stroll back out through the main entrance and head straight to her grandmother's house.'

'What did you do then?' Coral asked.

'I helped Irene fold up the paper and carpet that had been wrapped around the painting and put them on the trolley, then we both left the gallery in different directions. I went out through the main entrance. I don't think anyone saw me as the attendant wasn't at the front desk.'

'And I went out through the tradesman's entrance on Orange Street.' Irene's hand shook as she lit a cigarette. 'The doorman barely looked at me. I wheeled the trolley to the car and laid it across the back seat. When Penny came, I handed her the car keys and then walked up Charing Cross Road to Tottenham Court Road underground station and took a train home to Camden Town.'

'I drove the car back to the garage,' Penny added.

'I didn't see Marian, Penny or Irene again after I left the Westminster Gallery with Mr Norris, the attendant.' Coral closed her eyes for a moment, picturing the scene. 'We went into the Contemporary Gallery, and I was wondering how long I could keep him talking, when we heard Sid arrive. I followed Mr Norris out to the foyer, where the desk attendant was telling Sid and Luke they couldn't come in with a camera. They went to the Westminster Gallery, and I followed some way behind. I stood in the archway to the adjoining room, and when I saw Nathan Jennings and Charles Dean come in, I went through the Royal Gallery into the corridor.'

'Did you see anyone on your way out?' the countess asked.

'No one. The front desk attendant was still in the Westminster Gallery, and I think we were the only visitors until Sid and Luke showed up.'

Irene shook her head. 'When I was about to wheel the painting into the Westminster Gallery, I looked down the corridor to the foyer and saw a lady by the front desk. I thought I recognised her but only saw her for a moment before she headed in the direction of the galleries on the other side of the ground floor.'

'Who was it?' Harriet asked.

'I'm not certain.' Irene hesitated. 'I think it was Lady Carstairs.'

'Ronald Carstairs' wife?' the countess exclaimed. 'Did she recognise you?'

'I don't think so. She glanced towards me, possibly she heard the wheels of the trolley, but she didn't seem to take any notice of me.'

'I think I saw her, too.' Coral remembered the woman standing in the corner of the Westminster Gallery. 'A lady in her fifties with red-grey hair, wearing a black coat over a purple gown?'

'That's her.' Irene drew hard on her cigarette.

'How strange,' the countess murmured. 'Why was she there at that time? Could it have something to do with the fire at Riverside Lodge? You don't think she could have attacked Marian in revenge?'

'How would she know?' Penny's voice became shrill. 'About any of it?'

'Mrs Pankhurst announced publicly that the WSPU was responsible for the fire,' Harriet pointed out.

The countess reached for her silver cigarette box. 'Emmeline has been arrested for inciting arson, although the newspapers haven't picked up on it yet, as she's out on bail. She's due to stand trial in the new year.'

'I can't think how Lady Carstairs could possibly know what we had planned for that morning. But the police should be told she was there.' Coral watched the countess stroke Sultan or Seraphine – she could never tell them apart – remembering how Marian used to love fussing over the cats. It seemed impossible they'd never see her again.

Irene pushed one of the newspapers towards Coral. 'I suppose you should speak to this policeman in charge. This Flynn they mention.'

'Flynn?' Coral picked up the newspaper, trying to remember where she'd heard that name recently.

'Detective Inspector Guy Flynn of Scotland Yard,' the countess said with a slight smile.

Coral gaped, remembering the attractive man with the pretty daughter. 'The artist? The London scenes? He's a policeman?'

'He is indeed. A very pleasant gentleman, too, which is unusual for one in his profession. Quite humble about his talent. And I don't just mean for painting. He's risen through the ranks to become one of Scotland Yard's most respected detectives.'

Coral drew in a sharp breath. 'Then what the hell are we doing exhibiting his work?'

The countess shrugged. 'There seemed no reason not to. I was introduced to him by Oscar Lambourne. They're close friends. I thought it might be useful to count a senior policeman amongst my acquaintances.' Minerva ruffled the ears of one of the cats curled up on her lap, causing it to purr in appreciation. 'Besides, his paintings are magnificent.'

'Courting danger if you ask me,' Harriet remarked. At thirty-eight, she was twelve years younger than the countess yet was the one to rein in her partner's more reckless tendencies.

Irene lit another cigarette. 'A policeman who paints. I've never come across one of those before.'

'He has an office at Scotland Yard. In the morning, go there and ask for Detective Inspector Flynn,' the countess instructed Coral. 'Refuse to speak to anyone but him.'

10

'On Monday morning, you visited Mr Scott at the National Portrait Gallery. He tells us that the reason for your visit was to warn him that the suffragettes were preparing to stage some form of protest there.'

When Bally told Flynn he'd arranged for him to meet with Nathan Jennings, he'd warned him to tread carefully with regard to questions about government spies.

Flynn now found himself in the bowels of Whitehall, in the ministerial department of the home secretary. He hoped the great man himself wasn't present – the image in the portrait currently leaning against his office wall was still fresh in his mind. He didn't relish coming face to face with the reality.

Nathan Jennings nodded. 'That's correct. I had no idea what form the protest would take. Or when it would occur. I certainly never dreamt that someone would end up dead.'

Jennings' office was as austere as the endless corridors Flynn had passed through to reach it. The walls were painted a dull beige with little decoration. A single picture, a view of the Houses of Parliament from Westminster Bridge, hung above the mantelpiece. There were no photographs on the walls or displayed on the wide oak desk Jennings sat behind.

The only colour came from the blue check tweed suit Jennings was wearing. The politician clearly liked to make sure he was seen. He was a pleasant-enough-looking chap of about thirty-five, although Flynn found his hair rather effeminate. The quiff above his forehead curled backwards, almost into a roll. Judging by the vanilla fragrance that was tickling Flynn's nostrils, it had been styled with pomade, as had the neat, curling moustache that was identical in shade to the pale blond of his hair.

'Your private secretary, Mr Charles Dean, has confirmed the body is that of his sister, Miss Marian Dean.'

Jennings pulled a face. 'Lovely girl. The poor fellow's distraught.'

Flynn and Goodspeed had spent some time with Marian Dean's family shortly after her death. It was never an easy job and this occasion had been no different. Her brother confirmed her involvement with the Women's Social and Political Union but had no knowledge of her activities with them or what she'd been doing at the National Portrait Gallery.

'You knew Miss Dean?' Flynn asked.

'I'd met her a few times at social events. I liked her. She was pretty young thing, and good company. She'd have made any man a decent wife, if she hadn't got involved with those women. What a waste.'

Flynn refrained from commenting on this, wondering what Marian Dean had made of Nathan Jennings. Flynn suspected his unmarried status was due to his pomposity of manner; he clearly thought a lot of himself and probably expected his female companions to do the same.

'Did you or Mr Dean know Miss Dean was at the gallery on Monday morning?'

'No. I did not. And I'm certain Charles didn't either.' Jennings folded his hands together and stared at Flynn from across his desk as if daring him to contradict. 'We were only there for a short time before they discovered the Churchill portrait, and we left when Mr Scott sensibly decided to ask everyone to leave and closed the gallery.'

This echoed what Charles Dean had told him. 'Were you with Mr Scott all the time?'

'Yes. The chap at the front desk showed us to the boardroom, and Mr Scott met us there. We went into the boardroom and chatted for a few minutes, then Mr Scott went out to fetch some coffee. I took the opportunity to go to the cloakroom and then returned to the boardroom.'

Mr Scott had told him that Nathan Jennings had gone to the cloakroom and

Charles Dean had been on his own for some minutes in the boardroom. So far, Jennings had been the only person to admit using the cloakroom in the hour and a half between the gallery opening and Marian Dean's body being found.

'Did you see anyone when you went to use the cloakroom?'

'No. I was only in there for a minute or two, and I didn't see anyone. We had no idea what was going on until an attendant came to fetch Mr Scott.'

'How did you know something was going to take place? And why didn't you inform the police?' Flynn asked, trying not to let his temper show. The prime minister had the gall to blame the police for failing to prevent suffragette protests, yet one of his own MPs hadn't bothered to inform them of what he knew.

'It's a delicate situation. I can't tell you how I knew, and I was by no means certain that the information was correct. I decided the best course of action was to have a quiet word with Mr Scott and advise him to warn his staff to be on their guard.'

'You were a little late,' Flynn said drily.

Jennings bristled. 'As I said, I had no idea when, or even if, such a protest would take place. It was nothing more than a rumour, and I didn't think it a pressing concern. Suffragette protests are taking place all over the country.'

'This one was more unusual than most and guaranteed to generate headlines.'

'Yes, the painting was a shock.' Jennings' lips twitched. 'That was a sight I hadn't expected to see that morning.'

Flynn might have shared Jennings' amusement if the image of Marian Dean's lifeless body wasn't imprinted on his mind.

The smirk on Nathan Jennings' face suggested that the MP wasn't as supportive of his parliamentary colleagues as his public statements would suggest. This prompted Flynn to try a different approach.

'When did you last see Lord Carstairs?' He'd hoped to wrong-foot the man by this change of questioning and succeeded. Up until this point, Jennings had maintained a cool aloofness, but now he seemed flustered.

'Oh, er, on Bla... on Friday, the eighteenth of November.'

He'd been about to say Black Friday, Flynn was sure of that. Not a name any politician would publicly use to label the events of that afternoon.

'Where did you see him?'

'In parliament. I suppose that would have been at around five o'clock.

Under normal circumstances, we might have gone for a drink somewhere, but we were advised not to go out in public that night for fear of repercussions. I think Ronnie went to the House of Commons bar. I just wanted to get out of there, so I drove home.'

Bally had told Flynn that Jennings was the Member of Parliament for a constituency in Lincolnshire, which he rarely visited. He was a Londoner, preferring to stay in the comfort of his luxurious townhouse in Belgravia.

'Do you know where Lord Carstairs was going?'

'I believe he was staying at his London residence.'

This was a townhouse in Leinster Gardens, which Flynn was itching to visit but was unable to without permission from Bally. If he could just interview the staff there, it would give him some idea whether he should be taking the politician's disappearance seriously or not.

'And you haven't seen Lord Carstairs since then?'

'No.'

Flynn thought he detected a note of hesitation. 'Are you sure?'

'I didn't see him again after that day.' Jennings' eyes narrowed, and although Flynn wanted to press harder, he wasn't in a position to accuse the man of lying.

'A picture was stolen from the National Portrait Gallery on Monday. A self-portrait by Sylvie Blanchet gifted by Lord Carstairs. Are you familiar with the painting?'

Jennings shook his head. 'Art's not really my thing. Ronnie was a big collector, liked all sorts of foreign stuff.'

'Where do you think Lord Carstairs might be?'

Jennings took a moment or two to mull this over. 'I don't know. At first, I thought he'd hopped on a passenger ship and gone to the continent for a week or so to get away from all the trouble here. By here, I mean Whitehall.' He glanced around as if the walls could be listening. 'Since the prime minister's announcement to dissolve parliament and hold another election, things have been rather tense. Many of our members think it was the wrong thing to do, including Ronnie and me. I'm telling you this in the strictest confidence. There are enough stories being fed to the newspapers from in here.'

'I appreciate your frankness, Mr Jennings, and I can assure you of my discretion. Can I take it that you no longer believe Lord Carstairs has gone abroad to lie low, as it were?'

'It's been over two weeks since anyone saw him. He would have reappeared by now, especially after the fire at Riverside Lodge. It's not fair to leave Violet, I mean Lady Carstairs, to deal with it on her own.'

'You're friends with the Carstairs family?'

'I've known them for years. Ronnie's quite a character. Well, you probably know that from some of the things he says to the press. He can be bloody unpredictable at times.' Jennings shifted in his seat. 'It makes things difficult for all of us when we have to react to some outrageous statement he's made.'

'He ruffles feathers?' Flynn prompted diplomatically.

'That's exactly it.' Jennings nodded vigorously. 'Don't get me wrong, he's a great fellow, very charming and witty, but you never know what he's going to say next. I think the prime minister has had enough of his volatility. If Ronnie doesn't reappear soon, that's his cabinet career over.'

Jennings didn't appear to be too upset by this.

'How do you think the suffragettes knew that Riverside Lodge was empty?'

'That's the question, isn't it?' Jennings stroked his oily moustache. 'Did you hear what happened to me at Ascot? A spy in our midst, that's for sure. Churchill gets hit by that mad woman with the horse whip, then Lloyd George has a bag of flour poured over him when he's visiting a... a friend.'

By friend, Flynn knew he meant mistress. And Jennings was right. Only someone in government could have known where each of these politicians would be when the attacks took place. In June, the suffragettes had been waiting when Jennings arrived at Ascot races and pelted him with eggs the moment he'd stepped out of his car. The previous year, they'd known which train Churchill had been on when they attacked him on the platform of Bristol Temple Meads railway station. It was even more extraordinary that they were aware of the address of the woman Lloyd George was seeing behind his wife's back and doused him in flour when he was leaving her home.

'Could your private secretary, Charles Dean, have been passing on information to his sister?' Flynn asked.

'No. I trust Charles.' Jennings sounded unequivocal. 'Besides, I'm not sure he'd have access to that level of information, although I suppose he could have picked up gossip in parliament. But he was trying to persuade Marian to leave London and return to Yorkshire. That's where the family is from. He thought she'd be safer there, away from those harpies. And this has proved he was correct.'

That depended on why Marian was killed, Flynn mused. If it was because she was a suffragette, then it was probably true. But if someone had targeted her personally, she could have been killed wherever she'd been, though he couldn't understand why they would choose the National Portrait Gallery. It was certainly a strange place to commit murder.

11

Back at Scotland Yard, Flynn called Goodspeed into his office and told him about his meeting with Jennings.

'We need to find out why someone would want to kill Marian Dean.' Flynn stroked his beard as he stared at Goodspeed. 'As if arson attacks and missing politicians weren't enough, what chain of events leads us to have a stolen painting and a murdered suffragette on our hands?'

'And a naked Winston Churchill.' Goodspeed motioned to the portrait that was propped up on a filing cabinet, facing the wall. 'I see you prefer to look at the back side of the picture rather than Churchill's backside.'

Flynn laughed. 'I was checking to see if there were any clues as to who the artist is. It's well executed.'

Goodspeed grimaced. 'Executed is a bad choice of word under the circumstances.'

'That's the question, though. Was Marian Dean targeted, or did someone decide to kill a suffragette, and she was in the wrong place at the wrong time? It's possible the murder was a revenge attack for the fire, but the killer had to have known a protest was going to take place that morning. That's why we need to find out who was responsible for that.' Flynn indicated the Churchill portrait.

'And did they steal the other one?' Goodspeed asked. 'The one by Sylvie Blanchet.'

'They must have. One group draws everyone's attention to the Westminster Gallery, while another goes into the Contemporary Gallery and steals the Blanchet painting. Why that picture, though?'

'Unless the suffragettes didn't steal it, and Marian Dean was killed because she spotted the thief or thieves,' Goodspeed suggested.

The thought had occurred to Flynn. 'Let's take another look at that cloak-room. It's possible they passed the painting through the window to someone waiting outside. Though if I'd stolen it, I'd have left by the fastest route, which would be through the main entrance. Why go in the direction of where all the people were gathered?'

'Unless Marian Dean was the thief. You said Nathan Jennings went into the cloakroom. Perhaps he saw what she was doing...' Goodspeed trailed off with a shrug, seeming to acknowledge the flaws in this hypothesis.

Flynn raised his eyebrows. 'How likely is it that he would take a knife with him on the off chance of meeting a suffragette or a thief in the lavatory?'

Goodspeed smiled. 'Put like that, not very likely.'

'Let's go over what we know about Marian Dean. Did she have a boyfriend?'

Goodspeed took out his pocketbook. 'Not according to her family. She was twenty years old and moved to London six months ago from her home in Bradford, West Yorkshire. Her parents still reside in Bradford, where her father owns several cotton mills. Marian has been living at her grandmother's home on Porchester Terrace. She has one brother, Charles, who's five years older than her. He's been living with his grandmother, too, for the last couple of years. He came to London after he got a job as a junior secretary at Whitehall and worked his way up to become a private secretary. Apparently, he has political ambitions himself. Here's the interesting thing – for a short time, he worked as a private secretary to Lord Carstairs until he got a permanent position with Nathan Jennings.'

'Carstairs again.' Flynn rapped his fingers on his desk in frustration. 'We keep coming back to that bloody man.'

Goodspeed closed his pocketbook. 'Can we talk to Lady Carstairs? I reckon this could be connected to what happened at Riverside Lodge.'

'Bally's working on it. Lady Carstairs claimed to be too upset to talk to the police after the fire. She stays mainly in the country at Biddenden House, their estate in Kent. They don't have any children. It was Lord Carstairs' secretary who told us about the plans for Riverside Lodge. Bally's informed this secretary that it's imperative either Lord or Lady Carstairs talks to me. One way or another, there's a connection.' Flynn just wished he knew what the hell it was. 'I want a list of everyone present at the gallery that morning – staff and visitors.'

'Jack's already taken statements from all the staff. There were three attendants on the ground floor, one in the foyer and one in the galleries on either side of the entrance. Upstairs, there were two attendants on the first floor and one on the top floor. The director was in a meeting with Nathan Jennings and Charles Dean in the trustees' boardroom. His secretary was away that day, and there was a doorman at the back entrance. On busier days, such as weekends, there would generally be more attendants on duty.'

'The suffragettes knew what they were doing, which suggests a familiarity with the gallery,' Flynn mused.

Goodspeed ran a pen down his notes. 'The doorman at the tradesman's entrance reports only one caller, the young deliveryman who brought the painting in on a trolley. And according to the front desk attendant, the only visitors that morning until the reporter and photographer arrived were four well-dressed ladies: Marian Dean, with an auburn-haired companion, followed by a blonde lady, who also went into the Westminster Gallery. These three must have been responsible for hanging the Churchill portrait. Another lady, aged about fifty with reddish hair, went to the Actors and Dramatists Gallery on the other side of the ground floor. She doesn't appear to have been involved with what happened.'

'Unless she sneaked into the Contemporary Gallery and stole the Blanchet painting. We need to know who she is. And what made the attendant leave the Westminster Gallery?'

'The blonde lady asked him to direct her to a particular picture. As there were only the two other well-dressed ladies present in the Westminster Gallery, he thought it safe to leave it unattended.'

Flynn shook his head in exasperation. 'Well-dressed ladies have been setting fire to pillar boxes, smashing windows and assaulting politicians for the last five years. We need to find the auburn-haired woman who was with Marian Dean, the blonde woman who distracted the attendant, and the young man who delivered the Churchill portrait.'

'If we turn up at Clement's Inn and start questioning the WSPU, we could spark a riot,' Goodspeed observed.

'That's what Bally's afraid of. The prime minister has told him to avoid any unpleasantness. How the hell can we avoid unpleasantness when we're investigating the murder of a young woman?'

It wasn't just Bally who was causing Flynn's temples to throb. Teresa had implied that if the police failed to catch the murderer, it was because they didn't take the death of a suffragette as seriously as other crimes. No doubt this view would be shared by women across the country.

Flynn knew he needed to act quickly to catch the killer. God forbid, they should strike again and attack another woman. Yet he couldn't risk making the wrong move and igniting a powder keg. The antipathy between the Metropolitan Police and the suffragettes had to be cooled, and Marian Dean's murder was only likely to inflame current tensions.

Or, if he played things tactically, could he contrive to bring about some sort of conciliation? After all, both parties would want to find out who killed this young woman. And why.

To achieve this, he needed an ally within the WSPU. Someone to act as an intermediary and get the suffragettes to talk to him. But how the hell was he going to engineer such an alliance in the present circumstances?

'Sir.' Detective Constable Hall poked his head around the door. 'There's a lady in reception who wants to speak to you. Her name is Mrs Fairbanks.'

'What does she want?' Flynn frowned, trying to remember where he'd heard that name recently.

'She says she wants to talk to you about what happened at the National Portrait Gallery. She says she was there when...' Jack seemed to have to force out the words. 'When the young lady was murdered.'

Flynn noticed the lad's pallid expression. Finding Marian Dean's body had obviously affected him badly. More than Flynn would have expected. Jack had been in the force long enough to have seen plenty of nasty crimes on the streets of London. Was it the fact that this victim was a pretty young female rather than a grizzled old drunk or a petty criminal?

He pushed these thoughts aside and indicated for Goodspeed to accompany him to the interview room.

12

Coral saw Detective Inspector Flynn falter when he recognised her. And she knew why. The countess had told her that he'd requested anonymity when it came to his paintings. She guessed being an artist wasn't something the higher-ups in the Metropolitan Police looked for in their detectives.

'Detective Inspector Flynn. I hope you don't mind me calling on you like this. I read your name in the newspaper and—'

Flynn cut in. 'You were at the National Portrait Gallery on the morning Miss Marian Dean was murdered? Please take a seat. This is Detective Sergeant Goodspeed.'

Flynn was brusque. Was he afraid she would mention their meeting at the Stanmore Gallery?

Coral sat on a hard wooden chair across a desk from Flynn and his sergeant. She'd been escorted into the interview room by a young man who'd introduced himself as Detective Constable Hall. He now stood guard by the door, which seemed unnecessary since she was here voluntarily.

Although Scotland Yard was only a twenty-minute walk from Coral's home – she must have passed the red-brick and white Portland stone building on Victoria Embankment on hundreds of occasions – it had been an intimidating experience to walk through its doors.

With misgivings, she said, 'I'm a member of the Women's Social and Political Union. We were responsible for hanging the portrait of Winston Churchill in the Westminster Gallery.'

Flynn's hazel eyes rested on her for an uncomfortably long time before he responded. When he did, his question surprised her.

'Were you the decoy who lured the attendant away from the gallery?'

She nodded, wondering how much the attendant, Mr Norris, had told him. Had Flynn seen *Dawn Beauty* and recognised her? She'd dressed that morning in a green high-necked gown with a brown velvet wide-brimmed hat to try to look as respectable, and covered up, as possible.

'Who were the other two? Marian Dean's companion in the Westminster Gallery and the man who delivered the Churchill portrait. I want their names and addresses,' Flynn demanded.

So they still thought Irene was a man. That was all for the better.

'I'm not going to give you their names as they had nothing to do with Marian's murder.' Coral didn't like the way Flynn was firing questions at her. If he imagined she'd come here just to offer up information, expecting nothing in return, he had another think coming.

'This deliveryman came and left by the rear entrance?' Goodspeed had a pocketbook in front of him and was making notes.

Coral nodded. The doorman would already have given them this information. 'We all left the way we came in. The deliveryman through the tradesman's entrance. The rest through the main entrance.'

Except that wasn't what Marian had done. Someone or something had taken her into the cloakroom.

On cue, Flynn asked, 'Why did Miss Dean go into the cloakroom?'

'We don't know. She was supposed to have left before us by the main entrance, carrying the bag with the hammer and nails.' Coral took a deep breath. 'Could you tell me how she died? The newspapers are saying she was stabbed.'

'A pathologist is examining Miss Dean's body. I've yet to receive his report.'

'Did you see her?'

Flynn nodded. 'It appears someone attacked her with a knife; however, no weapon was found at the scene.'

Coral gulped, fighting back tears as she pictured Marian's terror. Why? It was all she kept asking herself. Why would someone do that to Marian? She scrutinised the drab room that smelled of stale tobacco, trying to focus on something to distract her. But it was featureless, with bare, white-painted walls and no windows.

She caught the eye of the detective constable standing motionless by the door. He looked away, though not before she'd seen the expression of pain on his face. It made her warm to him, glad to see someone else was horrified by what had happened to Marian.

Flynn was showing no such emotion. 'Did Miss Dean have a boyfriend?'

'She never spoke of one. Her grandmother might know more about that.'

'I'll be speaking to the Dean family again. I'm trying to find out who knew where Miss Dean was going to be that morning. When did you first devise the plan to hang the Churchill picture in the National Portrait Gallery?'

'Only a week before. The artist had worked on the painting over the summer with no fixed idea of what they would do with it.'

Flynn raised his eyebrows as if he didn't believe her. 'Who else apart from the four of you present that morning knew of the plan? You obviously arranged for the arrival of a reporter and photographer from the *Daily Mirror*.'

'I'd told Sidney Watson that if he turned up at the gallery just after nine o'clock with a photographer, he'd get a story none of the other newspapers would have.' She'd actually given Sid a little more information than that, but she didn't want him to get into trouble for not informing the police of what was going to happen. She'd also forewarned him of her visit to Flynn. 'He was the only person I told.'

'And that was your intention? To gain publicity?'

Coral nodded. 'And to embarrass Mr Churchill.'

She noticed Detective Sergeant Goodspeed's lips twitch. Flynn remained impassive.

'What about the painting by Sylvie Blanchet? Was it also your intention to steal a valuable work of art?' Flynn asked.

'We had nothing to do with the theft of that picture,' Coral replied warily. Although she'd known this wouldn't be easy, she hadn't expected Flynn to be quite so intimidating.

'Maybe you didn't. But perhaps another suffragette group was present. Perhaps they'd heard about what you had planned, and while everyone's attention was in the other gallery, they took the painting,' Flynn suggested.

'Not to my knowledge,' she answered truthfully, though the same thought had occurred to her. After all, she hadn't known about the plan to set fire to

Riverside Lodge. Could another suffragette group have been there without her realising? Had Marian seen what they were doing and confronted them? But why would they kill her?

'Were any of you carrying bags?' Detective Sergeant Goodspeed asked.

'Marian was the only one with a bag. I had a small purse similar to this one.' Coral placed her brown velvet purse on the table. 'I don't see how any of us could have taken the Blanchet picture without someone seeing us walking out with it. However, I'll be frank with you. I'm not privy to everything that goes on within the executive committee of the WSPU. But, as you've seen recently, Mrs Pankhurst isn't afraid of claiming responsibility for the union's actions. On this occasion, she denies any knowledge of the missing painting.'

Coral couldn't help admiring Mrs Pankhurst's willingness to get her hands dirty. The Pankhursts were the public face of the suffragettes and, as such, were the ones to endure repeated arrests and incarceration. There were other women, like the countess, who held considerable sway within the organisation but preferred to stay in the background.

'Was Mrs Pankhurst aware of your plan to hang the Churchill portrait in the gallery?'

According to Penny, Emmeline Pankhurst had laughed uproariously when she'd seen Irene's painting. But Coral just shrugged as if she didn't know.

'Alright. Let's put that aside for the time being. I want to establish who was present that morning. Who did you see when you were there?'

'We were the only visitors when the doors opened at nine o'clock, apart from Charles Dean, Marian's brother, and Nathan Jennings, the MP. They went into a meeting room with a man who I think must have been the director of the gallery.'

Flynn nodded. 'Mr Dean told me he was there that morning.'

'Did he see Marian?'

'He says not.'

Coral wondered if this were true. 'What were he and Nathan Jennings doing there?'

She saw by Flynn's pursed lips that this was one question too many. He didn't reply, instead, he asked, 'Did you see anyone else while you were in the gallery?'

'The man who delivered the portrait thinks he saw Lady Carstairs enter the building shortly after we did.'

Goodspeed whistled. 'Ronald Carstairs' wife?'

Coral nodded, noticing the warning hand Flynn placed on his sergeant's arm.

'What was she doing there?' Flynn asked.

'Looking at paintings, I suppose,' Coral replied, trying not to sound sarcastic. 'She was seen in the foyer before going into the galleries on the left-hand side of the ground floor. Then I saw her in the Westminster Gallery shortly before I left.'

Flynn stared at her as if doubting what she said. For a few moments, the room was silent apart from the sound of Detective Sergeant Goodspeed making notes.

Then Flynn asked, 'Why did you come here today?'

'To give you our account of what happened that morning. We want to help you find out who did that to Marian. And we want you to keep us informed of what's going on with your investigation.'

Flynn seemed to take an age to consider this, then he said, 'If you want to help me find the killer, you need to tell me the names of the man who delivered the portrait and the auburn-haired lady with Miss Dean.'

'So you can arrest them?' Coral shook her head. 'Believe me when I say we had nothing to do with Marian's murder or the stolen painting.'

'You've already told me you're not privy to everything that's discussed within the WSPU,' he retorted.

Their eyes locked, and Coral could sense his frustration at her lack of cooperation. This was a very different man to the one who'd visited the Stanmore Gallery with his pretty daughter. That morning, she'd found him to be charming and courteous. Today, he was stony-faced and much colder than she'd expected. She stayed silent, wondering if he planned to arrest her. It was a risk she was prepared to take, but she didn't want to be responsible for Irene and Penny ending up in prison.

Flynn cleared his throat and seemed to be trying to curb his irritation. When he spoke, it was in a calmer tone. 'I will arrest anyone if I suspect they had something to do with Marian Dean's death. Or the theft of the Sylvie Blanchet painting. However, in exchange for information, I'll overlook the matter of the Churchill portrait.'

The countess had predicted this would be his response.

'I appreciate you might not want to give me their names right now,' Flynn continued. 'Go and talk to the people you need to and then come back to me. Leave a message for me at the front desk, and if I'm not around, I'll call on you at home. What's your address?'

Coral told him and saw the slightest raise of his eyebrows. Houses on Adelphi Terrace weren't cheap.

'Do you live there with your husband? Is he aware of your activities?' Flynn asked in what she considered to be a rather pompous manner.

Coral saw him glance at the fingers of her left hand and wished she hadn't removed her gloves when she'd sat down. She forced herself not to touch the space where her wedding ring had once been.

'I'm a widow. I have a lodger, Miss Lacey. She's an actress and works mainly at night. You can always leave a message with her if I'm not around during the day.'

'Lavender Lacey? The one in *The Chocolate Soldier*?' Judging by his wide eyes, Sergeant Goodspeed was an admirer. And with his piratical good looks, she had no doubt Lavender would be delighted to flirt with him.

Coral nodded and smiled. This could work to their advantage.

Flynn must have had the same thought as he gave his sergeant a stern glance before abruptly standing to indicate their meeting was over.

'Thank you for coming here today, Mrs Fairbanks. We'll speak again in the next day or so.'

Coral rose from her seat. 'You can also find me at the Stanmore Gallery on Pall Mall,' she said with just enough of a smile to indicate a conspiracy between them. 'I work there most days.'

The flicker of annoyance that crossed Flynn's face told her he'd understood the message.

13

Flynn sat alone in the interview room, noticing the faint waft of floral perfume Coral Fairbanks had left behind. An unusual aroma in this all-male establishment.

He guessed the reason she'd been chosen to act as an envoy was because she knew his secret. She intimated as much when she said he could find her at the Stanmore Gallery.

Flynn didn't like this connection that had been forged between them. He'd done nothing wrong by allowing Countess Stanmore to sell his paintings through her gallery. And if Mrs Fairbanks or her suffragette comrades thought they could influence him in any way, they'd soon find they were mistaken.

He trudged up the stairs to his office where he found Goodspeed slumped in a chair in front of his desk. Flynn was grateful to see he'd brought a pot of coffee and two cups with him. He was less pleased by the ashtray and cigarette clamped between Goodspeed's lips, but he couldn't begrudge the man a smoke just because he didn't indulge.

'I'm surprised you didn't arrest her,' his sergeant commented.

'Before she arrived, I was thinking we needed to find an ally within the suffragettes. Someone who can act as an intermediary. Coral Fairbanks is our best chance of that.'

But could he trust her? There was only one way to find out. He had a feeling that without inside help, he wouldn't find the answers he needed to track down Marian Dean's killer.

'Did you believe her?' Goodspeed asked.

Flynn nodded. 'I believe what she told us was true. I'm more interested in what she wasn't telling us.'

'How do you think she managed to distract the attendant for so long?'

Flynn was trying to decide how to answer this when he saw the twinkle in his sergeant's eyes. He laughed.

Goodspeed poured the coffee. 'Do you think that's why Mrs Fairbanks was chosen to come to us? They may be feminists, but they're not above using their charms to try to get what they want.'

'I hope we're made of sterner stuff than to fall for a pretty face,' Flynn replied with a joviality he didn't feel. 'I get the impression you're a fan of Miss Lavender Lacey. What do you know of her?'

'She's gorgeous. Twenty-seven years old. Long dark hair, big brown eyes, pale skin. And a beautiful soprano voice. I was in tears when she sang—'

'I meant, is she an active suffragette?' Flynn rolled his eyes in mock exasperation, playing along with Goodspeed. But inside, he was still ruminating over Coral Fairbanks' last comment.

Goodspeed must have sensed his mood because he said, 'You seem angry? What is it?'

'This bloody case.' Flynn gave a dismissive wave of his hand. 'And those bloody suffragettes.'

Goodspeed blew out a curl of cigarette smoke. 'I can't see them killing one of their own.'

'No, neither can I, although we can't rule it out.' Flynn shuffled through the pile of statements on his desk. 'What about stealing a work of art? The doorman at the tradesman's entrance corroborates what Mrs Fairbanks told us about the deliveryman arriving and leaving that way. When he left, a piece of stiff carpet was lying open, resting on the spine and prongs of the trolley, and he was holding some loose brown paper in his hand. The doorman is adamant there was nowhere to conceal a picture the size of the Blanchet painting. It was taken on its wooden mount, which measures sixteen by sixteen inches. It couldn't be removed from that without destroying the painting.'

'What about Mrs Fairbanks or the auburn-haired woman? No one saw them leave. Could one of them have stolen the picture?'

'I don't think Mrs Fairbanks did, but I'm not so sure about the other one.' Flynn smiled. 'And neither is she. Did you see the look on her face when I asked if other suffragettes could have been there playing out a different crime? The same thought had occurred to her.'

Goodspeed stubbed out his cigarette and began to flip through the statements he'd taken from the staff. 'Out of the four women who entered the National Portrait Gallery that morning, the front desk attendant said that only Marian Dean had a shoulder bag, the one we saw in the cloakroom. The others were carrying small purses. If one of them did steal the picture, they'd have had to walk out with it under their arm.'

'There could have been someone waiting outside to whisk it off them as soon as they stepped out the door. Also, Nathan Jennings and Charles Dean were both carrying briefcases. They'd be about the right size to hide the painting.' Flynn pondered for a moment. 'There's something else that's bothering me. How did the deliveryman recognise Lady Carstairs? It's not as though she's often pictured in the newspapers like her husband.'

'The deliveryman was clearly working with the suffragettes. And they make it their business to know the faces of anyone prominent in politics. Lady Carstairs must have been the red-haired lady the desk attendant described. Didn't he say he was sure he'd seen her in the gallery before?'

Flynn nodded. 'I'll have a word with Bally. We need him to force Lady Carstairs to speak to us. The fire at Riverside Lodge would have made her angry. Angry enough to kill?'

Goodspeed tutted. 'Bally won't like you accusing her ladyship of murder.'

'I won't do that, but he must see we need to talk to her. And not just about Marian Dean's death. Ronald Carstairs has been missing for too long. I don't like it.' Flynn reached for his coffee. 'Get Jack to find a photograph of Lady Carstairs and ask him to take it to the gallery and show it to the staff to see if anyone recognises her.'

Goodspeed nodded. 'The Carstairs name has cropped up too many times now for it to be a coincidence. There must be a link between his disappearance, the fire and the murder.'

Flynn was silent for a moment, not liking where his thoughts were taking him. 'Did you notice Mrs Fairbanks wasn't wearing a wedding ring?'

'She said she was widowed. Perhaps she decided not to wear...' Comprehension dawned on Goodspeed's face. 'You're thinking of the wedding ring we found at the Hurlingham Club.'

Flynn took the ring from his top drawer and twirled it between his fingers. It was a silver band engraved with a Celtic design of love knots. He needed to find out more about Coral Fairbanks. And her late husband.

'She was involved in this latest protest, so why not that one?' Flynn placed the ring on his desk and fingered his own wedding band. It had been four years since Julia's death, and it had never occurred to him to take his ring off. They'd been married for thirteen years and would always be man and wife as far as he was concerned. Perhaps Coral Fairbanks hadn't felt the same way about her husband. Or perhaps she had and was grieving the loss of her ring.

'I want you to go and see Lavender Lacey,' he told Goodspeed. 'You might catch her at home – if not, go to the theatre. Find out whatever you can about Coral Fairbanks. I want to know who she associates with. Does she have people back to her home? Adelphi Terrace is known for writers, theatrical types and artists – does she mix with them?'

Goodspeed couldn't disguise his delight at being set this task. 'It will be a—'

He was interrupted by a knock at the door, followed by the appearance of Detective Constable Hall.

'The pathologist has sent over some preliminary notes. He's still examining Mar... Miss Dean's body. He said it will be a couple of days before he'll issue his formal written report, but...' Jack looked queasy. 'He said she was stabbed in the cloakroom and died only a short time before she was found.'

'Well, we knew that,' Goodspeed remarked. 'Presumably, she was attacked shortly after leaving the Westminster Gallery.'

'She was killed by a single stab wound to the chest.' Jack's voice held a slight tremor. 'The pathologist thinks the weapon was a serrated knife. Not a large one, some sort of utility knife.'

Goodspeed took the notes from Jack. 'Could our thief have been carrying a knife? They clearly had a chisel of some kind and might have used a knife to prise the wooden mount out of its frame.'

Flynn nodded. 'You could be right. We need to go back to the gallery to see if it would be possible for the Blanchet painting to fit through the cloakroom window. Marian Dean might have caught the thieves in the act.' He paused. 'But if that is how they got the picture out, the suffragettes didn't steal it.'

Goodspeed considered this, then nodded slowly. 'They wouldn't draw everyone to that end of the building if that's the way they meant to remove the painting. It doesn't make sense.'

Flynn growled in exasperation. 'Nothing about this makes sense.'

14

Coral's eyes flickered open as she heard movements from downstairs. It was light outside, which must mean it was after eight o'clock. She lifted her head to look at the small clock on her nightstand and was shocked to see it was nearly half past nine. She never slept in this late. Why had she today?

For those first few delicious moments on waking, she would often believe that Ernest was still with her. She'd yearn to stay under the covers and hold on to that belief, but then she would remember – and grief would wash over her. Today, there was something more. It wasn't just Ernest; something else had happened.

She let her head sink back into the pillows until the previous few days' events hit her with such force, she sat upright. Marian had been murdered – and she felt responsible.

Why had she gone along with that stupid scheme to publicly display the Churchill portrait? The answer was because it had seemed harmless – a practical joke to embarrass someone who'd behaved badly. But it had proved to be far from harmless.

The springs creaked as she staggered out of the bed she'd once shared with Ernest, and her legs ached as she planted her feet in her slippers. When she reached for her dressing gown, her arms felt weak.

Coral decided she needed food. She'd barely eaten for the last three days. It was time to put aside her anger and grief at Marian's death and start to think about how she could help Flynn catch her killer.

She washed and dressed, pondering on her two very different encounters with Detective Inspector Guy Flynn. Coral decided she preferred the artist to the policeman. But right now, she needed a detective, and the countess had said he was a good one.

In the kitchen, she found Lavender sipping coffee and flicking through the pages of *The Tatler*.

'You'll be late for work. How are you feeling, darling?' Lavender got up to fill the teapot from the kettle she'd kept hot on the stove. She'd already placed Coral's big rose-patterned teacup and saucer on the table. 'I didn't know whether to wake you.'

On impulse, Coral went up behind her and gave her a hug. When she'd first decided to advertise for a lodger, Coral had seen some appalling applicants and almost given up on the idea of sharing her beloved home with someone. Then she'd been introduced to Lavender by an actor who'd worked with them both, and that had been that. Lavender had moved in the following week, and three years later, they still rubbed along very well together.

'It's been dreadful for you, hasn't it, darling?' Lavender generally shied away from affection, but this time she squeezed Coral back. 'I'm so sorry about Marian.'

Coral let her go and nodded. 'I'm not working in the gallery this morning. I'm going to visit Marian's grandmother.'

'That's decent of you. I'm sure she'll appreciate it.' Lavender stirred the teapot and then picked up the strainer and poured the dark brown liquid into Coral's cup. 'Shall I cook you one of your disgusting breakfasts to give you sustenance?'

Coral smiled. 'I'll make it.' She knew Lavender found it easier to show affection through action, not words, and though she appreciated the younger woman's efforts to look after her, it did make her feel rather old at times.

Lavender poured herself another cup of coffee. 'Darling, you were right about that detective sending one of his officers to quiz me. The most adorable policeman came to the theatre yesterday evening. Detective Sergeant Goodspeed. I told him I couldn't possibly remember such a mouthful and insisted he told me his first name.'

Coral went to the larder and took out eggs, a packet of beef dripping and slices of bacon. 'I've met him. What did he ask?'

'He wanted to know who your friends are, do you have people back to the house, that sort of thing. I told Evan – that's his name by the way – that we were very private and respectable ladies who didn't entertain. He asked if I was a member of the WSPU, and I told him I found the suffragettes complete bores.'

This was all true. Although Lavender supported the cause, she wasn't keen on 'all that earnest self-righteousness'. And the pair of them rarely entertained at home, seeing the house as a quiet place where they could escape from the bustle of city life.

'I'm sorry you got dragged into this. I hope it wasn't too embarrassing having him turn up at the theatre.' Coral cut a slice of the beef dripping and melted it in the frying pan. Then she added two slices of bacon and a couple of eggs. Taking her favourite wooden spatula with the burnt end, she began to flick hot fat over the eggs. 'Do you want something to eat?'

'Just a fried egg on toast.' Lavender wrinkled her nose at the aroma of sizzling bacon. She went to the larder and came back with a large loaf of bread and started to cut it into thick slices. 'It was a complete hoot. Everyone was rigging me about it. Some of the girls were even jealous. Evan is gorgeous. Those dark curls and long eyelashes. And that endearing broken nose. He got it in a boxing match. Apparently, his right hook is legendary. I squeezed his arms – they were like rocks.'

Coral could picture the scene and felt a pang of nostalgia for the backstage gossip the detective's visit to Lavender's dressing room would have generated. Lavender loved to flirt, though contrary as it sounded, she did it to keep men at a distance. It was an act designed to prevent anyone from getting too close. Lavender harboured ambitions to star on Broadway and wasn't about to be distracted by a handsome man, no matter how endearing his broken nose. You couldn't be married and be a successful actress, as Coral knew to her cost.

'The thing is, darling. Evan asked if you usually wore a wedding ring.'

Coral paused, spatula hovering in her hand. Did that mean Flynn had found her ring? In normal circumstances, she would have marched straight to Scotland Yard and demanded it back. However, these weren't normal circumstances. Coral knew she couldn't afford to antagonise Flynn. She'd have to follow the countess's advice and watch and wait for the right moment to tackle him.

'What did you tell the adorable Evan?' Coral tried to sound light-hearted, though she was anything but.

'That I thought you'd put it away for safekeeping.' Lavender joined her by the stove. 'Do you think this Detective Inspector Flynn intends to arrest you?'

'I'm not sure. He said we should talk again soon.'

'Evan said the same.' Lavender winked at her. 'And not because he wants to arrest me.'

'I wish I could say the same for Flynn.' Coral turned her attention back to the frying pan. 'He's only interested in catching Marian's killer, which is fine by me. As long as he catches the right person.'

Once the eggs and bacon were cooked, Coral ladled them onto a plate, then added a slice of white bread to the frying pan, pressing it down to absorb the fat before flipping it over to cook both sides evenly. 'Do you want fried bread?'

Lavender pulled a face. 'Too disgusting. I'll do toast.' She believed eating greasy food was bad for the complexion. 'You're afraid he's going to go after one of you?'

'We're the obvious suspects,' Coral replied.

'Well, Detective Sergeant Evan Goodspeed seemed a decent man to me and a handsome devil to boot.' Lavender pretended to fan herself with a slice of bread. 'I think he'll carry out a proper investigation. What about this Detective Inspector Flynn? What's he like?'

Coral considered this. 'The artist and the policeman feel like two different men. I liked the artist more, but I need the help of the policeman. I'm just not sure I can trust him.'

* * *

Florence Dean resided in a Georgian townhouse on Porchester Terrace. The interior was as dated as the exterior, furnished with heavy, high-quality furniture and family portraits adorning the walls.

Coral had once called on Marian, anticipating her grandmother would be as staid as the house. It had been a pleasant surprise to find Mrs Dean was as lively as her granddaughter. With her soft grey hair and sparkling blue eyes, it was like looking at the Marian of the future. Only that future had now been destroyed.

The Deans' butler, George, answered the door to a house that was clearly in mourning. He wore a sombre expression as he left Coral in the hall while he ascertained whether Mrs Dean was accepting visitors. It appeared she was, as he returned and took Coral's coat before showing her into the drawing room.

Charles Dean, who was seated beside his grandmother on a chintz sofa, stood when she entered. A quick glance told Coral he didn't welcome her visit. He hadn't been pleased to see her on the last occasion, and this time around, he had every reason to resent her presence.

'Thank you for coming, Mrs Fairbanks.' Mrs Dean managed a half-smile. 'George, perhaps you could bring us some tea?'

The butler gave a slight nod and withdrew.

Feeling awkward, Coral perched on the edge of an armchair by the fire. 'I'm so sorry for your loss.'

Mrs Dean inclined her head in a gesture of acknowledgement, but Charles gave her a hostile stare as he sat back down. He had a clean-shaven boyish face that was at odds with the formal tweed suit he wore. Coral got the impression his choice of dress was an attempt to give him more gravitas.

'If there's anything I can do to help at this difficult time...' Coral felt the inadequacy of the words, knowing there was little she could do to help Marian's grieving family.

'Charles is looking after me.' Mrs Dean patted her grandson's hand. 'We'll be travelling to Yorkshire soon to be with my son and daughter-in-law.'

'We want to take Marian back home,' Charles said stonily. 'Once the police have... have finished what they have to do, we'll arrange for a funeral at the village church where she was christened.'

'Would it be possible for me and a few of Marian's friends to attend?' Coral asked.

'No.' Charles' response was final. 'We don't want you there. It would be too upsetting for my parents. They want no reminders of Marian's time in London.'

Coral nodded. Who was she to argue with grief? Clearly, Marian's family preferred to remember her as the lively girl who'd charmed everyone in the village where she'd grown up. Not the young woman who'd been thrilled with the life she'd made for herself in London, discovering a whole new world and embracing new friendships.

'If she hadn't got involved with your lot—'

'Charles,' his grandmother said sharply. 'Marian was a grown woman. She chose to become a suffragette, and I respect her for that decision.'

Charles scowled. 'Were you with her in the gallery?'

'Yes, I was,' Coral admitted.

'Then you should tell the police.'

'I've been to see Detective Inspector Flynn and told him everything I can.' This was a rather ambiguous statement. She could have told Flynn more but had chosen not to reveal Penny and Irene's names to him.

Charles stared at her in surprise. 'Why hasn't he arrested you?'

'I'm not sure.' Coral decided to be frank. 'I think because he believes I can help him. As you know, tensions are running high after what happened on Bla... what happened outside parliament a few weeks ago.'

Charles flushed but said nothing.

Encouraged that he wasn't rushing to defend the police's actions, Coral continued. 'Marian's friends want her killer to be caught. But they don't trust the police. I went to see Detective Inspector Flynn as a sort of peacemaker, I suppose. I believe we have more chance of finding out what happened if we can put our differences aside and work together.'

Mrs Dean nodded and dabbed watery eyes with a lavender-scented handkerchief.

Charles covered his face with his hands. 'Why?' he said in a muffled voice. 'I just don't understand why.'

'Neither do I,' Coral said softly. 'What were you doing at the gallery that morning?'

Charles glanced up sharply. 'Mr Jennings had received information that the gallery was a proposed target for the suffragettes. He went to warn the director.'

Coral was startled by this. How could Nathan Jennings have known? 'Information from whom?'

'Someone in government. I don't know who. I never dreamed Marian would be involved in such a ridiculous...' Charles waved his hands, seeming at a loss to know how to describe what had occurred.

'It wasn't supposed to be dangerous. It was a stunt designed to attract publicity, nothing more.'

'It was designed to humiliate the home secretary,' Charles retorted.

'He deserved it,' Coral couldn't help saying.

Charles gave her a withering look. 'It might surprise you to know that the government has more pressing matters to deal with than getting distracted by the same old arguments from Mrs Pankhurst.'

Coral tried to suppress her irritation. Now was not the time to remind him that if the government had done what it promised and allowed women to have a say in the democratic process, then this whole problem would go away. If this was the attitude Marian had faced at home, it was no wonder she'd turned to the WSPU.

The butler entered with a tea tray, and Charles stood as if this was a cue for him to leave. Muttering something under his breath, he strode from the room.

Mrs Dean nodded at George, who poured the tea before discreetly withdrawing.

'I apologise for my grandson's behaviour, Mrs Fairbanks.'

'There's no need. I can see he's upset.' Coral added milk and sugar and picked up the fine porcelain cup. The tea had a delicate floral taste, not like the strong bitter tea she was accustomed to.

'Charles loved Marian very much. And he's upset because he was at odds with her before she died. He's keen to make a name for himself in parliament and believed Marian's involvement with the WSPU would hamper his chances of promotion.'

It was a valid fear. Not many politicians would tolerate a private secretary with links to the suffragettes.

A thought occurred to Coral. 'Did Nathan Jennings know Marian?'

'Yes. In fact, I got the impression he rather liked her. When Charles tried to keep Marian away from him, I assumed it was because he didn't want Marian haranguing him about politics. Then I realised it was because he doesn't fully trust Mr Jennings and didn't want Marian getting involved with him.'

Could Nathan Jennings have spotted Marian that morning? If he had, would he have realised why she was there? And would he have tried to dissuade her from getting involved in a suffragette protest? Perhaps they'd argued...

Coral wondered why Flynn had refused to tell her the reason for Nathan Jennings and Charles Dean's visit to the gallery. No doubt, because the Metropolitan Police would prefer the murderer to be a suffragette than a member of parliament.

'Did Marian have a boyfriend?' Coral asked.

'Detective Inspector Flynn asked me that question. I told him no, but the answer is I'm not sure. Marian had become secretive of late, though I think that was for fear of getting into an argument with Charles.' Mrs Dean bent over and reached into a knitting bag by the side of her chair. She took out a small blue leather-bound book and handed it to Coral. 'This is Marian's diary.'

'Oh.' Coral took it, unsure what Mrs Dean expected of her.

'It felt too disloyal to Marian to give it to the police. She would have hated her friends, particularly you, to have got into trouble because of something she wrote. I'd like you to read it in case there's anything in it that could help identify her killer.' She patted Coral's arm. 'I feel happier knowing you're working with Detective Inspector Flynn.'

Coral hadn't exactly said she was working with Flynn, but if it gave Mrs Dean comfort, who was she to argue? And she would tell him if she found out anything that might help catch Marian's killer.

'I want you to know that Marian's friends truly cared about her. And I will do everything I can to find who did this to her. No matter who it is.'

'I thought you would.' Mrs Dean smiled. 'Marian said she'd never felt so alive as when she was with you all. Her life in Yorkshire had been too sheltered for such an intelligent and lively girl. I'm sorry you can't come to the funeral, but Charles is right. I think it's best we protect Marian's parents from any more hurt. That's another reason why I'm giving the diary to you. I don't want them to be upset by anything it may contain.'

Coral nodded. What good would it do for Charles and his grieving parents to read about Marian's illegal activities? And if she'd mentioned the fire at Riverside Lodge in her diary, it could mean a prison spell for Penny and Irene.

'I understand, and I promise I'll be discreet.'

'Thank you, my dear.' Florence Dean's eyes filled with tears. 'I admire what you and your friends are doing. I wish I was as brave as my granddaughter was. It made Charles angry when I said that I supported the cause. But I'm glad I told Marian I was proud of her.'

This made Coral reach for her own handkerchief. Marian had been brave. She'd also been a caring friend and loyal suffragette. Had she died because of this? Coral realised she didn't just need to know who murdered Marian; she had to know why.

15

'How was the divine Miss Lacey?' Flynn asked Goodspeed as they strode across Trafalgar Square.

'Even more gorgeous close up. I went into her dressing room. It was full of clothes and make-up and stuff. She was lovely, very friendly. Kept calling me darling, which was a bit off-putting at first, but I got used to it.'

Flynn saw to his amusement that Goodspeed actually had a dazed expression on his face. 'She's an actress. They call everyone darling. I hope you made it clear you were there in your capacity as a police officer. Not one of her admirers.'

Goodspeed smiled. 'I told her my rank, and she asked me what it was like to be a detective. She seemed fascinated by me.'

'Did you manage to ask her any questions?'

'Of course.' Goodspeed looked affronted. 'She said she supports the cause, though claims not to be a member of the WSPU as she finds their meetings too dreary. She knows Mrs Fairbanks is a member but is positive that she wouldn't get involved in anything illegal.'

Flynn grunted. 'I wouldn't be too sure about that. Who does Coral Fairbanks socialise with?'

'It sounds like mainly theatrical or arty types. She said Mrs Fairbanks sometimes meets her at a bar called Teddy's on Shaftesbury Avenue, where the cast go for after-show drinks. They both like their privacy and don't often entertain at home.'

'How long has Miss Lacey lived with Mrs Fairbanks?'

'Three years. She says they get on well together and that Mrs Fairbanks is more like her best friend than her landlady.'

'Did you ask about the wedding ring?'

'Lavender said she thought Mrs Fairbanks had put it away for safe-keeping.'

'Recently?' Flynn noted his sergeant's familiarity in calling her Lavender. God forbid he'd told the woman his first name.

'No, she didn't think it was that recent.'

Flynn wasn't sure what sort of an answer that was, but didn't pursue the matter. Lavender Lacey seemed to have avoided telling Goodspeed anything of interest. Or perhaps there really was nothing to tell.

When Goodspeed went to mount the steps of the National Portrait Gallery, Flynn stopped him.

'Before we speak with Mr Norris, let's go around the back. Based on what Mrs Fairbanks told us, I want to go through the sequence of events before Marian Dean's death, starting with the delivery of the painting.'

He and Goodspeed walked to Orange Street and entered the gallery through the tradesman's entrance. They made a tour of the Westminster, Royal and Contemporary galleries before examining the trustees' boardroom, the director's office, the secretary's room, the library and trustees' cloakroom.

It was only a few steps from the trustees' boardroom to the cloakroom. Could Marian Dean have seen her brother or Nathan Jennings and been forced to hide? Or could someone have dragged her in there?

The cloakroom had been cleaned and held no traces of where the body had lain. Flynn examined the window with a tape measure. It was too small for a person to climb out, but it was wide enough for the Blanchet picture to fit through. Was it possible someone had been standing on Orange Street, waiting to take it?

They left the cloakroom and went to the Westminster Gallery, where they'd arranged to meet Mr Norris. At their request, he told them everything he remembered about the morning of Monday the fifth of December.

'In your statement, you said one of the ladies asked to see a particular paint-ing, and that's why you left this gallery. Could you take us to the Contemporary

Gallery, following the same route you took that morning to the same picture the lady asked to see,' Flynn instructed.

'Of course.' Mr Norris answered politely enough, but for some reason, colour suffused his cheeks.

Flynn exchanged a quizzical glance with Goodspeed as they followed him down the corridor.

At the entrance to the Contemporary Gallery, Mr Norris hesitated. 'I realise I should have mentioned this earlier, but the lady is in the painting.'

'In the painting?' Flynn frowned. 'What do you mean?'

Mr Norris had now turned a deep shade of red. 'It's best I show you.'

Flynn looked at Goodspeed, who appeared equally confused. When they reached *Dawn Beauty*, they understood the reason for his embarrassment.

'Ahhh.' Goodspeed made a strangulated noise. 'Mrs Fairbanks.'

'The lady said she'd sat for the artist, Algernon Posner. She told me she'd only recently found out it was on display here. I guessed this was the painting in question, so I was able to take her right to it.'

Flynn could appreciate why Mr Norris had been so easily lured away from his post. It must have given him quite a thrill to stand beside Coral Fairbanks and admire her curves on display in this picture. Since meeting her, she'd plagued his thoughts, and this portrait was as if someone had taken an image from his mind and put it on canvas.

Flynn dragged his attention away from the picture in case it seemed as though he were staring at it too intently.

'*Dawn Beauty* by Algernon Posner,' he read aloud, glancing around to find Goodspeed still gaping at the painting while Mr Norris had turned away as if he couldn't bear to look at it.

'I had no idea what was going to happen,' Mr Norris muttered.

Flynn's eyes roamed the rest of the gallery. The Sylvie Blanchet self-portrait had been on the opposite wall, on the same side as the door, so the thief wouldn't have been seen by anyone walking along the corridor. A simple job to wrench it from the wall and make their escape while everyone was preoccupied in the Westminster Gallery.

'What did you do once you'd showed the lady this picture? Did you leave her here?' Flynn asked Mr Norris.

'I... er... we chatted for a few moments about the artist, then I heard voices in the foyer and went out to see what was happening. I have a feeling the lady followed me into the foyer, but I can't be sure. I didn't see her again after that. My attention was taken by the two gentlemen from the press. One of them had a camera, and when they went towards the Westminster Gallery, I went after them.'

Flynn asked Mr Norris to walk them back to the Westminster Gallery and describe the actions of Sid Watson and Luke Chaplin. It became clear that in the chaos, no one had noticed what had happened to the four women who'd entered the gallery that morning. Only the young man who'd delivered the Churchill portrait had been seen leaving by the doorman at the tradesman's entrance. Coral Fairbanks, Marian Dean's companion and even Marian herself, could have been involved in the theft of the painting. And so could Lady Carstairs.

* * *

Flynn had booked a table at L'Escargot on Greek Street. The small French restaurant was a favourite of Oscar Lambourne's, and his old friend was already seated when he arrived.

Oscar was dressed in his customary distinctive style in a fitted green velvet smoking jacket over slim-leg black velvet trousers that highlighted his svelte figure.

'What's this all about then?' Oscar asked after the waiter had left them to browse the menu.

'I told you in my note. I wanted to thank you for introducing me to Countess Stanmore. She's sold three of my paintings already.'

Oscar brushed this aside. 'If that's the reason, I shall walk out. If, however, you wish to discuss recent events at Trafalgar Square, I would be delighted to accept your offer of dinner. And, of course, provide what assistance I can.'

Flynn smiled. He was hoping Oscar could shed some light on Coral Fairbanks' character. 'I had a visit from a Mrs Fairbanks. How well do you know her?'

'Coral? I've known her for years. She's appeared in some of my productions, as did her late husband, Ernest.'

'She's an actress?' Had Coral Fairbanks been putting on a performance in his interview room, Flynn wondered. 'How long has she been on the stage?'

'About twenty years. She started in her youth and had a few memorable roles in her salad days. Mostly hired for her looks. Producers made her the ingénue or the femme fatale. I always put her in comedies. She could have the audience in stitches. Her last big part was as Barbara Undershaft in Shaw's *Major Barbara*. The casting director originally thought she wasn't serious enough for the role, but Coral proved him wrong. She was excellent and got rave reviews.'

'Does Mrs Fairbanks still act?'

'Not so much. She stopped work to nurse Ernest when he became ill with tuberculosis. I know Minerva paid some of their doctors' bills, so Coral could stay at home with him until the end. He was only thirty-four when he died. Taken far too soon. He could have been one of the greats. He was a fine actor with a wonderfully melodic Scottish accent.'

Flynn thought about the Celtic symbols on the wedding ring he'd found at the Hurlingham Club.

'And she didn't go back to acting?'

'Producers have short memories. By the time she was ready to return, the parts had dried up. She's thirty-six now – a tricky age for an actress. Past the ingénue stage but not quite an old hag.'

'Nearly an old hag at thirty-six!' Flynn exclaimed. 'I'm glad I was never drawn to the acting profession. I'd have been put out to pasture by now.'

'A man of forty? You'd be considered in your prime.'

Flynn was glad Teresa wasn't there to hear this imbalance between the sexes. She needed no further encouragement to enter the fight for equality.

When the waiter appeared to take their order, they opted for familiar dishes they'd enjoyed many times before. Oscar chose oysters, followed by côte de veau in a sage and caper sauce with asparagus, while Flynn ordered langoustine bisque, followed by roast rack of lamb with a herb crust and haricots verts – and a large dish of dauphinoise potatoes to share.

'So Mrs Fairbanks is reliant on her job at the gallery?' Flynn asked once the waiter had poured them each a glass of Bordeaux.

'Ernest left her a nice house on Adelphi Terrace. He was able to ensure she had a roof over her head, and one that could provide her with income as she can take in lodgers. But he wasn't wealthy enough to leave her any sort of nest egg. Coral works for Minerva at the gallery and still gets offered the occasional acting role, mainly bit parts. Oh, and she's also somewhat of an artist's muse.' Oscar smiled as he picked up his glass to admire the rich red hue of the wine.

'An artist's muse,' Flynn repeated as the waiter placed a bowl of langoustine bisque in front of him. He'd never been entirely sure what was meant by this phrase. Until today.

'She's modelled for a few painters.' Oscar carefully covered his green velvet jacket with a napkin before tackling his oysters. 'She's a particular favourite of Algernon Posner. You can't have failed to notice that curvaceous figure.'

'I've tried very hard not to notice it. However, this morning I saw more of it than I expected.' Flynn told him how Coral had lured Mr Norris away with the help of *Dawn Beauty*.

Oscar's shout of laughter caused the other diners to look in their direction. 'I'm sorry. I know I shouldn't find it amusing under the circumstances. But that's priceless.'

Flynn was glad their table for two was tucked away in a corner. He had no desire to be overheard.

'Coral Fairbanks and at least two other suffragettes, Marian Dean being one of them, were responsible for displaying the Churchill portrait.'

'Dreadful what happened to that poor girl.' Oscar dabbed at his lips with a napkin. 'In case you suspect her, I would swear Coral wasn't involved.'

'I suspect anyone who was in the National Portrait Gallery that morning. Mrs Fairbanks was there, engaged in an illegal activity.'

Oscar made a dismissive gesture. 'Was it that illegal?'

Flynn wasn't entirely sure on this point. 'It offended public decency,' he hazarded, with no clear idea if this were true. 'And damaged the wall.'

Oscar laughed again. 'You don't have enough room in your cells for all the people in London who offend public decency. Coral's a moderate. Committed to the cause but wary of the militants. She's a member of the WSPU, though not in the inner circle. She's not the type to get involved in anything too illegal.'

'Too illegal? In my book, there's only legal and illegal.'

'I don't believe Coral is capable of murder. But I suppose your job would be easy if we knew what murderers looked like.'

'What about Countess Stanmore?'

'Minerva?' Oscar chuckled. 'I wouldn't like to get on the wrong side of her, although I think she'd draw the line at murder.'

'I meant... is she involved with the WSPU? After all, Mrs Fairbanks works for her.'

Oscar shook his head. 'She knows all the key players. But then Minerva's well connected in all walks of life.'

'Would she ever take part in a suffragette protest?'

'Not a chance. Besides, I was with her that morning. We were invited to a breakfast at Irving's to celebrate the unveiling of the Henry Irving statue.'

Flynn felt somewhat reassured by this. 'Could she have been involved in the theft of the painting? After all, she's a dealer and was nearby at the time.'

'So was I.' Oscar finished his oysters and removed the napkin from his front. 'I'll swear it wasn't Minerva. I don't see how it could have been.'

'She isn't one of your paramours, is she?' Flynn knew Oscar, a confirmed bachelor at forty, engaged in a lively but discreet love life.

'I'm not her type,' Oscar replied with a twinkle. 'Minerva prefers the fairer sex.'

'Oh.' Flynn was somewhat taken aback. 'But she was married to Earl Stanmore.'

'Very happily. Her husband preferred his own sex, too. It made for a harmonious marriage. She was devastated when he died; comforted only by the large fortune he left behind.'

They paused their conversation while a waiter removed their plates and another delivered their main course, garlic and herb-scented steam rising from the dishes.

Once they'd been served, Oscar attacked his côte de veau with relish, his serrated knife reminding Flynn of the wound sustained by Marian Dean. His rack of lamb suddenly didn't look as appetising.

Flynn spooned dauphinoise potatoes onto his plate. 'It's possible Marian Dean witnessed the theft of the Sylvie Blanchet painting. Do you know what it's likely to fetch?' Oscar was an avid art collector and frequented most of the galleries in London.

'Possibly thousands to the right buyer. The artist died fairly young, if I recall. There aren't many of her works around. Minerva would be able to give you a more accurate answer. But there are far more valuable and sought-after pictures in the National Portrait Gallery. Only a collector of Blanchet is likely to be interested.'

'Do you know of any collectors?'

Oscar shook his head. 'I'll ask around and see what I can find out. Honestly, it's really not a painting to murder for. I'd look for other motives. Isn't it always love, sex or money?'

'The Dean family is well off, but no one had anything to gain financially from Marian Dean's death. She was a pretty young woman, so if the killing was personal, it's more likely to be a crime of passion. A jealous lover or something like that.'

Oscar smiled quizzically. 'When is murder not personal?'

'When it's war. *Deeds not Words*. That's the suffragette motto. The Pankhursts have created a military-style operation. They even award their members medals, for goodness' sake. They're waging a war, and when that happens, the other side will retaliate.'

Oscar raised his eyebrows. 'In this case, surely the opposition is the British government. Or even the police.'

'Or someone who hates the suffragettes – some unknown.' Flynn prayed this wasn't the case for two reasons. The first was because they were likely to strike again if that was their motivation. And second, they would be extremely hard to find if they had no connection to their victims. If he failed to catch the killer soon, Flynn would be facing difficult questions, and not just from Bally. The pride Teresa had shown that morning at the Stanmore Gallery was indeed proving to be short-lived. He said as much to Oscar.

His friend just laughed. 'You'll catch them – I have no doubt about that. What you need to find out is what made them go to the National Portrait Gallery that day? How did they know what was going to happen that morning? I presume it couldn't have been a member of staff?'

Flynn shook his head, touched by Oscar's faith in him. 'No one had the opportunity, and from what I can tell, none of them had a motive. You're right. Why choose there when it was the focus of so much attention with that ridiculous portrait?' Flynn finished his meal, refusing the waiter's entreaties to inspect the dessert trolley but accepting the offer of coffee.

'The *Daily Mirror* photograph made it look like a glorious work of art,' Oscar observed.

'It is an impressive piece in its way.' Flynn watched him tuck into a pear and almond tart topped with cream, wondering how he stayed so slim. 'It wasn't some amateur, whoever did it knew how to paint. You wouldn't have any idea who the artist might be?'

'The WSPU count a few artists amongst their members. There's Ethel

Wright, Irene Grayson and Marion Wallace Dunlop. I've seen pictures by all of them. It didn't look much like Marion Wallace Dunlop's style, however, I'd have a better idea if I could see it in the flesh, pun intended.'

Flynn stirred his coffee and considered this. He didn't see any harm in showing it to him; after all, he needed all the help he could get. Oscar had a good eye and might spot something Flynn had missed.

'If you're free, come to Scotland Yard on Saturday afternoon, and you can take a look. *But...* don't tell anyone that's why you're there. I don't want Bally getting wind of it.'

'I can't wait.' Oscar gleefully finished the last of his dessert and then called over the waiter and ordered a brandy.

16

Coral glanced up to find Nathan Jennings and Charles Dean staring in at her.

The countess had positioned her desk close to the door of the Stanmore Gallery, so Coral could greet visitors as they came in and use her charm to entice those who lingered hesitantly outside. Coral thought the countess over-rated her charm, as often one look from her sent prospective customers scurrying away. However, that could be due to the exorbitant price tags under each painting.

Coral stood up and ushered the two gentlemen inside. 'Can I help you?'

'Good morning, Mrs Fairbanks. Mr Jennings and I were wondering if we might have a word about...' Charles Dean's youthful face flushed, and he seemed unable to continue. Jennings patted him on the arm.

'Of course,' Coral replied. It didn't need saying that they were there to talk about Marian.

Nathan Jennings removed his hat, carefully caressing a quiff of pomaded hair back from his forehead. Coral watched the movement, wondering if he knew how vain it made him appear.

'Charles tells me that you were at the National Portrait Gallery on the morning of Miss Dean's death. And that you participated in that rather unsavoury protest.' Jennings wagged a finger at her as if she were a child.

'That's correct,' she replied. 'Although the only unsavoury aspect was Marian's murder.'

Jennings ignored this. 'It's to your credit that you've admitted your involvement to the police. Charles and I have also been speaking to Detective Inspector Flynn, offering him every assistance. And it struck us how important it was to find out who was responsible for the picture.'

'I'm not sure I understand,' Coral replied, knowing precisely what he was after.

Jennings smiled condescendingly. 'Who painted it?'

'Who painted what?' she asked, feigning ignorance.

'The Churchill portrait,' Jennings replied through gritted teeth. 'Who was the artist? Is it someone Countess Stanmore represents?' His eyes flitted around the gallery, as if he expected the artist to materialise from one of the pictures.

'Of course not. It was a prank that in hindsight I realise I shouldn't have taken part in. The countess knew nothing about it.' Coral had adopted her haughtiest tone but softened her voice as she addressed Charles Dean. 'I'm sorry for what happened that morning and wish I could turn the clock back.'

Charles nodded but didn't reply. He'd stayed silent throughout this exchange, which made Coral think it hadn't been his idea to come here. Like her, did he suspect Nathan Jennings had his own reason for asking these questions? And it had nothing to do with finding out who killed Marian.

Jennings gave her another patronising smile. 'I don't doubt your remorse at what happened. However, we must all now play our part in getting to the bottom of it.'

Coral had no idea why he was so keen to find out Irene's identity but he wasn't going to learn it from her. Instead, he could answer one of her questions.

'How did you know a suffragette protest was planned at the gallery?'

The question seemed to fluster Jennings. 'That's confidential information.'

He replaced his hat and seemed to be about to leave, then hesitated. Reaching into the inside pocket of his jacket, he took out a card and handed it to her. 'If you should change your mind, this is where you can reach me.'

Coral noted the residential address in Belgravia. She'd guessed Jennings was here for some reason of his own; nevertheless, it was a relief to have it confirmed that he wasn't on official government business.

'I've told Detective Inspector Flynn that I'll talk to those involved and ask them to visit him at Scotland Yard.' She turned to Charles. 'I'm sure he'll inform your family of any developments in the investigation.'

Coral opened the door to show them out, and as he passed, Charles shot her a strange look.

'I don't know what happened to my sister, but I wouldn't want it to happen to anyone else,' he muttered.

This statement could almost be construed as a threat. However, Coral decided they were the clumsy words of a grief-stricken young man unable to express what he felt, particularly in front of someone like Jennings.

She watched them walk along Pall Mall before dropping into her chair and reaching under the desk for her bag. She tucked Nathan Jennings' card inside and took out Marian's diary, preparing to scour every page for any reference to the politician.

An hour later, she jumped at the sound of the countess's voice.

'I hope that's a racy novel.' Minerva swept into the gallery, dressed in a regal-looking purple silk dress covered in a layer of fine matching lace. Sultan and Seraphine were at her heels, playing with the lace trim that trailed behind her.

'It's Marian's diary.' Coral closed the book and leaned down to replace it in her bag. She didn't like prying into Marian's secret thoughts – the girl deserved more respect than that. But then, whoever killed her hadn't shown her any respect, and as the diary might help Coral discover who that was, she had to pry. 'Her grandmother gave it to me.'

'Ah. Probably not very racy then.' Minerva swirled her skirts, sending the cats skidding across the polished teak floor, much to their delight. 'Does it reveal any secrets? Was she leading a double life as a government spy?'

Coral rose from her desk to gaze out at the traffic on Pall Mall. 'Funnily enough, I was looking for any mention of Nathan Jennings.' She told the countess about her earlier visitors.

'Why would Jennings want to know who painted Churchill? Unless he intends to commission a similar portrait of himself.' Minerva smiled wickedly. 'I can imagine him reclining naked in front of a mirror, admiring his erect quiff.'

For the first time since Marian's death, Coral let out one of her long gurgles of laughter. This made Minerva cackle, and a passerby shot a bemused glance at the pair of women holding on to each other, tears rolling down their cheeks.

As they wiped their eyes, the countess murmured, 'Poor, sweet Marian,' and Coral knew that for her, too, their sudden mirth had released a wave of sorrow.

'Why Marian?' Coral asked for the millionth time.

'I don't know, but when I find out...' Anger flashed in the countess's eyes. 'Are there *any* clues in the diary? Was Marian keeping something from us?'

Coral shook her head. 'The Marian in the diary is the Marian we knew.'

'No secrets?' Minerva seemed surprised that anyone could live a life without having at least one skeleton in their cupboard.

'There is something she never told me about. She'd been meeting a man called Jack.'

'A lover?'

'Nothing serious – it doesn't seem to have amounted to more than a few walks in Hyde Park before she tells him she doesn't want to see him any more.'

'Why?'

'She doesn't give a specific reason, but I suspect it's because he's a policeman.' Coral paused. 'Is it possible he's stationed close to the National Portrait Gallery and saw her there that morning?'

'You think he could have been involved in her death?' Minerva contemplated this. 'Uniformed officers turned up later that morning, though she would have been dead by that time. The first policemen to arrive were in plain clothes. Detective Inspector Flynn was one of them. Are you going to tell him about this?'

Coral hesitated. 'I'd have to explain how I found out. I suppose I could make something up, but first I'd like to find out who this policeman is. If I tell Flynn, I don't know how he'll react. He might want to cover it up.'

One line in the diary had read, *Hope Sherlock Holmes doesn't find out about the Hurlingham Club.* If Marian's policeman friend had discovered her involvement, would he have been angry enough to lash out?

Minerva turned away from the window to look at Coral. 'Guy Flynn doesn't strike me as the type of man to cover things up. I think he's more likely to take you into his confidence.'

Coral wasn't so sure about that. 'I'm going to see Penny and Irene tomorrow. If they agree to talk to him, and he keeps his word about not arresting them, then I might tell him.' She'd held a faint hope the case would be solved before having to ask them to trust Flynn. It had gone without saying that no mention must be made of the countess's involvement. 'Of course, he might arrest me too, especially if he has found my wedding ring.'

Coral told her about Goodspeed's visit to the theatre and the questions he'd asked Lavender.

Minerva picked up one of the cats and began to stroke its ears. 'If Detective Inspector Flynn is foolish enough to arrest any of you, then you'll be represented by the best solicitor in London. One way or another, we will get your ring back. And we will find out who killed Marian.'

Coral nodded, knowing the countess meant what she said. 'Thank you, I appreciate that.'

'I can't have you going to prison. I need you to take care of things here while Harriet and I are in Nice for Christmas.'

Coral smiled at this typical Minerva comment. 'Perhaps you should go earlier than planned.'

The countess raised her thin eyebrows. 'You think the police might suspect my involvement?'

'It's not the police I'm worried about. Why did the killer attack Marian? And how did they know we would be at the gallery?'

'You're concerned I might be in danger?' Minerva hugged the cat closer to her chest.

'We could all be in danger. Anyone known to be a suffragette...' Coral held up her hands in despair.

The countess nodded. 'It's something I've discussed with the Pankhursts. They don't want to spread panic, but they're going to warn their members to be vigilant.'

Coral's despair changed to anger. This could affect the union badly. Women would shrink back into the shadows, too afraid to speak out. Is this what the killer wanted?

Minerva placed the cat on the floor, then squeezed Coral's arm. 'I appreciate your concern. Harriet and I won't alter our plans, but we will be careful, and you must, too. I want the killer to be caught before we leave, and our best chance of that is cooperating with Guy Flynn. Tell Penny and Irene, I would appreciate it if they'd speak with him right away. He's made it clear he's not interested in prosecuting them for the Churchill portrait, so they have nothing to fear.'

'Speak of the devil.' Coral blinked at the sight of Detective Inspector Flynn about to push open the door of the gallery.

Minerva swept her skirts behind her as she went to greet him, wafting Guerlain perfume in her wake. 'Mr Flynn, how lovely to see you.'

Coral noticed she didn't use his professional title, respecting his request for confidentiality.

'Good morning, Countess Stanmore.' Flynn removed his hat, then nodded at Coral. 'Mrs Fairbanks.'

'I wasn't expecting you this morning. I'm afraid my business partner is using my office for a meeting with our bookkeeper. It's just me and Mrs Fairbanks here.' Minerva indicated the empty gallery. 'But I can take you upstairs to my apartment if you'd prefer to speak in private.'

Flynn turned his derby hat over in his hand. 'That won't be necessary. Mrs Fairbanks is aware of my occupation, and the information I seek is of a general nature. It's regarding the self-portrait by Sylvie Blanchet that was stolen from the National Portrait Gallery.'

'How can I help?' The countess looked intrigued. 'I can assure you no one has been here offering it for sale.'

'I'm curious to know what someone would do with it. If no reputable gallery will buy it, why steal it?'

Coral had wondered the same thing. The story had been covered by the national press and probably been reported in some international newspapers. What could you do with a painting that was known to have been stolen from a famous London art gallery?

'Only a private collector of Blanchet's work would be interested,' the countess replied. 'Someone who wants it purely for themselves. You couldn't risk putting it on public display.'

'Are there any such collectors around?' Flynn asked.

'Plenty. Sylvie Blanchet was only thirty-five when she died. Her pictures are few in number and hard to come by. Collectors will pay a great deal for one. Her own family would be keen to get hold of the self-portrait.'

'Really?' Flynn's attention had obviously been caught. 'How do you know?'

'I met Sylvie's daughter, Rosalind, at an exhibition in Paris last year. She has a few of her mother's paintings and would particularly like the self-portrait. She told me she'd once written to Lord Carstairs asking if he'd sell it to her. He didn't reply, and I believe she was rather hurt when he chose to donate it to the National Portrait Gallery.'

'Do you think the Blanchet family could have something to do with the theft?' he asked.

The countess shook her head. 'I doubt it. Sylvie's husband, Henri, is an invalid, and Rosalind cares for her father. They never leave Paris.'

Coral was surprised by Minerva's knowledge of the Blanchet family, but then she did spend a great deal of time in France and had contacts with many overseas art dealers.

'Perhaps they paid someone to steal it for them,' Flynn suggested.

'It's possible,' the countess conceded. 'Henri sold one of his wife's paintings to the Louvre for a considerable amount, so they're not short of money.'

Coral was intrigued by this, and from his expression, so was Flynn. Perhaps their fears that someone was targeting suffragettes were unfounded. Marian could simply have been in the wrong place at the wrong time.

Whatever the truth, the uncertainty was doing untold damage. Coral knew she wouldn't stop being afraid for herself and her friends until they knew who the killer was – and why they'd stabbed Marian.

17

That evening, as Coral turned into Adelphi Terrace, she felt the prickling of fear when she spotted a shadow by the steps leading up to number five.

She hesitated, glancing around to see if anyone else was about, but the street was deserted. As if sensing her unease, the figure moved to stand directly under the lamp post. It was Flynn.

Coral walked towards him, a different kind of apprehension replacing her fear. Was he here to arrest her? She hadn't expected to see him again so soon after his visit to the Stanmore Gallery.

'Mrs Fairbanks. I hope you don't mind me calling on you at your home. Would it be possible for me to come in?'

She nodded, taking the key from her purse and walking up the steps. Inside, she was greeted by the sight of Lavender twirling in front of the full-length mirror in the hallway, wearing what looked like a new navy winter coat.

'Darling, I...' Lavender stopped when Flynn followed her into the house.

'This is Detective Inspector Flynn.' Coral shot her a warning glance before turning to address Flynn. 'And this is Miss Lavender Lacey.'

Flynn removed his hat and nodded at Lavender.

'A pleasure to meet you.' Lavender held out her hand. 'Your sergeant, Evan, is such a darling. All the girls at the theatre are wild about him. Tell him he's welcome to call on us whenever he's in the area, although we're finishing at the Lyric at the end of the year, so he'd better hurry.'

'I'll mention that to him,' Flynn assured her.

'Did you want to speak to me? Only I'm just on my way to the theatre.' Lavender touched Coral's arm. 'I can stay if you'd like.'

'That won't be necessary, unless Mrs Fairbanks would prefer you to be present while we talk,' Flynn replied.

Coral checked the hall clock. 'You're late already. You'll miss curtain up if you don't get going.'

'If you're sure, darling.' Lavender pulled on her gloves and tied the bow of a ridiculously perky navy hat under her chin, before winking at Coral, then saying to Flynn, 'Do give Evan my love.'

'Evan,' Flynn muttered as the front door closed behind her.

Coral smiled as she removed her coat and placed her hat and gloves on the hallstand. Lavender's performance reminded her that this was her house, and she controlled what went on inside it.

'Would you like a whisky and soda?' She walked into the drawing room without waiting for a reply. To her relief, Lavender had lit a cedarwood fire, and the room was warm and cosy with the comforting smell of pine. She poured herself a large whisky, then added a splash of soda from the siphon.

When she turned, Flynn was standing uncertainly by the door. He hesitated a moment before disappearing into the hall and returning without his hat and coat.

Coral poured another whisky and soda and handed it to him, motioning him to take a seat. She settled into an armchair by the fire, wondering if she should turn the tables and start to question him. The interview room at Scotland Yard had been his territory; this was hers. And she was desperate to know if he did have her wedding ring. However, there was no way she could ask without incriminating herself. On reflection, she decided to say nothing and wait for him to speak.

Flynn sat down and took a sip of his drink, seeming unsure where to begin. Coral let the silence drag on, happy to examine him from the comfort of her chair. He was a handsome man, perhaps older than she'd first thought, as she now noticed the grey hairs around his temples. His face was strong, his eyes the best feature, although there was sadness in them. He gave the impression of being a man who'd lived a longer life than his years would suggest.

Eventually, he spoke. 'This is a lovely house. I've always admired the architecture of the terrace.'

'Most of these houses had views of the river before the embankment was built,' she replied.

He nodded. 'Yes, I suppose they would have.'

Not the most scintillating conversation, but she supposed he would get to the point soon.

'I considered selling it after my husband died...' She gazed around. 'But it holds so many happy memories.'

'I feel the same about our house. So many memories of Julia, my wife. And, of course, Teresa when she was just a child.'

Her eyes drifted to his gold wedding band. 'You lost your wife?' she asked tentatively.

'Cancer. Three years ago.'

'I'm sorry.' Coral thought of his pretty daughter. How tragic to lose her mother at such a young age. It had been evident from the pride she'd shown in her father that she was close to him, and it made Coral soften towards Flynn a little.

He cleared his throat. 'There are a few questions I want to ask you about Marian Dean, but I didn't want to mention the subject earlier, in front of your employer, Countess Stanmore. I wasn't sure if she was aware of your... suffragist sympathies.'

Coral was amused by his choice of words but didn't let it show. That day, she and Minerva had discussed how to portray their relationship to Flynn.

'I've told the countess about my involvement in what happened at the National Portrait Gallery. And apologised for doing something that could bring the Stanmore Gallery into disrepute.' Coral looked down into her lap as if repentant. 'The countess has been kind to me over the years, and I was sorry for betraying her trust.'

'How did Countess Stanmore respond?'

'She was understanding, especially when I told her that Marian Dean was a friend. She has suffragist sympathies herself.' Coral enjoyed repeating his phrase back to him. 'Although she advocates peaceful protest only.'

Flynn seemed pleased by this response. 'I was interested in what Countess Stanmore had to say about the Blanchet family and private collectors of Sylvie Blanchet's work. Do you think Marian Dean could have witnessed the theft of the painting or recognised someone she knew in the gallery? Perhaps that's what got her killed.'

'It's something I've considered. But it seems strange that the thief would be anywhere near the cloakroom. They'd be more likely to encounter staff at that end of the building, and there was a doorman at the tradesman's entrance. It would seem more sensible to me to go directly out of the front.' Coral was sure Flynn must have worked this out for himself.

He nodded. 'Did you see anyone in the Contemporary Gallery while you were there with Mr Norris?'

Coral eyed him warily. Did he know about *Dawn Beauty*? She decided on caution. 'As Mr Norris has probably told you, there was no one else in that gallery when we were there.'

'I have a feeling Mr Norris was oblivious to what else was going on in the gallery at that time, as I'm sure was your intention.' There was a hint of amusement in his voice. 'Perhaps he failed to notice the thief in his eagerness to show you the painting by Algernon Posner that you'd modelled for.'

So he had seen *Dawn Beauty*.

She smiled. 'Algernon is a great artist, but I'm not sure the portrait is captivating enough to render a man oblivious to a thief walking out with a canvas under their arm.'

'It added to the confusion of the situation.' Flynn's tone was now accusatory, and Coral wasn't sure if her crime was luring Mr Norris from his post or posing for the picture in the first place.

'What did you think of the painting? As an artist, I mean,' she added, enjoying his obvious discomfort at the question. If he thought she was embarrassed by the picture, he was very much mistaken. She loved *Dawn Beauty* and so had Ernest. He'd even persuaded Algie to sell him one of the smaller preliminary works he'd painted. It still hung on the wall of their bedroom, a reminder of a happy time in her life.

'It's an accomplished piece of work,' Flynn replied impassively.

Coral wondered what he'd really made of the portrait. To her annoyance, what concerned her most was how he thought she compared to that earlier version of herself. She'd been thirty when she'd posed for Algie. In the six years that had passed, she'd lost her husband and struggled to reclaim her place on the stage. She was no longer the uninhibited woman who'd posed in a blue silk robe in that chilly flat in Chelsea.

There was an awkward silence, then Flynn asked, 'Have you thought any more about telling me the names of the man and woman who were with you and Miss Dean at the gallery that morning?'

'I haven't had the opportunity to talk to the people involved. When we spoke before, you said that you wouldn't seek to prosecute them over the Churchill portrait. Is that still the case?'

'I've spoken to my senior officer and he's agreed that we won't charge them with any offence relating to the hanging of the portrait. I'm only interested in finding Miss Dean's killer and the thief who stole the Sylvie Blanchet painting. If they had nothing to do with those crimes, then they have nothing to fear.'

'I'll speak to them.' Coral paused to sip her drink, wondering how far she could push Flynn. 'If you tell me how Nathan Jennings knew we were planning a protest at the gallery.'

Flynn didn't look pleased by this ultimatum. 'Who told you that's why he was there?'

'Charles Dean. I visited his grandmother to pay my condolences. I told them I'd been to see you and promised Florence Dean I'd do everything I could to help you find who killed Marian. She seemed to take some comfort from that,' Coral replied, aware that she hadn't cooperated as fully as he would have wished. She should tell Flynn about the visit she received from Charles Dean and Nathan Jennings, but that would only lead him to ask the same question – who did paint the Churchill portrait?

Flynn stared into his glass. 'Nathan Jennings refused to tell me how he knew a protest was planned.'

Coral scrutinised his expression. Was he lying or had Jennings really refused? 'Can't you force him to tell you?'

Flynn shook his head. 'He's a government minister, and I'm under orders to tread carefully. Do you think Marian Dean could have told her brother what was planned?'

'No. I'm sure she didn't.'

'How can you be certain?'

'She was shocked when I told her he was at the gallery that morning.' Coral also thought Marian would have mentioned it in her diary if she'd been confiding in Charles. The only references to him were the arguments they'd had over her involvement with the suffragettes.

She knew she ought to tell Flynn about the diary, but it contained too much damning information regarding their activities. And it mentioned the countess, though not directly. Marian had used codenames for each of them, but it hadn't been difficult to work out who she was referring to. It would be dangerous to allow Flynn to study it too closely.

It occurred to her that there was someone beside Charles Dean who might have known what was afoot that morning. 'Have you spoken to Lady Carstairs? After all, her husband is in government. What was she doing at the National Portrait Gallery at that time?'

'I've yet to confirm her presence there.' Flynn stroked his beard. 'Have you heard anything about Ronald Carstairs? He's been gone for some weeks now.'

'I've heard the rumours that suffragettes are somehow involved in his disappearance, but I don't believe them. To my knowledge, no one in the WSPU knows where he is. Of course, there are plenty of suffragettes acting independently.' Coral dreaded the repercussions of this. There'd been enough bloodshed already. 'Has Lady Carstairs confirmed her husband is missing?'

'She's reluctant to speak to us.' Flynn must have noticed her look of surprise because he added, 'Unless a crime's been committed, it's difficult to persuade people to talk to us, especially when they're well connected.'

'Her lack of cooperation must mean she has something to...' Coral stopped, realising the implications of what she'd been about to say.

'Something to hide?' Flynn finished the sentence. 'Lady Carstairs refuses to speak to me, Nathan Jennings won't tell me how he came by his information, and you won't give me the names of the two other people with Marian Dean at the gallery that morning.' His voice had risen in frustration. 'As you can imagine, this lack of cooperation, especially from someone who describes herself as a friend of Marian Dean, makes it extremely difficult for me to catch her killer.'

His words stung, and Coral was shocked into silence. When he'd told her he was a widower, she'd felt an affinity between them. But the atmosphere had deteriorated rapidly during the course of their conversation, and she now sensed his hostility.

It wasn't as if she didn't want to trust him. Part of her longed to confide in him and share the burden she carried. What stopped her was the comment he'd made about well-connected people.

He'd practically admitted that the Metropolitan Police gave special treatment to people like Lord and Lady Carstairs and Nathan Jennings. Flynn had been warned to tread carefully with them. So, instead, he'd come to her demanding the names of her friends.

Is that what Jennings and Lord and Lady Carstairs wanted? Were they biding their time, waiting for the blame to be put firmly at the door of the suffragettes, so their secrets could remain hidden?

'I should warn you, Mrs Fairbanks, that I may be forced to arrest you if you don't tell me who was with you on the morning of Marian Dean's murder.'

18

Flynn felt like he was entering a lion's den as he stepped into Sidney Watson's office.

He'd been tempted to get Watson and his photographer, Luke Chaplin, to come to him at Scotland Yard rather than face a grilling by the reporter in the *Daily Mirror* building. Then he'd thought better of it, deciding not to risk letting them loose in the offices of the Metropolitan Police.

'What's the latest on Marian Dean's murder? Do you have any suspects? Can you be more specific about the weapon that was used to kill her? It was a knife, wasn't it?'

Flynn and Goodspeed had been directed to Watson's office on the first floor and hadn't even been offered a seat before the reporter started firing questions at them. It was Luke Chaplin who hastily wheeled over a pair of office chairs and invited them to sit down.

Watson's desk was covered in papers, but they were gathered together in neat piles, and Flynn noted a precise list of questions in the notebook lying in front of the reporter. The man clearly had an orderly mind, which might prove useful.

'I'm here to ask the questions, Mr Watson.' Flynn took out his own notebook, which felt embarrassingly like one-upmanship. 'When did you find out the suffragettes were planning to enact some form of protest at the National Portrait Gallery?'

'It would have been a few days before. Coral Fairbanks came to see me on the morning of Friday the second of December. We go way back. I used to do theatre reviews, and I got to know Ernest and Coral Fairbanks well.'

'Did you know what was planned?'

Sid grinned. 'Not exactly. She said to get there shortly after nine and go straight to the Westminster Gallery if I wanted to see a new portrait of Churchill go on display. Oh, and she told me to bring Luke as we'd definitely want to get a photograph of it.'

'You didn't think to inform the police of what was planned?' Flynn already knew the answer to this but thought he should at least make the point.

Sid shrugged and lit a cigarette. 'Seemed harmless enough to me. What laws were they breaking?'

'Offending public decency.' Flynn repeated what he'd said to Oscar, still with no clear idea if it were true. 'And criminal damage.'

Sid laughed. 'It was a piece of work, wasn't it?'

'Apart from Mrs Fairbanks, did you know who else was present in the gallery that morning?'

'Didn't see any of them. They did a smart job – in and out fast. Shame more people couldn't have seen the portrait.' Sid drew on his cigarette and let out a long breath. 'Tell you who I did see. That politician, Nathan Jennings. What was he doing there?'

'As I said, Mr Watson, you're required to answer my questions, not the other way around. Did you see Marian Dean at any point?'

'No. I told you, I didn't see any of them, not even Coral.'

'What about any other visitors to the gallery that morning? Did you recognise anyone?' Flynn didn't want to name Lady Carstairs.

'There weren't any, as far as I could see. That's why they chose that time on a Monday. Shame really. Best painting I've ever seen hanging in a gallery.'

'What about you?' Goodspeed asked Luke Chaplin, who was perched on the corner of Sid's desk.

'I wasn't really looking. I knew I had to get the camera out quick before they kicked us out. I got a cracking shot. Do you want to see it?' Luke twisted his long, thin body to reach for a photograph lying on top of the filing cabinet behind him.

'Yes, please,' Goodspeed replied, then added, 'you might have caught someone in the background.'

Flynn suspected this last comment was for his benefit. He leaned forward, and, like Goodspeed, couldn't help but smile at the image Luke held up.

The young photographer had captured the scene perfectly. The precariousness of the way the picture was hung on the wall, the sloping canvas and frame – and there, in pride of place in the centre, was a vain-looking Winston Churchill. Robbed of colour, the portrait had a more authoritative appearance, as though it were a work of art to be studied and appreciated for its subtle nuances.

Goodspeed nodded appreciatively. 'Impressive photograph.'

Flynn refrained from comment, wondering if he ought to confiscate the film. But what was the point? The image had already appeared on the front page of the *Daily Mirror*.

Goodspeed was right. It was an excellent photograph, which unfortunately meant there was nothing superfluous in the picture, such as the faces of bystanders.

'If you do pick up any information, come and see me. And in your next article, perhaps you could ask anyone who was present in the gallery that morning to attend Scotland Yard.'

'Of course. Always happy to help the police.' Sid gave him a look that said he expected something in return. 'Perhaps you can help me. I'm keen to know what's happened to Ronnie Carstairs. Any sightings?'

Flynn had anticipated the question. 'I'm not privy to the details of Lord Carstairs' social diary.'

'Neither is the prime minister, it seems,' Sid replied. 'Rumour has it, Nathan Jennings is in line to replace Lord Carstairs as Secretary of State for the Colonies.'

'Really?' Flynn couldn't keep the surprise from his voice.

Sid nodded. 'Something odd going on, isn't there? The suffragettes set fire to Riverside Lodge, then one of them is killed. A painting gifted to the National Portrait Gallery by Ronald Carstairs is stolen, and yet there's still no sign of the man himself. But Nathan Jennings was at the gallery that morning.'

Flynn was glad he hadn't mentioned the sighting of Lady Carstairs. That would give Sid Watson even more to think about. Jack Hall had shown a photograph of her to the front desk attendant at the National Portrait Gallery, and he'd confirmed she was the other visitor that morning.

'What do you think happened to the girl?' Sid stubbed out his cigarette. 'Do you think she was killed by the thief who stole the Blanchet painting? Or was it a reprisal on the suffragettes?'

Flynn rose from his chair and picked up his hat. 'Thank you for your time, gentlemen.'

Back at Scotland Yard, he found a message on his desk from Bally.

'At last.' He showed the note to Goodspeed. 'We've got an appointment to see Lady Carstairs at her London home on Monday.'

'Bally must have told her she was seen at the gallery.'

'Interesting what Sid Watson said about Nathan Jennings being in line to replace Carstairs as Secretary of State for the Colonies. Politically, he gains from Ronald Carstairs' disappearance.'

'It's getting very murky,' Goodspeed agreed. 'Why do I feel we're being taken for fools? It's either the suffragettes or the politicians. Or both. Someone is toying with us.'

As usual, his sergeant had voiced exactly what Flynn was feeling.

After Goodspeed left his office, he spread out all their case notes and witness statements on his desk, trying to find a connection between the disparate events, starting with Ronald Carstairs' disappearance on Black Friday, the fire at Riverside Lodge a week later, followed by the theft of the Blanchet painting and Marian Dean's murder just over a week after that.

Having spent a fruitless hour attempting to link the crimes, he welcomed the interruption of a constable telling him Mr Lambourne was in reception. As Flynn had hoped, it was a quiet Saturday afternoon, with few officers present and no sign of Bally to witness him greeting Oscar and whisking him up the stairs and into his office.

In their years of friendship, Flynn had often enjoyed privileged peeks into Oscar's fashionable world: tickets to the opening of a new play, the occasional theatrical party. But this was Oscar's first glimpse into Flynn's working life, and the drab headquarters of the Metropolitan Police were a far cry from the splendour of the London Palladium.

However, Oscar seemed fascinated by everything, and Flynn dreaded to think what his creative mind would make of it. He could just picture a new musical set in Scotland Yard with dancing policemen.

Flynn indulged his friend and let him peer around his office, even allowing him to study the diagram he'd been working on. Oscar picked it up and pointed to the arrows between the stolen painting and the disappearance of Ronald Carstairs.

'I've been asking around about Sylvie Blanchet and a friend of mine knew her – spent some time with her in Paris in 1896.'

'Is that relevant?' Flynn asked.

'It was the year Sylvie Blanchet painted the self-portrait she gave to Ronald Carstairs.'

'She gave it to him? I must admit, I assumed Carstairs had bought it.' Flynn saw the glint in Oscar's eye and knew there was more to come. 'A self-portrait is quite an intimate gift.'

'Precisely. According to the lady I was speaking to, Ronald was thirty-six at the time, two years older than Sylvie, and a very dashing fellow. He was already a lord and married when he met Sylvie, and they became close.'

'Lovers?'

Oscar nodded. 'She was married, too. It seems to have been a passionate affair while it lasted, resulting in the self-portrait she gave him. Her family believe it's the only self-portrait she ever did.'

'Who is this lady you've been speaking to?'

'An old friend, who doesn't want to be named. I can vouch for her honesty. She only told me the story because I said it could be important. She didn't want to be thought of as a gossipmonger, especially as she's still on friendly terms with Lord and Lady Carstairs. She was at pains to point out that she doesn't know all of the facts. However, Sylvie did confide in her about the affair and said she was in love with Carstairs.'

'Does your friend know when the affair ended?'

'She remembers Sylvie looking dreadful when she saw her early the following year and Sylvie's husband, Henri, telling her his wife was suffering from depression. The next she heard, Sylvie had taken her own life. This was in the spring of 1897. When she went to the funeral, Henri Blanchet blamed Ronald Carstairs for Sylvie's death, saying he'd treated her like a whore. Poor man was left to bring up his eleven-year-old daughter on his own.'

'Suicide.' Flynn tutted, feeling sympathy for Henri Blanchet. 'The more I learn about Ronald Carstairs, the less I like him. Have you ever met him?'

'Yes. A few times at art exhibitions. I confess, I liked him. He was good company. He has a genuine love of the theatre and arts and is very knowledge-able about a range of subjects.'

Flynn sat at his desk and began to add notes to his diagram, trying to work out if this new information had any bearing on the case.

Oscar coughed gently. 'Have you forgotten the real reason for my visit?'

Flynn smiled at his eager expression. He was tempted to make his friend wait but decided he'd earned his reward. Flynn got to his feet and went to unlock the cupboard where he'd hidden the Churchill portrait from prying eyes. Bally had ordered him to keep it under lock and key as, heaven forbid, the home secretary should be embarrassed any further by this piece of impudence.

When he turned the painting around, Oscar let out a bellow of laughter that made Flynn wince. Goodspeed and any officers still at work on this floor were certain to have heard it.

'Wonderful. Completely wonderful.' Oscar clapped his hands together. 'What's going to happen to it? Can I buy it from you?'

'No! I don't own it. Neither does the Metropolitan Police or the National Portrait Gallery. Once this case is over, it will either be destroyed or returned to its owner if we can establish who that is.'

Oscar shook his head in dismay. 'Such a shame. I'd happily pay a considerable sum for it. What a talking point it would be at parties.'

'I'm not showing it to you for your entertainment,' Flynn reminded him. 'You said you might be able to recognise the artist?'

Oscar began to scrutinise the brushwork more closely. 'It's not by Marion Wallace Dunlop, that's for certain. I think I'd rule out Ethel Wright as well. I can't be sure, but the impressionistic style is more in keeping with some of the works I've seen by Irene Grayson.'

19

Coral was still stinging from Flynn's words. Would he arrest her if she didn't give him the names he wanted?

She suspected he would, given the obstacles he was up against. She'd spent most of the night going over their conversation and knew she couldn't shield Penny and Irene any longer. Hopefully, the countess's request that they speak to Flynn would be enough to persuade them to go to him voluntarily, although both had their reasons for avoiding the police.

Coral understood their fears. And, to her surprise, so had Marian. The diary contained shrewd observations about each member of their gang, revealing the girl had been more intuitive than Coral had given her credit for.

Marian had realised Penny's bossiness was due to her eagerness to please the Pankhursts, who'd become her family since she'd left Manchester to live in London. Penny was entirely dependent on them, living in a flat with three other suffragettes that was rented by the WSPU and located just a few doors down from its headquarters at Clement's Inn. She also officially worked for the union and was paid a wage.

Like Marian, Penny loved the life she'd made for herself in London and had no desire to return to the north. Unlike Marian, if Penny were to go back, it would be to the harsh hours of working in a paper mill. Marian had seen how scared Penny was of being forced to resume her old life. Perhaps it was a fear she shared?

Reflecting on this, Coral decided Penny was more likely to be at the garage on a Saturday afternoon, so instead of going to her flat, she headed to Long Acre.

Once famous for its coach and carriage makers, in recent years, motor car dealerships had begun to take up residence on the long road that ran behind Covent Garden market. The double garage was tucked away on the corner with Endell Street, not far from the WSPU headquarters at Clement's Inn – but not near enough for anyone to suspect a connection. However, it was a little too close to Bow Street police station and magistrates' court for Coral's liking.

Sure enough, Penny poked her head around the side door after Coral knocked five times on the double-front doors in quick succession. This was the code to indicate it was friend, not foe.

Penny beckoned her in and pulled out two mismatched chairs from an odd assortment of furniture. Coral sat on one of them, hoping it wasn't as grubby as it looked. Penny took the other, brushing down her long skirt, which seemed to be dotted with grease stains. Her black laced-up boots were covered in a fine grey powder, and a sulphuric odour, like fireworks, hung in the air.

Coral decided not to ask what the smell was – or stay too long. She told Penny about her interview at Scotland Yard.

'As we expected.' Penny flicked her auburn hair over her shoulder in a defiant gesture. 'Did he say why Nathan Jennings and Charles Dean were at the gallery that morning?'

'No. But Charles Dean did.' Coral recounted the information Nathan Jennings had received. 'I don't understand who told him. When was it decided to hang the Churchill portrait there?'

Penny screwed up her face, trying to remember. 'It began months ago and sort of evolved over time. Irene had been dabbling with the painting for a while. I saw it at her flat and thought it was funny. I said she had to show it to Mrs Pankhurst when it was finished. So she did. I believe the original idea was to try to smuggle it into parliament, but it just wasn't feasible. The picture was too big, and Mrs Pankhurst said it would be confiscated and destroyed before anyone clapped eyes on it. I think it was the countess who came up with the idea of hanging it in the National Portrait Gallery.'

It was certainly Minerva's style. 'When was that?'

Penny frowned. 'I'm not sure. I suppose about a month ago, around the beginning of November. Irene had finished the painting, and we started to discuss doing it in December when the gallery would be quiet. Only a few people were in on it: Mrs Pankhurst and Christabel, Minerva and Harriet, and me and Irene. Then you and Marian.'

'But others could have been told?' Coral suggested.

'Not by me.' Penny looked indignant. 'I suppose it's possible one of the others told someone. Do you think whoever killed Marian knew about the plan?'

'I don't know. And neither does Flynn. But it's strange that Nathan Jennings and Charles Dean chose that particular morning to be there.'

Penny bit her lip. 'I guess Flynn asked about me and Irene?'

Coral nodded. 'He knows there were four of us and what each of us did. The countess thinks you should go to him voluntarily. He promises there will be no charges over the Churchill portrait. He's only interested in who killed Marian and who stole the Blanchet painting.'

Penny sighed. 'I suppose I'll have to speak to him. For Marian's sake.'

Coral was relieved to hear it. She hoped Irene would be of the same mind. But Marian's connection to a policeman was still troubling her.

'Did Marian ever mention a boyfriend? Someone called Jack?'

'No. Though I once saw her walking with a young man in Hyde Park. That would have been back in September. They looked sweet together, and I wondered if he might turn her head.' Penny sniffed and reached for a crumpled handkerchief. 'I thought we wouldn't see so much of her after that, but our Marian was made of sterner stuff.'

'She seems to have stopped seeing him because he was a policeman.'

Penny's eyes widened. 'A policeman? Do you think he could have found out about us? That must be it. He must have found out and... and killed her because of it.'

Coral held up her hand. 'There's no evidence of anything like that. It probably has nothing to do with what happened.'

But Penny wouldn't be dissuaded. She began to gabble about a conspiracy by the Metropolitan Police to discredit the Pankhursts and try to force them to leave London.

'They've been told to rid the city of suffragettes,' she said in a shrill voice. 'They want the Pankhursts to return to Manchester so it will be someone else's problem.'

Coral thought this complete nonsense as the Pankhursts were capable of causing trouble in London from wherever they were based. She stood to leave, telling Penny she needed to calm down before they went to see Flynn on Monday. At this rate, they were all going to end up behind bars. And she would never get her wedding ring back.

With relief, Coral left the sulphuric-smelling garage and walked to Tottenham Court Road underground station to take a train to Camden Town. It was only a short walk from there to Irene's basement flat.

In contrast to Penny, Irene was more realistic about the WSPU's attempts to influence the government and openly critical of some of the methods it used.

She had an underlying good sense that Coral respected, which led her to ask, 'What do you think happened to Marian?'

Irene placed her brush in a pot of turpentine and started to clear away her paints, taking her time to consider the question before answering.

Coral watched her from the comfort of an ancient armchair. She always enjoyed her visits to Irene's flat, which was tiny but interesting. It contained a few decent pieces of furniture – two stout armchairs, a sofa, and a heavy pine table – supplemented by objects that had been transformed with paints and fabrics into something colourful and unique. What was once an old crate was now an eccentric coffee table.

Coral noticed that Irene became more attractive when she was creating something. With her short hair and narrow figure, it was easy for her to pass as a young lad when she put on her deliveryman's uniform. But when she was focused on a painting, her features were more animated. A natural beauty seemed to emanate from dark brown eyes that were seeing something more than this shabby basement flat.

In her diary, Marian had commented on the two sides of Irene's personality: the sensible young lady who campaigned for women to get the vote but was pragmatic about their chances of success, and the unconventional painter, who shared the countess's love of art and was equally knowledgeable.

Marian had observed that although Irene was often the most practical one of their gang, there was a part of her that was *dreamy, and she sometimes seems a little lost*'. Coral knew what she meant. Irene did sometimes seem to be separate from everyone else – and this made her judgement less clouded.

Irene sat on the sofa and took a packet of cigarettes from her pocket. 'I get the feeling that what happened to Marian wasn't planned. Could the intention have been to kill a suffragette? And it didn't matter to the killer who it was?'

Even though Coral had similar thoughts, it still filled her with dismay to realise how many others had come to the same conclusion.

Irene lit one of the long French cigarettes she favoured and offered the packet to Coral. Tempted though she was, Coral didn't want to get back into the habit. She hadn't smoked for years, not since Ernest's illness, when smoke would have been bad for his breathing. She'd been dissuaded from starting again by Lavender, who didn't like people smoking in the house as she thought it detrimental to her singing voice.

'Flynn wants to talk to everyone who was at the gallery that morning, including Lady Carstairs.'

Irene let out a long plume of smoke. 'That was odd, although I suppose she might have been going to the unveiling of the Henry Irving statue later on. It's the type of thing she'd be invited to.'

'Do you know her?'

'A little. Lord Carstairs was acquainted with my father. He and Lady Carstairs came to dinner a few times; this was a couple of years ago, when I was living at home. I think Lord Carstairs wanted my father's advice. He'd made one of his outrageous comments, and someone was threatening to sue him.'

Irene's father, Sir Leonard Grayson, was a famous barrister. His speciality was libel, and his cases often made headlines in the newspapers.

'What were they like?'

'Both lively characters. I remember my mother found Lady Carstairs rather shocking. I was brought up in a house where men had interesting conversations and women made small talk and looked decorative. The only thing my parents liked about them were their titles. They're snobs like that. It was around that time I knew I had to leave home if I was to have any sort of life.'

Coral noticed that Irene still called it home, even though she'd been estranged from her family for over two years. She wondered if setting fire to Riverside Lodge had been an act of defiance or perhaps even revenge on her parents.

'Do you ever see your family?'

Irene shook her head. 'My father has forbidden my mother and sister from contacting me unless I renounce the suffragettes.'

Coral wanted to reach out and hug her. This made her recall an observation

Marian had made in her diary that had caused her throat to tighten. Even though Marian had used codenames, it had been obvious she was referring to Coral when she'd written about: *a mother hen who likes looking after us because she's lonely and misses the love she once shared with her husband.*

Coral's eyes had misted over when she'd read this, and they did so again now. To hide her emotion, she stood up to examine the painting Irene was working on. It was of a dramatic, rugged coastline, which was unusual for Irene, who tended towards portraiture or still life rather than landscapes.

'Where is that?'

'Cornwall. I used to go there every summer with my family.'

'And you're painting it from memory?'

Irene shrugged. 'It's more a feeling than an accurate depiction. I haven't been there for a few years, though I'm thinking of going back, and I don't just mean for a holiday.'

'To live?' Somehow Coral couldn't imagine Irene in the country.

'There's an artists' community in St Ives. I haven't made up my mind yet, but I think it's where I should be. Sometimes my work tells me what I want. I seem to be yearning for wild coastlines and endless sea.'

Coral shivered, already imagining the cold wind in such a setting. 'I could never leave London.'

'I thought I couldn't.' Irene glanced around the tiny room she could barely afford on what she earned from selling her paintings. 'It's not much, but I'm fond of this place and of Camden Town. After my family home, it felt good to be living in a working community. Being here and part of the gang was like finally taking part in real life. Marian felt the same about leaving Yorkshire and coming to London. I can't believe her life ended the way it did. There should have been so much more to come for her.'

It was unusual to see the normally composed Irene so emotional, but Coral understood. They'd all found a family in their eclectic little gang and losing Marian was an end to that. No one had said it, though Coral guessed they all knew they couldn't carry on without her. For Irene, it must feel like losing her family for the second time.

Coral sat back in the armchair and asked Irene about the Churchill portrait. 'We need to try to work out who knew we were going to be at the gallery that morning.'

'I started the painting over the summer. I had this bizarre idea to create a voluptuous male in the style of Rubens – you know, all those plump women – and began to experiment with the flesh tones. Then, God knows why, it turned into Winston Churchill and became a sort of male version of the *Rokeby Venus*.'

Coral smiled at her description. 'Who knew about the painting?'

'Penny came over one evening and saw it. I think it was around September. She persuaded me to show Mrs Pankhurst, and of course, the countess got involved. We joked about hanging it in the House of Commons, though we knew that would be impossible. Then, somehow, one thing led to another, and it became the National Portrait Gallery, and even then, we weren't completely serious. But after Black Friday, the whole thing seemed to make sense.'

Coral nodded. It was pretty much what Penny had said. 'Did Marian ever mention a boyfriend? Someone called Jack? They used to meet in Hyde Park. We think she might have ended it because he was a policeman.'

'A policeman boyfriend?' Irene's eyebrows rose. 'No. I got the impression Marian's passions lay in a different direction, in line with the countess's, if you get my drift.' She added with a smile, 'Well, perhaps she hadn't made up her mind on that one. I think the last six months were a series of revelations for Marian.'

Coral knew the truth of this from Marian's diary. Although the girl had shown insight when it came to her friends, she was more naïve about her feelings towards the countess. She seemed to have been in awe of Minerva and intrigued by her relationship with Harriet. The girl obviously suspected they were lovers, and it had made her question her own desires. Coral wondered if Irene was right and that was the real reason Marian had ended her relationship with Jack.

Irene took a final draw of her cigarette and exhaled a long breath. 'I take it Flynn wants names?'

Coral nodded, breathing in the pungent aroma of tobacco and longing for a drag. 'The countess thinks it's best if we all cooperate with him. Penny's agreed. I'm going with her to Scotland Yard on Monday to try to stop her from making a scene. She's got it into her head that this Jack is part of a Metropolitan Police conspiracy to banish the Pankhursts from London. I have a horrible feeling she's going to accuse Flynn of being part of it.'

Irene rolled her eyes as she stubbed out her cigarette. 'I'll come with you for moral support. I'm willing to tell Flynn I was the deliveryman and responsible for painting the Churchill portrait.' She gave a grim smile. 'He might take pity on a fellow artist.'

Coral thought it highly unlikely Flynn would welcome any reference to his life as a painter.

'I'm not sure you should—' Coral was interrupted by the appearance at the window of two pairs of trousered legs coming down the steps to the basement flat.

20

Irene Grayson opened the door as though she'd been expecting them. Flynn entered the flat, Goodspeed at his heels, only to come face to face with Coral Fairbanks, seated in an armchair with a quizzical look on her face.

Irene removed some clutter from a sofa, and he and Goodspeed sat awkwardly on the too-small seat. Their combined bulk seemed to fill what little space was remaining in a tiny room that smelled of cigarettes and turpentine.

There was an awkward silence, then Flynn cleared his throat to begin. But before he could say anything, Irene cut in.

'By your visit, I assume you know I was with Coral at the National Portrait Gallery on the morning of Marian Dean's death. What you may not realise was that I was the one who delivered the picture to the gallery.'

'Ahh,' Goodspeed said in surprise, giving away the fact that they hadn't known the deliveryman was a woman.

Flynn didn't respond immediately. His attention was captured by the paintings covering the walls. Propped on an easel was Irene's latest work, a seascape depicting a rough sea and rugged cliffs. He noticed her landscapes were more conventional than her portraits, which tended towards the abstract.

But all were highly accomplished and, in some ways, unexpected. As was Irene Grayson herself. She had a deep voice and was wearing a fitted dress suit that was severe in its cut. The impression was almost masculine, though not quite. She was feminine in a very precise way with high cheekbones and intense brown eyes.

'Irene and I were just discussing the situation. We had planned to call on you at Scotland Yard on Monday morning to make a statement.' Coral gave him a direct look. 'Along with Miss Penelope Bright. She was the auburn-haired lady with Marian.'

At last, he had all their names. 'Thank you.' Flynn held her gaze. 'I appreciate your cooperation.'

'What gave me away?' Irene asked, lighting a cigarette. She didn't seem perturbed by their presence in her home.

'Oscar Lambourne thought he detected your style in the Churchill portrait. Did you paint it?'

Irene nodded. 'What did Oscar think of it?' She offered the packet of French cigarettes in their direction. Flynn declined but Goodspeed accepted, then after one puff seemed to regret the decision.

'Mr Lambourne was most complimentary.'

Irene smiled. 'I bet he tried to buy it.'

'I'm afraid it's staying in my office for the time being,' Flynn replied, having no idea what he was going to do with the damn thing.

'Tell him that if I ever get it back, I'll sell it to him.'

'Do you sell much of your work?' Flynn ignored Goodspeed's look of surprise at the question. Her comment had made him curious about a possible connection between Irene and Countess Stanmore.

'Bits and pieces here and there. Coral sometimes gets the odd painting into the Stanmore Gallery where she works, if it's something that takes the fancy of Countess Stanmore. And there are a few other galleries in London that are happy to sell my pictures depending on the subject matter.' Irene grinned. 'Some of my paintings aren't to everyone's taste.'

Flynn nodded, satisfied that she didn't seem to be aware of his own connection with the Stanmore Gallery. He turned to more relevant matters.

'Mrs Fairbanks mentioned you saw Lady Carstairs in the National Portrait Gallery when you delivered the painting.'

Irene nodded. 'I was waiting to wheel the picture into the Westminster Gallery and looked down the corridor to see if anyone was coming. I saw her by the front desk in the foyer.'

'Do you know her well?'

'I met her a few times when she and Lord Carstairs visited my family home. That would have been a couple of years ago.'

'Do you know when your father last saw Lord Carstairs?' Oscar had told him a little about Irene's background, and he knew her father was the prominent barrister, Sir Leonard Grayson.

'No idea. I left home two years ago, and I'm estranged from my family. They don't approve of my politics.'

It was a simple statement that held no bitterness. Nevertheless, it saddened Flynn. He knew he could never bear to be apart from Teresa, no matter what she did. Of course, he would fear for her if she became a suffragette and would do all he could to protect her, but he would never cast her out.

Coral interrupted his thoughts. 'Is Lady Carstairs still refusing to speak to you?'

'I have an appointment to see her on Monday. I also plan to talk to Nathan Jennings and Charles Dean again.' Flynn felt some sympathy for Coral and her friends. They'd agreed to speak to him even though they were incriminating themselves while others in more protected positions had yet to be as frank.

'Nathan Jennings and Charles Dean visited me at the Stanmore Gallery,' Coral told him. 'Jennings wanted to know who painted the Churchill portrait.'

'Why would he want to know that?' Flynn asked sharply. 'Did he give a reason?'

Coral shook her head, but Flynn noticed her lips twitch as if she was remembering a joke. He'd have to ask her about it when they were next alone together. Would it be too inappropriate to call at her home for a second time?

He pushed the thought away and turned to Irene. 'Do you know anyone who may have revealed your plans to someone in government?'

Irene shook her head. 'I started working on the painting in late summer with no clear idea of what I was going to do with it. Then someone came up with the notion of hanging it in the National Portrait Gallery. We only decided on the date about a week before.' She glanced at Coral for confirmation.

Coral nodded. 'Irene, Penny, Marian and I had dinner together at my house. That would have been on the twenty-sixth of November, and that's when we came up with the plan.'

'Was your lodger, Miss Lacey, there?' Goodspeed asked, stubbing out his half-smoked cigarette.

Coral shook her head. 'Lavender would have been performing, as it was a

Saturday. She's not involved with the suffragettes and knew nothing of our plans.'

Flynn thought Goodspeed was a little too eager to establish Lavender Lacey's whereabouts. Was he worried his idol might not be the woman he imagined her to be?

After a few more questions, Flynn stood, eager to leave the confines of the claustrophobic flat. It hadn't been built for a man of his size.

'I look forward to seeing you and Miss Bright on Monday.' He gave Coral a smile that he hoped conveyed his appreciation for her help, then turned to Irene. 'As you've already given us your account of events, there's no need for you to attend, unless you think of anything else that might be relevant.'

Irene nodded, opening the door to show them out. Goodspeed mounted the steps ahead of him, and as Flynn went to follow, she touched his arm.

'Coral is innocent in all this,' she said in a soft voice, barely above a whisper. Before he could respond, she closed the door.

What was that supposed to mean? That the others were guilty? But guilty of what?

He caught up with Goodspeed, and they strode along the pavement towards their carriage.

'Do you want me to call on Miss Lacey and ask her about the night of the twenty-sixth?' Goodspeed asked.

'That won't be necessary, Evan,' Flynn replied. 'We'll take Mrs Fairbanks' word for it for the time being.'

Goodspeed appeared momentarily confused by this use of his first name, then reddened. 'I didn't say she could call me that. She—'

'I've had the pleasure of meeting Miss Lacey and appreciate your predicament.'

'Do you think she's involved?' Goodspeed asked anxiously.

'Not directly, but I think she's loyal to Coral Fairbanks. I think all of Mrs Fairbanks' friends are loyal to her, which makes me wonder if she's the ringleader in all this, despite her protestations at being on the sidelines.'

Goodspeed didn't seem convinced. 'Can't see it myself.'

Flynn sighed. 'You're probably right. Perhaps I'm becoming too suspicious, imagining some shadowy figure in the background pulling the strings. Let's call it a day and try to enjoy the rest of the weekend. On Monday, we'll get to meet Miss Penelope Bright, and in the afternoon, we need to go over to

Leinster Gardens to talk to Lady Carstairs. Things might look clearer after that.'

They headed back to Scotland Yard, then went their separate ways. But despite what he'd told Goodspeed, Flynn didn't go home, although his temples were throbbing, and he felt a headache coming on. His usual remedy would have been to hide himself away in his attic studio and paint until the tension had lifted. But today, some impulse seemed to compel him to return to the National Portrait Gallery.

'We're closing soon,' said the attendant on the front desk as Flynn entered.

'I won't be long,' he promised. The man wasn't a member of staff he'd seen before and he felt safe to browse the Contemporary Gallery without arousing comment.

The gallery was empty, so he made his way directly to the one picture he'd come to see. *Dawn Beauty*.

He'd been too embarrassed to stare at it for long in front of Goodspeed and Mr Norris. Without an audience, he leaned in to study it in detail, telling himself it was the painting he admired, not the model.

And it was a fine piece of work, worthy of its place on these walls. The precision of the brushwork, the use of light and shade, and – he had to confess – the allure of the woman, all combined to make it a captivating portrait.

He dwelt for some time on the areas of the body that were on display – the contours of the breasts and the curve of the buttocks enticing you to imagine the areas that were hidden – before examining the composition, which led you to believe the first light of dawn was pouring through the window.

Sunlight glinted on Coral's gold hair and on the pale blue silk robe she held to her left breast with her left hand. And on one slender finger of that hand was a wedding ring. His breath caught when he noticed it.

Flynn moved in closer, then rested his head in his hands and groaned. It was a simple silver band engraved with Celtic love knots.

21

Scotland Yard had once been a place of mystery to Coral. Now she'd visited twice in the space of a week and was becoming familiar with its unwelcoming reception, grey interview room and scent of disinfectant.

She wondered where Flynn's office was in the building. It amused her to think that the Churchill portrait was there. Had he hung it on his wall or hidden it away? Probably the latter, although he'd obviously shown it to Oscar Lambourne.

Coral and Penny were escorted to the interview room by the young detective constable who'd stood by the door the last time. It seemed he was going to perform the same duty again.

Flynn and Detective Sergeant Goodspeed were seated when they entered, and Flynn thanked them for coming. He got straight to business and asked Penny to give her account of what happened on the morning of Marian's death.

Penny sounded a little rehearsed, but that couldn't be helped. Coral had guided her through what to say to avoid unnecessary references to the Pankhursts, the countess and police conspiracies.

'And you left before Sidney Watson and Luke Chaplin arrived?' Flynn asked.

'Not quite. I heard them in the foyer and left the Westminster Gallery by going through the Royal Gallery. When everyone had gone to look at the portrait, I went out of the front entrance.'

'What did you do then?'

'I walked around to Orange Street where Irene Grayson was waiting by the car. She handed me the keys, and I drove back to Clement's Inn.'

'Is that where the car's normally kept? Is there a garage there?'

'Not exactly. The yard behind the WSPU offices is covered, and we park it there.'

It was perfectly true that the car was parked there when it was being used for official business. More often than not, it was in Penny's garage, where it was kept when being used for unofficial business.

'What model is the car and who does it belong to?' Flynn asked.

'It's a Vauxhall landaulette owned by Mrs Pankhurst. She doesn't drive, but there are a few of us who can, so we take it in turns to be her chauffeur.'

'Did Mrs Pankhurst know what you were using her car for that morning?'

'She wasn't around. She was in Manchester that day. The car keys are kept in the office, and we have permission to use it for WSPU business.'

If Flynn noticed the ambiguity of her answer, he didn't pursue it. Coral thought it was because he was only interested in murder and not suffragette protests. She thought wrong. His next question came like a punch to the stomach.

'Did you use the car on the night of Friday the twenty-fifth of November? On WSPU business?' Although he addressed the question to Penny, Flynn's eyes locked with hers – and she didn't like what she saw.

The twenty-fifth was the night of the fire at Riverside Lodge. Without meaning to, she touched the empty space on her ring finger.

'Er, I... No. I don't think I did.' Penny wasn't as rehearsed with her answer this time.

'Are you sure?'

'The twenty-fifth?' Penny now took her time to consider. 'That would have been the night of a public meeting we held in Lambeth. I remember, I walked there with Irene Grayson. So, no, I couldn't have used the car that night.'

Clever girl, Penny. Coral's heart began to beat more normally.

'I presume other people can vouch for your attendance at this meeting?' Flynn asked with a hint of mockery.

Penny agreed, a retaliatory glint in her eye. 'There were quite a crowd of us.'

Penny and Irene's alibis would come from suffragettes who'd been at the meeting and would happily claim the pair were with them. Flynn suspected this, but he couldn't prove they were lying, and that was all that mattered.

He turned to Coral. 'Were you at this meeting?'

Was it her imagination, or had he just looked at her left hand? She was fairly certain he had found her ring at the Hurlingham Club and suspected her involvement; otherwise, why would he have asked Lavender if she wore a wedding ring? She knew she needed to be careful with her answers. There was nothing on the ring to indicate it was hers, but she would want to reclaim it at some point. Preferably, when she could prove she was innocent of murder and arson.

'I think I was at home.' She had been at home for some of that night, and she preferred to tell a half-truth than to lie and say she'd been at the same meeting as Penny and Irene.

'Alone?' Flynn asked.

'Yes. I was supposed to meet Lavender for after-show drinks at Teddy's Bar, but I didn't go in the end.'

'Why not?'

'I was tired.'

Flynn rubbed his beard, seeming to deliberate over his next question. When it came, it made her heart lurch.

'I noticed you just touched the ring finger of your left hand. Do you normally wear a wedding ring?'

He knew. Or at least he suspected. A battle raged in Coral's head. If she admitted to being at the Hurlingham Club, it might be enough for him to charge her with involvement in the arson attack. But if she denied being there and denied owning the ring, she'd scupper any chance of getting it back.

An uncomfortable silence fell, and Coral withered under Flynn's hostile gaze. She glanced towards the door, desperately wanting to leave this miserable, grey room and have time to think about what she should say.

Her throat was tight when she replied in a hoarse voice. 'I lost it recently.' Coral lifted her eyes to Flynn's in desperate appeal. 'I should very much like it back.'

She waited for a reaction, but none was forthcoming. He sat motionless, his face like stone.

Then suddenly, he stood up. 'Thank you for coming to see us, Miss Bright.

Would it be possible for Detective Sergeant Goodspeed to call on you at Clement's Inn and see the motor car in question?'

Penny was out of her chair in an instant. 'Of course. I'll try to ensure he receives a warm welcome.'

Coral almost smiled at how Penny managed to make this sound like a threat. Her own fight was gone, and she got slowly to her feet, trying desperately not to cry.

'Thank you,' Flynn said in a low voice, his expression softer. 'Detective Constable Hall will show you out.'

The young constable stood aside, holding open the door, and Penny shot out like a greyhound from its trap. Coral was fast on her heels when she heard Flynn say, 'Then come up to my office, Jack.'

Penny must have heard, too, because she stopped in her tracks, causing Coral to walk into the back of her.

They both turned to stare at Detective Constable Hall. Could this be Marian's Jack? Coral remembered Marian had called him Sherlock Holmes – and this young man was a *detective* constable.

'Is everything alright?' he asked nervously. Flynn and Goodspeed were watching in confusion.

Coral was tempted to demand there and then if he'd known Marian, but suspected Flynn wouldn't like her questioning one of his officers. Penny had no such scruples.

'Jack?' She peered at him. 'You're the man I saw in Hyde Park with Marian.'

Bright spots of pink appeared on Detective Constable Hall's cheeks, and his eyes darted towards Flynn. 'I... I knew her a little.'

Coral saw Goodspeed's mouth drop, and Flynn's face turn back to stone.

'Come here and sit down,' Flynn ordered. 'All of you.'

They did as they were told, Flynn dragging over another chair for Jack to sit on, so all five of them were huddled around the table.

Penny was about to speak, but Coral put a hand on her knee and shot her a warning glance. Fortunately, Penny got the message to shut up and let the policemen do the talking this time.

Jack sat upright in his chair; his eyes fixed on Flynn. 'I should have said something sooner—'

'Yes. You should,' Flynn barked. 'Why didn't you?'

'I don't know.' Jack ran a hand through his dark blond hair. 'At first, I was in shock.'

'Did you know Miss Dean was at the gallery that morning?' Goodspeed asked. He spoke gently, giving Coral the impression he was fond of the lad.

Jack shook his head. 'No, of course not, sir. I had no idea. When I arrived, only staff were there.'

'Were you the first policeman to arrive?' Coral ignored the sharp look Flynn gave her.

'Yes,' Jack said in a whisper. 'At about ten o'clock.'

Goodspeed came to his rescue. 'After the desk sergeant received a message from Mr Scott, the director of the gallery, I sent Detective Constable Hall to see him, saying Detective Inspector Flynn and I would be along shortly.'

'What happened when you got there, Detective Constable Hall?' Flynn had obviously decided to take back control of the questions.

'I was shown to the Westminster Gallery by Mr Scott, who told me that they'd closed the doors to the public. I went to the front entrance to wait for you and Detective Sergeant Goodspeed to arrive and to make sure no one else entered. They hadn't discovered a painting was missing at that stage.' Jack paused. 'After you told me to check each room in the building, I decided to start at the top and work my way down. The cloakroom was the last place I looked.'

'You saw it was Marian?' Coral felt some sympathy for Jack but couldn't understand why he hadn't identified her immediately.

'I just saw a woman's body, the face half hidden by a hat.' Jack's voice became hoarse. 'I suppose I had no reason to think it was her. I ran to fetch Detective Inspector Flynn and Detective Sergeant Goodspeed from Mr Scott's office. I stood outside the cloakroom, and when they came out and said they thought the lady was Miss Marian Dean, I couldn't believe it.' Tears filled his blue eyes. 'I waited for the stretcher to arrive and offered to help. I had to know for sure. When they lifted her, I could see that it was Marian.'

Jack pulled a handkerchief from his pocket and wiped his face. 'I'm sorry.'

Coral looked at Flynn. 'How did you know the body was Marian's?'

'I found a letter in the pocket of her coat,' Flynn replied. 'It was from her mother. I called on the Dean family, and Charles Dean attended the mortuary with me to confirm it was her.'

Coral saw the pain in Jack's eyes, and asked, 'How did you meet Marian?'

'I was in Hyde Park with two of my sisters. They wanted to listen to Mrs

Pankhurst at Speakers' Corner. It was the last Sunday in August, and I ended up standing beside Marian. We got chatting, and I said I'd be there again next Sunday. We met a few times over the following months.'

This fitted with what Marian had written in her diary. 'When did you last see her?'

'Towards the end of October in Hyde Park. It was starting to get colder, and I said we'd have to find a warmer place to meet.' He sniffed. 'That's when she said she couldn't see me any more.'

'Were you keen on her?' Coral felt sorry for the boy. Marian hadn't wanted to hurt his feelings but was too confused about her own to carry on the relationship.

He gave a rueful smile. 'Keener on her than she was on me. When I asked why we couldn't meet, she said that she was too busy and had to focus on her work for the WSPU.'

'You knew she was a suffragette?' Flynn's face was still like granite.

'She didn't make a secret of it. I told her she should be careful. I warned her not to get mixed up in anything...' Jack's voice shook '...illegal.'

Penny gave a derisive snort. 'I think you were using Marian to spy on the WSPU.'

'I... I wasn't,' Jack stammered. 'I liked her.'

'Penny.' Coral gripped her arm, willing her not to make the situation worse. 'I don't think Jack had anything to do with Marian's death.'

If he had killed Marian, he must have done it as soon as he'd arrived at the gallery. But that was nearly three-quarters of an hour after Marian should have left the building. Coral thought it more likely that Marian had been killed earlier, when she was trying to leave, and that she was already lying dead in the cloakroom by the time Jack Hall got there.

Jack looked almost pathetically grateful at her words.

'Maybe not. But he's part of the conspiracy to lay the blame at our door. And so are they.' Penny pointed at Flynn and Goodspeed. 'They're acting on the home secretary's orders to try to discredit the Pankhursts and the WSPU when we haven't done anything wrong.'

Apart from arson, Coral thought. She'd hoped that she and Flynn would be able to bring opposing sides together with the common goal of finding Marian's killer. The meeting at Irene's flat had been cordial enough, and she got the impression Flynn had rather admired Irene and her paintings.

But Penny was a different kettle of fish. She was bringing all their differences to the fore, and any chance of reaching an understanding was looking remote. Perhaps it had been naïve of her to have believed it was possible. Flynn obviously knew they'd been involved in the fire at Riverside Lodge – a far more serious crime than displaying a silly portrait of a politician – and not one he could overlook.

If he had found her ring, and it was almost certain that he had, Coral didn't think she would ever get it back.

22

'That turned into a complete bloody fiasco.' Flynn gripped the carriage door as the wheels hit a pothole. 'They ended up interviewing us. Jack should have told us straightaway that he knew Marian Dean.'

Flynn had escorted the two women off the premises, Penelope Bright muttering about conspiracies all the way. Coral had tried to shut her up with little success.

'It sounds like he got himself into a bit of a state after he found the body.' Goodspeed leapt to the lad's defence as Flynn had known he would. 'It doesn't seem to have amounted to more than a few strolls around Hyde Park. He didn't know her well.'

'Not for the want of trying,' Flynn retaliated. 'She was the one to end it. How often has that been a motive for a male to act violently towards a female? Rejection and jealousy are always reasons for murder.'

'Mrs Fairbanks doesn't think Jack killed her,' Goodspeed pointed out.

'No,' Flynn conceded, calming a little. 'It doesn't really make sense that he came across her in the cloakroom and decided to stab her. However, it is possible.'

Goodspeed shook his head. 'I can't see it. But let's speak to him again in the morning.'

They'd been late leaving and were now in a hackney carriage hurtling towards 22 Leinster Gardens to speak with Lady Carstairs before she journeyed back to her country home of Biddenden House in Kent.

On arrival, they discovered that Leinster Gardens was actually a long road of Victorian townhouses running off Bayswater Road. The door to number twenty-two was opened by a butler aged about sixty, wearing a formal black suit with tails, who introduced himself as Mr Treadaway. He had the air of a man who'd been in service for a long time, and by the way he examined Flynn and Goodspeed, saw it as his duty to protect his master and mistress from any unpleasantness.

Satisfied that they had an appointment, he showed them into the drawing room where Lady Carstairs was seated, announcing their arrival with solemn formality.

The luxurious townhouse was as different from Irene Grayson's shabby basement flat as it was possible to be. Had she once lived in a place like this with her rich family, Flynn wondered? It was a lot to give up for your political beliefs.

Lady Carstairs gestured for Flynn and Goodspeed to sit in two high-backed leather chairs that appeared to have been positioned in preparation for their visit. As he examined her, Flynn reflected that, as with Irene Grayson, his expectation was proving contrary to the reality.

He'd imagined Irene to be a dramatic young woman, affecting to live the life of an impoverished artist while enjoying a comfortable allowance from her family. What he found was a sensible young woman who seemed content with the choices she'd made despite her reduced circumstances.

By contrast, he'd pictured Lady Violet Carstairs as a haughty, primly dressed prude who considered it beneath her dignity to talk to lowly policemen. The sight of her wild red curls tinged with grey and her vivid purple silk gown with silver embellishments led him to think he might have been mistaken for a second time.

This was confirmed when she greeted them with the words: 'Don't scold me, but I've had a gin already. The last few weeks have been beastly.'

'I can imagine.' Flynn exchanged a glance with Goodspeed. Given what they knew of Ronald Carstairs, perhaps it shouldn't have come as such a surprise to find his wife was equally forthright.

'Would you like a gin? Or whisky? Or aren't you allowed? Treadaway will get you a tea or coffee if you'd prefer.'

'A coffee would be most welcome,' Flynn replied, and Goodspeed nodded his agreement.

Mr Treadaway gave a slight bow and left the room.

'Is this about the fire? I'm absolutely furious.' Lady Carstairs waved a wrist heaving with silver bangles, sending wafts of jasmine in their direction. 'Don't get me wrong, I'm all for women getting the vote. I just don't see how setting fire to my new house will achieve it.'

'I'm sorry for what happened at Riverside Lodge. The fire brigade tells me that they managed to put out the blaze before it did too much damage.'

'The outside is still structurally sound, the builders are just assessing what needs to be done inside.'

Mr Treadaway entered the room with a coffee pot and two cups on a silver tray. Flynn waited until the butler was right in front of him before he asked, 'Has your husband been to see the property?'

He saw Mr Treadaway's mouth tense and his eyelids flicker.

'Ronnie leaves that kind of thing to me,' Lady Carstairs said breezily. Perhaps a little too breezily. 'He's not the most practically minded man.'

'Is he here today?' Flynn glanced pointedly towards the door that Mr Tread-away had just opened. The butler caught his eye for the briefest of seconds before leaving the room and closing the door behind him.

'No. I'm sure you've read the newspapers. Ronnie's being very naughty. But can you blame him? Black Friday wasn't his fault, yet it's our house they decide to set fire to. It wasn't Ronnie's idea to go for another election.'

Flynn couldn't help noticing that she seemed more upset about the damage to Riverside Lodge than her absent husband. He'd been warned not to push the matter; after all, Ronald Carstairs hadn't been reported missing. But something odd was going on here.

'When you say naughty, what do you mean? Where is your husband, and when did you last see him?'

Lady Carstairs took her time before answering. 'Do you know, I'm not entirely sure.'

'About where he is or when you last saw him?' Flynn asked patiently.

'Both. I think he may have gone to Bruges. Or Paris. Things have been so stressful for him recently in Westminster, he needed to get away from it all for a while.'

'When did he go?'

'A few weeks ago. I spend most of my time at our country estate. This is Ronnie's domain.' She gestured around the room. 'It's fine for somewhere for him to stay when he's sitting in parliament but far too small for entertaining. That's why we were building Riverside Lodge. My father died recently and left me some money. It was my big project.'

Although most people wouldn't consider 22 Leinster Gardens small, Flynn could see her point. It was a modest house that was stylish but not lavish. Flynn rather liked the eclectic décor – Ronald Carstairs clearly favoured Middle Eastern art and colourful Persian furnishings.

Lady Carstairs followed his gaze. 'Ronnie and I love collecting unusual pieces. Art is a shared passion. It's what brought us together.'

'That brings me to another matter I'd like to ask you about. Were you at the National Portrait Gallery on the morning of Monday the fifth of December?'

Lady Carstairs seemed to freeze for a moment and then regained her composure. 'Yes, I was. Early too – it must have been when that poor girl was murdered. I met her once when her brother worked for my husband as a private secretary.'

'Did your husband meet her?' Flynn felt a flicker of excitement tinged with exasperation at yet another connection between Marian Dean and Ronald Carstairs.

'Yes, we invited Charles Dean to bring the girl and her grandmother over to tea. Ronnie found her charming. You know what men are like.'

Could Lady Carstairs have killed Marian out of jealousy? Perhaps she thought the girl was her husband's mistress, though from what he'd learned of Marian, this seemed unlikely.

'We did ask that anyone who was at the National Portrait Gallery that morning should contact us at Scotland Yard,' Flynn informed her, an edge to his voice.

By her shrug, he could tell that Lady Carstairs cared little for this. 'I didn't read about what happened until later that night when I was back home at Biddenden House. And I didn't see any point in speaking to you as there was nothing to tell.'

Flynn tried not to let his irritation show. 'Why did you go to the gallery that morning?'

'I'd been invited to the unveiling of the Henry Irving statue,' she replied promptly.

'That wasn't until eleven o'clock.'

'There was a breakfast beforehand.'

'And did you go to that breakfast? It was at Irving's restaurant, I believe.'

She seemed a little put out by his knowledge of the event, as Flynn had hoped. He wanted her to know that if she lied to him about being there, he would find out.

'I didn't,' she admitted. 'Nor to the unveiling of the statue. I'd popped into the National Portrait Gallery as I didn't want to arrive at the breakfast before anyone else. When I came out, I remembered I had some urgent correspondence to deal with from the insurers of Riverside Lodge, so I came back here.'

Flynn wondered why she was lying about her reason for visiting the gallery. It wasn't something he could accuse her of outright, so he asked, 'Who did you see when you were there?'

'The attendant on the front desk and the one in the Actors and Dramatists Gallery. Oh, and there was another attendant in the Westminster Gallery when all the fuss kicked off.'

'So you went into the Westminster Gallery?' Goodspeed had his pocketbook out and was making note of her comments.

'I heard a noise in the foyer and went to see what was happening. The attendant seemed to be objecting to a gentleman coming in with a camera. They were talking about a new Churchill portrait, so I followed them to the Westminster Gallery.' She tittered. 'I'm glad I did. That painting was an absolute hoot. I suppose I must be one of the few people who got to see it in all its glory.'

'Who was in the gallery?' Goodspeed asked.

Lady Carstairs thought about this. 'Two attendants and the gentleman with the camera and his companion, who I realised were probably from the newspapers. A blonde lady was standing in the archway that goes through to the Royal Gallery. I think she might have been a suffragette because when she saw Nathan Jennings and Charles Dean appear, she left in a hurry.'

'You saw Nathan Jennings? Did you speak to him?'

'No. Fortunately, he didn't see me.' Lady Carstairs took a gulp of gin. 'He'd only start lecturing me about Ronnie skipping town, so I decided to follow the blonde lady out through the Royal Gallery.'

'Did you go into the Contemporary Gallery or see anyone in there?'

She shook her head. 'I followed the lady into the corridor and then through the foyer and out of the main doors.'

'Did you see where she went?' To his consternation, Flynn felt a strange sense of relief that what she'd told them so far tallied with what Coral had said.

'I stood on the corner to hail a taxi, and she seemed to disappear into the crowd. She wasn't carrying a picture under her arm if that's what you want to know.'

Flynn did want to know and was delighted to hear it. Since discovering the wedding ring he'd found at the Hurlingham Club was Coral's, he'd come to realise how much he didn't want her to be involved in any of this. Lady Carstairs' testimony would seem to rule out Coral as the murderer or the thief.

'What can you tell me about the stolen painting? I believe your husband donated it to the gallery.' Flynn was glad Lady Carstairs had been the one to raise the subject of the Blanchet picture.

'We got to know the Blanchets around fourteen years ago when we spent the summer of ninety-six in Paris. Sylvie Blanchet gave Ronnie the painting as a gift.' Lady Carstairs related this information in hard, clipped tones before taking another gulp of gin.

Flynn guessed she knew about the affair. It would have been difficult to ignore the significance of a lady giving a gentleman a self-portrait as a gift.

'Why did your husband donate the picture to the National Portrait Gallery?'

'I encouraged him to. It was a way of honouring Sylvie. She died far too young, and we wanted more people to recognise how talented she was.'

The answer was too pat, as if this was something she'd said many times before. Flynn thought it more likely that she hadn't wanted a reminder of her husband's affair hanging on her walls.

'Why do you think someone would choose to steal that painting?'

'I have no idea,' Lady Carstairs murmured, staring into the distance. 'The last few weeks have been a complete mystery to me.'

'In what way?' Flynn spoke softly, feeling they might finally be getting closer to finding out what was really going on with Lord Carstairs.

As if realising she'd said too much, Lady Carstairs reached for the handbell by her side and rang it once. 'I'm afraid there's nothing more I can tell you.'

Mr Treadaway had obviously been waiting for the command, perhaps with his ear pressed to the door, as he appeared in an instant.

'Detective Inspector Flynn and Detective Sergeant Goodspeed are leaving. Thank you so much for coming. I do hope you catch those responsible for the damage to Riverside Lodge.'

Flynn nodded, noting again that her concern lay with her property rather than the whereabouts of her husband.

Mr Treadaway showed them into the hall, and Goodspeed – anticipating Flynn's intention to question the butler – made sure the door to the drawing room was firmly closed behind them.

'When and where did you last see Lord Carstairs?' Flynn asked abruptly, his tone indicating he expected the butler to give him an immediate and honest answer.

'Right where you're standing, on the morning of Friday the eighteenth of November,' Mr Treadaway replied in equally direct tones.

'He didn't come back here later that day?'

'I don't know. I wasn't here. Lady Carstairs had been in town for a few days and was keen to return to Biddenden House. There isn't a permanent staff here. Lady Carstairs' maid travels with her, and so do I, unless Lord Carstairs chooses to remain in town.'

'And he wasn't planning to remain in town on this occasion?'

The butler shook his head. 'We had expected him to return to Biddenden House later that night or at the very latest that weekend. It's not unusual for him to stay at his club in London if something comes up and he has to remain in town.'

'What clubs does he belong to?' Flynn asked.

'His lordship is a member of Brooks's on St James's Street and the Reform Club on Pall Mall.'

Flynn nodded to Goodspeed to make a note of this. 'He's not been seen at Biddenden House in these last few weeks?'

'No.' Mr Treadaway hesitated. 'Lord Carstairs can sometimes be unpredictable, but this... this isn't like him. I am now concerned that something untoward may have occurred.'

'Thank you for your frankness, Mr Treadaway. I have a feeling we'll be speaking again soon.'

'I fear so,' Mr Treadaway replied with a grave nod.

23

When Coral heard a knock on her front door that evening, she wasn't entirely surprised to find Flynn on the doorstep.

He didn't appear to be on the verge of arresting her, so she let him in and waited to hear the reason for his visit. He'd arrived a bit later this time, and she remembered him saying he had an appointment to see Lady Carstairs that afternoon. She was curious to know what her ladyship had to say, but the look on Flynn's face told her he wasn't in the mood for questions.

'When I first interviewed you, I asked if Marian Dean had a boyfriend and you said not to your knowledge.' His eyes flickered around the hall as if trying to ascertain whether Lavender was still at home. 'Yet you and Miss Bright seem to have known she was seeing someone called Jack.'

So that was it. He thought she was keeping information from him. After the scene at Scotland Yard, Coral had guessed he would expect some kind of explanation.

'I didn't know when you asked me. Later, when I talked to Penny, she told me she'd once seen Marian with a young man in Hyde Park.' Now Coral began her fabrication. 'When Penny mentioned it to Marian, she said his name was Jack and he was a policeman. Of course, Penny got it into her head that this man was spying and started to question Marian about their meetings. I've made notes of everything I've been able to find out from her, if you'd like to see them?'

'Miss Bright should have told me herself, instead of throwing accusations at my officers,' he growled, then said in a politer tone, 'Yes, I would like to see your notes.'

'I'll fetch them for you,' she replied with equal politeness.

Flynn suddenly seemed to notice she was wearing an apron. 'I'm sorry, were you preparing dinner?'

'I was just making a sandwich, I'm too tired to cook.' Coral had spent some time talking Penny into a more sensible frame of mind before spending the afternoon on reception at the Stanmore Gallery. She was tired, hungry and longing for a drink. Anticipating Flynn might be in the same mood, she asked, 'Would you like a sandwich? Lavender cooked a roast dinner yesterday, and there's some beef left over. Why don't I make it, while you look through my notes?'

He hesitated, then nodded. 'Thank you. I'd like that.'

Coral went to fetch the notes she'd prepared from her bag while he removed his hat and coat, and then she led him down the hall into the kitchen. She motioned to a chair and placed the papers on the kitchen table. They contained the times and dates from the diary of when Marian had met with Jack in Hyde Park, and she'd added the comment about Sherlock Holmes for good measure.

Coral went to the larder and took out a pat of butter, a loaf of bread and a plate of sliced beef. She began to cut the bread, feeling self-conscious at doing such a mundane task while Flynn sat nearby on one of her familiar old kitchen chairs.

She turned to glance over at him. 'Horseradish or mustard?'

'Horseradish, please,' he replied without looking up.

As he sat and read, she couldn't help thinking that, so far, she'd put her trust in Flynn by getting Penny and Irene to talk to him, but hadn't received much in return. And she doubted a roast beef sandwich would do much to loosen his tongue.

Her eyes drifted to the open bottle of red wine on the sideboard. She and Lavender had enjoyed a glass each the previous evening, and there was still plenty left.

'Would you like some red wine?' Coral held up the bottle. 'It was given to Lavender by one of her admirers. It's rather good.'

'That would be very pleasant, if you're sure Miss Lacey won't mind.'

Coral shook her head. 'She doesn't drink much, she says it's bad for her voice.'

She went to the cupboard and, ignoring the two small glasses she and Lavender had used, chose two larger ones. She filled a glass and took it over to Flynn.

'I'm sorry about what Penny said today. After Black Friday—'

He held up a hand. 'You don't need to explain. What happened that day was atrocious. It sullied the reputation of the whole police force. My intention is to find out the truth about Marian Dean's murder to try to help restore a little of the trust that's been lost. Perhaps we should drink to putting the past behind us and starting afresh?' Flynn held up his glass. 'To new beginnings.'

Coral held up her own glass, feeling a strange swirl of emotions at his words. 'To new beginnings.'

He took a healthy swig of wine, then gave her a quizzical look. 'There's something else I want to ask you.'

'Oh?' Coral queried, her heart sinking.

'At Miss Grayson's flat, you told me that Nathan Jennings had asked you who painted the Churchill portrait. You seemed rather amused. Why was that?'

Coral smiled with relief, surprised he'd noticed. 'When I informed Countess Stanmore of his visit to the gallery, she suggested Jennings might want a similar picture of himself. She joked that she should commission Irene to paint a series of portraits of politicians in the nude.'

She enjoyed his roar of laughter, feeling less self-conscious as she placed two plates and a pair of napkins on the table and sat opposite him.

Flynn pushed the notes to one side. 'I'm sorry Detective Constable Hall wasn't as honest as he should have been. I intend to speak to him again in the morning. Goodspeed and I had to go out this afternoon. Bally secured a meeting with Lady Carstairs, and we needed to move quickly.'

'Bally?' She smiled. 'Isn't that some posh euphemism for bloody?'

Flynn grinned, which made him look instantly younger. 'Chief Superintendent Ballantyne-Smythe is frequently referred to down at the yard as bally Bally.'

Coral laughed, remembering her days on the stage when they'd all had nicknames for each other. She hadn't imagined Scotland Yard would be the same. It made her wonder what the junior officers called Flynn behind his back. From what she'd seen of him, he was fully capable of scaring the hell out of them if he felt they deserved it.

Coral picked up her sandwich. 'Was it Lady Carstairs we saw that morning?'

Flynn nodded. 'She saw you too. When Nathan Jennings and Charles Dean appeared in the Westminster Gallery, she says she followed you through the Royal Gallery and out of the building as she wanted to avoid Jennings.'

'Why did she want to avoid him?' Coral asked, pondering on Lady Carstairs' statement. She supposed it corroborated what she'd told Flynn and gave her an alibi of sorts for the time of Marian's murder and the theft of the painting. Or could it be that Lady Carstairs was trying to give herself an alibi?

'Awkward questions are being asked in Whitehall as to the whereabouts of her husband. She didn't want Jennings quizzing her over it. The last public sighting we have of Lord Carstairs is in the House of Commons bar at around seven o'clock on Friday the eighteenth of November. Yet his wife doesn't appear to be the slightest bit concerned about him.'

Coral could understand why Flynn looked so perplexed. Ronald Carstairs had been missing for over three weeks. She would have been frantic if Ernest had disappeared for all that time.

'What was Lady Carstairs doing at the gallery that morning?'

'She says she often visits when she's in town.' Flynn's expression told her what he thought about this.

'You didn't believe her?'

He shook his head, swallowing a bite of his sandwich. 'This is delicious, and so is the wine.'

She smiled. 'Lavender is an excellent lodger. She can cook and brings home lots of lovely gifts.'

Flynn picked up his glass. 'Lady Carstairs said that she and her husband once met Marian Dean. Did Marian ever mention meeting them?'

'No, I don't think so. No, wait, yes, she did. It was when we were...' she'd been about to say when they were driving back from the Hurlingham Club. 'I think we were reading one of the newspaper stories on his disappearance, and she said she'd met him once, and he was rather sweet.'

Coral remembered the scene in the car. Irene had spotted a police wagon heading towards Riverside Lodge, and Marian had suggested they might be looking for Lord Carstairs. That was when Marian had made the comment about meeting him. Little did she know, Irene and Penny had just set fire to his house.

'Is that it?' Flynn seemed disappointed. 'It hardly sounds like they were having a torrid affair.'

Coral smiled. 'No. I think you can definitely rule that out. I assumed the meeting came about because her brother moves in parliamentary circles. The only possible boyfriend mentioned was Jack. Could he and Marian have been trading information? Maybe the spy isn't in the government. Perhaps he's in the police force.' She suddenly felt uncomfortable as she realised trading information was exactly what she and Flynn were doing at that moment.

He shook his head. 'We're not privy to what goes on in parliament. I can't see how someone at Jack's level would have found out those kinds of details.'

'What about Bally? You say he's a chief superintendent. Penny could be right. Bally could have encouraged Jack to strike up a relationship with a suffragette and tell her certain confidential information in return for details of WSPU activities?'

Flynn clearly didn't like this suggestion. 'Bally has regular meetings at Whitehall and probably picks up parliamentary gossip there. But I'm not sure he'd hear personal details such as the fact that Riverside Lodge would be empty that week.'

'I suppose not.' Coral let it go, having no desire to dwell on the fire at the Carstairs villa.

Flynn ran a finger down the dates listed in her notes. 'Why do you think Marian went off Jack? He's a good-looking young lad, and he obviously cared for her. I'm sure his feelings were genuine. Her death has affected him badly. Did Miss Bright tell her to stop seeing him?'

'No. I think Marian was in love with someone else.' Coral saw a glint in Flynn's eyes she was becoming familiar with. It was a sudden alertness that flared when he thought he had a potential new lead. However, she was going to disappoint him.

'Who? What's this man's name? Charles Dean seemed to think all Marian was passionate about was the Pankhursts and the WSPU.'

Coral smiled. 'Correct. Christabel Pankhurst in particular. She wrote an article for *The Tatler* a couple of years ago, and the magazine featured a rather fetching picture of her on the front cover. She was photographed with an outstretched hand and a beseeching look on her face. As a result, many young ladies succumbed and joined the cause, and Christabel became an object of desire amongst suffragettes. She's very pretty and persuasive.'

'She's a barrister, isn't she?' Flynn said, as if this explained everything.

'She would be if women were allowed to practise law,' Coral pointed out. 'But, yes, she has a first-class law degree.'

Flynn nodded as if to concede the point. 'I remember the photograph and the article. My daughter, Teresa, had a copy of the magazine and seemed rather taken with her, too.'

Much to your dismay, Coral thought. She felt some sympathy for Flynn. If she had a daughter, would she want her to become a suffragette? After all, hadn't she been worried by Marian's fervour for the cause?

Flynn finished his sandwich and drained the last of his wine. He didn't object when Coral filled up both their glasses.

He took a sip and then gave her a curious look. 'Has the king been to see my paintings again?'

Coral was about to ask what he meant, then, with a sinking feeling, it dawned on her. He was referring to the night of Friday the twenty-fifth of November. The night he suspected she'd been at the Hurlingham Club. The night she'd told him a private viewing was taking place at the Stanmore Gallery. And the night she'd later told him in the interview with Penny that she'd been at home by herself. She groaned, deciding that she'd never make a decent criminal. She was too bad at remembering her lies.

He smiled at her response. 'Rather than holding a private viewing for his majesty in the Stanmore Gallery, I think you were writing a rude word in the grounds of a private sports club frequented by royalty.'

Of course, the reason the blinds had been pulled down was that Penny and Irene had visited the gallery later that night to tell the countess what had happened. Coral felt a twinge of guilt that this secret meeting had taken place surrounded by Flynn's paintings.

'What makes you think that?' She was still reluctant to confess until she knew what evidence he had.

Her heart began to beat a little faster as Flynn reached into the inside pocket of his jacket and took out an unsealed brown envelope. Coral inhaled sharply as he tipped out her wedding ring and held it in the palm of his hand.

She reached across the table to take it from him, but he closed his fist. With an effort, she withdrew her hand, accepting she couldn't rush this.

'How did you know it was mine?'

'You're wearing it in *Dawn Beauty*.'

She groaned again. How could she have been so stupid not to remember she was wearing the ring in the portrait?

'I didn't notice it at first, but when I went back...' Flynn trailed off as if realising how this could be construed. He gazed down at her ring, turning it over in his fingers, and it gave Coral a strange sensation to see it in his hands.

So, he'd gone back for a second look. Coral would feel flattered if she weren't preoccupied with how to get hold of her ring. If Lavender were here, she'd flirt outrageously with him, but Coral decided she was too long in the tooth for that game and didn't think Flynn would respond anyway.

To her dismay, he dropped the ring into the envelope and returned it to the inside pocket of his jacket.

'I think one, possibly two, other suffragettes dropped you and Marian Dean at the Hurlingham Club while they went to Riverside Lodge. Did you and Marian know what they had planned?'

Coral shook her head, grateful that he hadn't named Penny and Irene. 'We thought they were going to smash a few windows and throw in some *Votes for Women* pamphlets so the police would know who was responsible. When we got back to town, I found I'd lost my ring and wanted to go to the Hurlingham Club to look for it, but the others wouldn't let me. That's when they told me they'd set fire to Riverside Lodge.'

'Why didn't they tell you before?'

'Because they knew I would have tried to stop them. I may write rude things on sports pitches and smash the odd window, but I don't do anything that might hurt people.'

'The windows in question being those of 10 Downing Street.'

'For which I was charged and spent six days in Holloway Prison.' Coral had in fact smashed the windows of other government offices before that; she just hadn't been caught on those occasions. This wasn't something she planned on sharing with Flynn.

The attack on Downing Street had been swift and satisfying. On that day, she'd worn a plain dark dress and low-brimmed hat and sprinted along the road, smashing every window in easy reach. It had been wonderful. A release of all the anger that had built up inside her after Ernest's death.

Even when she'd been arrested, she hadn't been sorry, she'd been elated.

But after those six long days in Holloway, she'd realised enough was enough. In other suffragettes, she'd seen how those initial, maybe seemingly harmless, criminal acts had escalated into more dangerous behaviour. She had no desire to follow in their footsteps. It had led her to worry how far Marian's enthusiasm for the cause might take her.

She tried to explain this to Flynn. 'I'm not in the confidence of those who control the WSPU. And I have no desire to be. As you'll have gathered, Penny is close to the Pankhursts, and Marian would have liked to have been. I tried to warn her that it could be dangerous, but she loved being a suffragette and was upset when... when she thought I wanted to leave.'

'Do you plan to leave the WSPU?'

'I've considered it.' His obvious approval of such a plan irked her, prompting her to add, 'I don't condone all their activities, though given the government's behaviour, they leave us with little choice.'

He nodded slowly as if conceding her point, but not enough to acknowledge it out loud.

'I regret going to the Hurlingham Club, and I certainly regret wearing my ring there.' She interlaced her fingers, feeling its loss. 'I've thought for a long time about keeping it safe in my jewellery box rather than risk losing it.' Coral couldn't keep the tremor from her voice. 'It just felt too big a step to take it off.'

'How long were you married?' he asked gently.

'Eleven years. I was lucky to have had all that time with Ernest, and I tell myself it would be greedy to ask for more. But it doesn't stop you wishing.'

'I know what you mean. I had fourteen years with Julia and still long for one more day.' Flynn stared down at his own wedding band. 'I don't just wish it for myself. It's Teresa. She was thirteen when Julia died, and I feel she's missed out on so much that only her mother could give her.'

'It must be hard bringing up a daughter on your own, though I'm sure she's a comfort to you.' Coral wondered what it would have been like if she and Ernest had been blessed with children. Ernest would have loved it, but it had never happened – not for want of trying, she thought with a smile.

'My sister helps out. She has two daughters of her own, and my nieces are more like sisters to Teresa than cousins. I just can't help feeling I should do more to fill the gap that Julia left.' Flynn drained his glass and stood up, evidently feeling he'd said too much. 'I must go.'

Coral rose, knowing that with him would go her ring. She followed him out into the hallway and watched him put on his hat and coat.

'Thank you for the sandwich and wine. And for showing me your notes.'

She nodded, feeling too drained to reply, and held open the front door, enjoying the coolness of the night air on her flushed face.

Then suddenly Flynn was in front of her, standing so close she could smell the citrus fragrance of his cologne. Her wedding ring was in his hand, and he held it out to her.

As she took it from him, his palm closed over her fingers. 'Be careful, won't you, Coral,' he murmured, then turned and left.

24

Flynn shouldn't have given Coral her ring back. He shouldn't have accepted the whisky and soda on his first visit to her home, and he shouldn't have sat eating sandwiches and drinking wine with her the previous night.

He felt the familiar throbbing in his temples and longed to be in his attic studio, with a paintbrush in hand. *Be careful what you wish for*, he thought. If he didn't solve this case soon, that's exactly what he'd be doing – a disgraced ex-detective, stuck at home with a disapproving daughter, relying on whatever income he could generate from his paintings.

But Coral had looked at the ring with such longing, he hadn't been able to resist. He knew how he would feel if he lost the wedding band Julia had placed on his finger the day they'd promised to love and cherish each other forever.

Flynn had justified it by telling himself that Coral didn't know about the fire at Riverside Lodge. Alright, so she had been guilty of criminal damage but she wasn't an arsonist. And Lady Carstairs had followed Coral out of the National Portrait Gallery, which meant she wasn't a murderer or an art thief either.

But he still shouldn't have given her the ring back. It was evidence – and he should tell Goodspeed what he'd done. But first, they needed to speak to Jack Hall.

'I went to see Coral Fairbanks last night,' Flynn said, as Goodspeed placed two cups of coffee on his desk and then shut his office door. 'She showed me her notes on everything she's learned about Marian Dean and her relationship with Jack.'

Goodspeed tutted. 'Mrs Fairbanks should have told us about it earlier and left the detecting to us.'

'Most of it came from Penelope Bright. Do you think we should get her back in for questioning?'

Goodspeed shuddered at the suggestion as Flynn had known he would.

'I get the impression Mrs Fairbanks felt maternal towards Marian Dean and was worried she was getting out of her depth. I think she's trying to find out what happened to her out of a sense of duty.'

Flynn thought he understood Coral a little better after their supper together. He wondered if she and her husband had wanted children. It was evident how much she loved him and tragic that she'd lost him at such a young age. He could imagine Coral in that house that was now too big for her, with a brood of children around her, laughing at their antics.

A knock at the door interrupted these thoughts, and Jack Hall's anxious face appeared.

'Come in and sit down,' Goodspeed ordered.

'You should have told us you knew Marian Dean,' Flynn said as Jack pulled up a chair. 'Why didn't you?'

'I was worried because of her being a suffragette. You know what they say about them in here.' Jack jerked his head towards the door, and Flynn knew exactly what he meant. How many times had he overheard the crude comments of officers who thought women were the weaker sex, purely there to service the needs of men? 'I don't think they're wrong, the suffragettes. Some of the things they do are wrong, but I used to agree with lots of what Marian said. Why shouldn't women have the right to vote?'

Flynn smiled, impressed by the lad's candour. 'I think you're right,' he said and was amused by Jack's look of surprise.

'But we shouldn't fraternise with them, should we?' Jack glanced between Flynn and Goodspeed, seeming unsure of their feelings on this.

'There are no rules to say that,' Flynn replied, wondering if eating a roast beef sandwich and drinking red wine could be considered fraternising. The answer to that was probably yes. He pushed thoughts of his cosy supper with Coral from his mind. 'However, if you believe someone is involved in a criminal act, then it's your duty to report it.'

Flynn was acutely aware of the hypocrisy of his words. He'd handed back a piece of evidence to a woman who'd admitted two criminal offences. Damage to a polo field and helping to display a controversial portrait might not be major crimes, but Coral was associated with people who committed arson.

How would he have reacted if Jack had come to him and told him about his relationship with Marian Dean? He'd warned his own daughter not to get involved with the suffragettes and would probably have said the same to Jack.

'Let's concentrate on solving this case for Marian Dean's sake,' Flynn said, wanting to end this conversation as much as his constable.

'Yes, sir.' Jack immediately took a notebook from his pocket. 'I spoke to a newspaper vendor on the corner of Trafalgar Square and Charing Cross Road. He said he saw two gentlemen, who we know to be Sidney Watson and Luke Chaplin, going into the National Portrait Gallery. He hadn't particularly noticed anyone going in before that, but they caught his eye because Luke was carrying a camera. He guessed they were reporters and started to keep an eye on the doors, hoping to spot someone famous. Shortly afterwards, he saw three ladies leave separately. One blonde and two with reddish hair. Then the two newspaper men came out, and the gallery was closed.'

'Good work.' Goodspeed slapped Jack on the back. 'That fits with what we know about Penelope Bright, Coral Fairbanks and Lady Carstairs all leaving the gallery.'

'I take it the newspaper vendor didn't mention if any of them were carrying a picture under their arm?' Flynn remarked drily.

'He's sure they were all empty-handed,' Jack replied. 'And he didn't see them meet with anyone.'

'What about Luke Chaplin? He was carrying a camera case. Was it big enough to conceal the Blanchet painting?' Goodspeed asked.

'I checked with staff at the gallery to see if Sidney Watson or Luke Chaplin could have entered the Contemporary Gallery at any time, but they were in sight of attendants from the moment they entered the building until they were kicked out.'

Goodspeed grinned. 'Thought that would be too much to hope for.'

Jack flipped over the pages of his notebook. 'I also went to Lambeth and spoke to the organisers of the public meeting that Penelope Bright and Irene Grayson supposedly attended on the night of the fire at Riverside Lodge. It's a local chapter of the WSPU, and three of their members have vouched for the fact that both women were there that night.'

'I bet they have—' Flynn was interrupted by a sharp rap on the office door. 'Come in,' he called.

To his surprise, Sergeant Donaldson from Fulham police station entered.

'What's brought you over this way?' Flynn hadn't seen Donaldson since the night of the fire at Riverside Lodge, and by the look on the sergeant's face, something significant had happened. Flynn's starched shirt suddenly pricked with sweat. If Donaldson had discovered new evidence that incriminated Coral Fairbanks, then he was going to be in serious trouble.

'Workmen have been inside Riverside Lodge, checking the structural integrity of the walls and floors, and one of them went down to the coal bunker to inspect the foundations. He found the body of a man there.'

25

In bright winter sunshine, Riverside Lodge looked charming. From the outside, there were no indications that anything sinister had happened there.

Inside, the effects of the fire could still be seen and smelt, with the odour of charcoal heavy in the air.

'Do you know who has keys to the property?' Flynn asked Sergeant Donaldson.

'A local agent and Lord and Lady Carstairs. The agent made sure the doors were locked after the fire brigade had finished and arranged for the two smashed windows to be boarded up. The builders collected the keys from him yesterday, and the foreman said the property was secure when they arrived.'

Sergeant Donaldson guided Flynn and Goodspeed to the end of a long hallway, through the kitchen and out to a scullery on the side of the house.

'Who found the body?' Goodspeed asked.

'The foreman went to examine the coal bunker this morning and saw it as soon as he lifted the trapdoor. He could see the man was dead, so he didn't go down.' Donaldson pulled a torch from his pocket. 'He sent one of his lads to the station, and I came to see it for myself. Then I left a message for Dr Jarvis to meet us here, before I came to tell you what had been found.'

In an alcove, the trapdoor to the coal bunker was lying open. Donaldson shone the torch into the shaft, and Flynn peered down steep wooden steps, grimacing at the sickly stench that was pungent enough to overpower the burning smell.

The young doctor stepped forward and introduced himself. 'I've been down there, and I can assure you he's dead.'

That much was obvious from the odour and a cursory glance at the body from above. The man was lying at an awkward angle, his head on the ground, touching the edge of the coal pile, while his legs were pointed upwards, caught on the steps.

'Not much room to get a body through,' Flynn observed, inspecting the trapdoor.

'I think it was tipped down,' Donaldson replied.

'Could he have tripped and fallen down the hole?' Goodspeed suggested.

Dr Jarvis shook his head. 'There's a stab wound to his chest. My examination would suggest that's what killed him, and he was already dead before he was put into the coal bunker. A pathologist might be able to tell you more. I'd say he's been down there for some weeks.'

It was three and a half weeks since the last sighting of Ronald Carstairs.

Flynn took the torch from Donaldson and trod gingerly down the wooden steps. It was a small opening, just enough room for him to squeeze through.

'I had to step over his legs,' Dr Jarvis called.

Flynn did the same and landed heavily on the stone floor of the cellar. The dead man was wearing a formal morning suit with a white shirt and blue cravat. Flynn studied the body with the torch, noting the dark stain on the front of the shirt. Although the face was bluish grey, Flynn had no doubt this was Ronald Carstairs.

He inspected every inch of the soot-covered floor with the torch and found nothing. With some difficulty, he manoeuvred himself back up the ladder, glad to emerge from the reeking cellar.

'Chief Superintendent Ballantyne-Smythe is arranging for a Home Office pathologist to come and examine the body before it's moved to the police mortuary. He should be here shortly. Would you be able to stay until he arrives?' Flynn asked Dr Jarvis. 'He might have some questions for you.'

'I'd be delighted. I mean... yes.' Dr Jarvis did indeed look delighted but seemed to realise this may not be an appropriate response under the circumstances.

'Your discretion in this matter goes without saying,' Flynn warned. 'I don't want the press reporting on this until we've identified the deceased and his next of kin have been informed.'

Dr Jarvis nodded. 'Of course.'

'We'll be outside,' Flynn told Donaldson, indicating for Goodspeed to follow him.

They walked through the scullery and out into the landscaped gardens, Flynn breathing in the clean air while Goodspeed immediately lit a cigarette.

'If the fire had caught hold, as presumably intended, the body would have been destroyed,' Flynn observed.

'All that coal would have seen to that. As it didn't, we know he died from a stab wound to the chest.' Goodspeed inhaled then breathed out a circle of smoke. 'The same as Marian Dean.'

Flynn put a hand to his stomach, feeling a wave of nausea. 'Three people are linked to both crimes. Lady Carstairs didn't report her husband as missing and was at the gallery when Marian Dean was killed. Then there's Penelope Bright and Irene Grayson. I think they started the fire here. The problem is, I can't bring them in for questioning because of the witnesses who claim they were at that bloody meeting in Lambeth on the night of the twenty-fifth of November.'

'Don't forget Coral Fairbanks,' Goodspeed added. 'The wedding ring puts her in the vicinity of the fire. And she was one of the last people to see Marian Dean alive.'

26

'Get upstairs quick,' Coral told Penny and Irene, hearing the doorbell chime to indicate a customer had entered the Stanmore Gallery. They'd arrived through the rear entrance just as she was about to lock up.

They hurried up the stairs, and Coral returned to the gallery to find Sid Watson resting his bulky frame on the edge of her desk while Luke Chaplin gazed in awe at the paintings. Or their price tags.

'Is it Ronald Carstairs?' she asked. The previous day's newspapers had reported on the discovery of a body at Riverside Lodge and speculation was rife.

Sid nodded. 'Flynn's not saying but I know a porter at the police mortuary and he said it's definitely him.'

Coral groaned.

'Did Marian Dean know him?' Sid asked, taking out his cigarettes. 'Her brother once worked as Carstairs' private secretary. Do you think she and Carstairs could have been in some kind of relationship?'

Coral shook her head, pushing an ashtray in his direction. 'You're barking up the wrong tree there.'

Sid looked disappointed. 'My gut's telling me there's a connection somewhere.'

Coral thought so too, though a sleepless night niggling away at the problem had yielded no answers. 'If there is, I can't figure out what it could be.'

Sid grunted. 'Me neither. It's a strange one. I never believed the rumours about a suffragette involvement with Carstairs' disappearance. Now I'm not so sure. Did you hear anything?'

'No one I've spoken to has the slightest idea what happened to him. Like you, I never believed in the Pankhursts' involvement, and I still don't.'

'But you do know who set fire to Riverside Lodge. Can you give me their names? Were they at the gallery when Marian Dean was killed?'

Coral sighed. She'd been expecting the question. 'They didn't know the body was in the cellar. That's all I can tell you.'

'If you say so, but I'd expect another visit from Detective Inspector Flynn if I were you. Did he ask you about the Sylvie Blanchet painting? Once owned by his lordship? He might suspect you nicked it to fence through this place.' Sid cackled at his own joke.

Coral gave a forced smile. 'Fortunately, I was seen leaving the Portrait Gallery with nothing more than a small purse in my hand.'

Her eyes flickered to Flynn's pictures, and she was alarmed to see Luke staring at them intently. The young man had an otherworldly quality, as if he wasn't paying much attention, yet Coral had noticed he could sometimes be more intuitive than Sid.

'These are good,' Luke announced to no one in particular.

Sid hefted himself off the desk and went to take a look.

'Artist is obviously a Londoner. Got an eye for detail.' Sid peered closely at the signature. 'Who's GF?'

Coral shrugged. 'I don't know much about them. A new artist the countess discovered. I think they prefer to stay out of the limelight.'

'It's someone who knows the streets of London well,' Sid observed.

'Perhaps they're a criminal,' Luke suggested.

'What's criminal is the cost of one of these.' Sid whistled as he pointed at a price tag. 'No wonder Countess Stanmore drives around in a Rolls-Royce.'

He and Luke sauntered to the door.

'If the ladies who set fire to Riverside Lodge would like to tell me their side of the story, you know where to find me.' Sid leaned in to kiss Coral on the cheek. 'And be careful, love. I don't think anyone really understands what's going on here.'

Coral thought he was right. She squeezed his arm, then locked the door after them, pulling down the blind.

She hurried upstairs to the countess's apartment to find Penny and Irene scouring the evening newspapers.

'They've just stopped short of accusing us of murder.' Penny tossed one of the papers onto the glass table.

Coral had read the article. It was carefully worded but implied that the body found in the cellar at Riverside Lodge was believed to have been there at the time of the recent arson attack. The implication was that the fire had been an attempt to destroy evidence.

Coral told them Sid was sure the dead man was Ronald Carstairs.

Penny groaned, and Irene reached for the silver cigarette box. Even the countess lost her customary poise, letting out a string of expletives.

Only Harriet seemed unperturbed. 'The police don't know Penny and Irene started the fire.'

'Flynn knows.' Coral was sure of that. 'He just can't prove it.'

'How? Did you tell him?' Penny demanded.

'I didn't need to tell him,' Coral said in exasperation. 'He's not stupid. He found my wedding ring and knows I was at the Hurlingham Club with Marian. Of course he's going to suspect you and Irene set fire to Riverside Lodge.'

Penny picked up the newspaper again and began to worry the edges of the pages with her fingertips, causing them to tear. 'I see you're wearing your wedding ring now. How did he know it was yours?'

Coral felt her cheeks grow hot. 'I'm wearing it in *Dawn Beauty*.'

The countess smiled. 'He must have looked closely at that painting. And he gave it back to you?'

Coral nodded, recalling how he'd placed his hand over hers. It had been a spontaneous act, one she was certain he was now regretting.

'He can't arrest us.' Penny still gripped the newspaper. 'Our friends will say we were with them at the Lambeth meeting that night.'

'Flynn's not a fool. He knows they're your friends, and he knows they're lying.' Coral's temper was beginning to flare. She wasn't the one who'd got them into this mess by setting fire to Riverside Lodge. She hugged one of the velvet cushions, trying to work out what Flynn would do next.

Penny's eyes narrowed. 'You seem to know an awful lot about what Flynn thinks.'

The countess intervened. 'That was rather the point, Penny. Coral's been getting better acquainted with him so we can find out what the police are up to.'

Coral wouldn't have put it quite like that, but wasn't in the mood to argue. Since he'd returned her ring, she'd started to feel confused by the nature of her relationship with Flynn and didn't want to dwell on it.

Irene, who'd been silent until now, asked a question that had long been on Coral's mind. 'Penny, how did you know Riverside Lodge was empty?'

'What's that go to do with anything?' Penny snapped.

'Because whoever put the body there wanted us to get the blame,' Irene replied before taking a long drag of her cigarette.

'By us, you mean the suffragettes?' Minerva queried.

Irene nodded. 'I think someone is setting us up.'

'I've been thinking the same thing,' Harriet murmured.

'Penny. Where did the information come from?' It was a command not a request, said in the silkiest of tones. The countess never raised her voice. She didn't have to. The glint in her dark eyes was usually enough to ensure compliance.

Penny played with the edges of the newspaper. 'Someone writes to me at Clement's Inn. I don't know who; I don't recognise the handwriting. My name and the address are printed on the envelope, and there's always a single sheet of paper inside. It's generally just a few lines. This time it said, "Wouldn't it be a shame if Lord Carstairs' newly built villa in Fulham was burned to the ground. It will be empty all of next week, so no one would be hurt".'

Minerva raised her arched eyebrows. 'And you act on these messages?'

'Not without checking first. But they've always been accurate in the past.'

'What have the previous ones said?' Coral's anger was simmering at the sheer idiocy of it all.

'They've given times and places of where a politician's going to be. That's how we were able to pelt Jennings with eggs at Ascot, flour Lloyd George at his mistress's house and attack Churchill at Bristol Temple Meads railway station.'

Coral winced as she remembered the incident the previous November when Theresa Garnett had hit Churchill across the face with a horse whip, inflicting a minor cut and knocking his hat to the ground. That had earned Theresa a month inside HM Prison Bristol.

Had the escalating antagonism and violence towards politicians led to Ronald Carstairs' death? And Marian's? After all, the growing hostilities had culminated in a full-scale battle on Black Friday. Was murder the next inevitable step?

'I went to Fulham and asked around first.' Penny sounded desperate to try to justify her actions. 'I found out from someone who was due to start working in the kitchens at Riverside Lodge that the builders had gone, and Lady Carstairs wasn't due to inspect the property until the following week. It seemed too good an opportunity to miss.'

The countess made a tssking sound. 'When did this message arrive?'

'On Monday the twenty-first.' Penny fiddled with a lock of hair. 'There was no postmark. Someone must have put it through the door the night before.'

Two days after Black Friday, when emotions were still running high. Coral's rage rose another notch. Irene was right; someone was setting them up – someone who wasn't afraid to kill. And if they weren't stopped, the WSPU would be destroyed and Mrs Pankhurst could end up being hanged for murder.

The countess reached for her cigarette box. 'Did you show the letter to Mrs Pankhurst?'

Penny flushed. 'No. I told her I'd heard some information, which I'd personally verified, and she was happy to go along with my plan.'

'And agreed to take responsibility for it,' Minerva said drily as she lit a cigarette, 'which she will no doubt be regretting. She's currently charged with abetting arson. Scotland Yard may try to change that to murder.'

Penny buried her face in her hands. At that moment, Coral felt little sympathy for her. She couldn't believe she'd been reckless enough to act on a tip-off from an anonymous letter writer.

'Ronald Carstairs hasn't been seen since around seven o'clock on the evening of Black Friday,' Coral told them. 'I think we're all going to need alibis for that night.'

'Coral's right. We should prepare.' Minerva turned to Harriet, who was perched on the end of her chaise longue. 'I doubt Flynn suspects my involvement in any of this, but what were we doing that day?'

Harriet thought for a moment. 'We were at Christie's that afternoon. Got outbid for that dull Renoir, which I wasn't sorry about. When we got back, Irene stopped by to tell us what had happened in Parliament Square and warn us she was going to try to get into the Reform Club.'

Minerva nodded. 'That's right. And we hopped in the car and had dinner at the Savoy, so we were out of the way when she was causing havoc across the road.'

Irene took a puff of her cigarette and exhaled slowly as she tried to remember.

'Penny and I left Parliament Square and went to Clement's Inn. Mrs Pankhurst was there and told us she was planning to call a meeting of the executive committee. I wasn't invited, so I suggested I cause some disruption at the Reform Club. She agreed, so Penny helped me take a bundle of pamphlets to the garage and load them into the car with the trolley. I put on the deliveryman uniform, drove to St James's Square and called here to tell you what I was up to. Then I wheeled the trolley over the road just as MPs were beginning to arrive from parliament. We'd covered *Votes for Women* pamphlets with that evening's newspapers, and they let me in without a word. I dashed around the club, throwing pamphlets on all the seats, and at some of the members, then got out quickly.'

'If asked, leave out the bits about the garage, the car and calling here,' the countess instructed.

Irene drew on her cigarette. 'Dozens of people saw me in the Reform Club... although I suppose what they saw was a deliveryman.'

'Mrs Pankhurst asked me to attend the executive committee meeting at eight o'clock that night.' Penny was unable to hide her pride at this. 'I went to the garage with Irene and helped her bundle up the pamphlets with that evening's papers. Then I went back to Clement's Inn and was there until past midnight. When I got home, the girls I share with were already asleep.'

The countess exhaled a long plume of smoke. 'Does anyone know what Marian did that evening?'

'A nurse tended to her at Caxton Hall after she'd been assaulted by those men,' Coral replied. 'It was just cuts and bruises, but I could see she was upset, so I walked her back to her grandmother's house. We got there at about seven o'clock. Then I went home, sank into a hot bath, had a good dinner and read a book until I fell asleep in my chair. Then I went up to bed.'

'Was Lavender there?' Harriet asked.

Coral shook her head. 'She was working. I'm not sure what time she got home.'

Harriet sighed. 'Not the best collection of alibis under the circumstances.'

27

Flynn caught a whiff of gin mingling with Lady Carstairs' jasmine perfume as Mr Treadaway showed him and Goodspeed into the drawing room of 22 Leinster Gardens.

It was only eleven o'clock in the morning, though he could forgive her the indulgence under the circumstances. She'd had the unenviable task of viewing the body and had confirmed that it was indeed her husband, Ronald Carstairs.

'I'm sorry to disturb you, Lady Carstairs,' Flynn said as he and Goodspeed sat in the high-backed leather armchairs. 'But I need to ask you some questions about your husband.'

'I understand,' Violet Carstairs murmured. Her eyes were bloodshot and swollen, and her cheeks looked dry and sore. 'I was stupid. Ronnie wouldn't have stayed away so long without letting me know where he'd gone.'

'Why didn't you report your husband missing?' Flynn asked.

'Because I wasn't sure he was missing. I certainly didn't imagine he was dead.' She shuddered, probably recalling her visit to the mortuary.

'Then what did you think?' Flynn still couldn't understand why she hadn't been concerned before now.

She gave a pinched smile. 'Ronnie could be impulsive, especially if people were making demands on him. He'd just up and go, and that's what I thought he'd done this time. He didn't like feeling hemmed in; that's why I gave him his freedom. He wasn't always faithful, but he came back to me because we had a good marriage.' She dabbed at her watery eyes with her handkerchief. 'We were friends, and we used to laugh together.'

'Is there any reason why he would go to Riverside Lodge?' Flynn asked gently.

'I can't think of any. He'd only been there once, and that was before the villa was built. It was just after I'd purchased the land, and we met the architect to discuss plans. Ronnie was a member of the Hurlingham Club and a keen polo player. We were looking forward to entertaining at the villa during the summer season. But I can't think of any reason why he'd go there at this time of year; the place hasn't even been furnished yet.' She wiped her cheeks, making them look redder and sorer. 'I pictured him in Paris or Bruges, holed up in some plush hotel, enjoying the nightlife.'

'You thought that's where he'd run to?'

She nodded. 'Ronnie knew his days in the cabinet were numbered. That bloody Jennings was snapping at his heels, and Ronnie was tired of toeing the line. He didn't agree with Asquith's decision to hold another election, and I assumed the mess Churchill made on Black Friday was the last straw for him. He'd talked about us going travelling for six months and coming back in time for the sporting season. I thought he'd hopped on a boat to the continent as a way of saying bugger off to the lot of them. And... and...' Lady Carstairs stared down into her lap. 'He'd sold a few things to get some ready cash.'

Flynn exchanged a look of astonishment with Goodspeed. 'What things?'

'Treadaway will show you. He noticed that some things were missing from Ronnie's study.'

'You didn't mention this the last time we spoke,' Flynn said in exasperation. 'And neither did Mr Treadaway.'

'I told him not to. I didn't want to cause Ronnie any embarrassment. The thing is, Ronnie's not good with money. We'd probably be on our uppers if it wasn't for my inheritance. My father died recently and left me quite a sum. It was thrilling to have funds to play with, and we decided to build the villa and sell this place.' She glanced around the room. 'The house was handy enough when Ronnie was working in Westminster, but he knew his parliamentary career wasn't going to last much longer. He'd been sailing close to the wind for far too long.'

Flynn followed her gaze, taking in the collection of art decorating the walls.

'Why would your husband sell his possessions? Did he have no money of his own?'

'Not much. I hold the purse strings. I would have given him anything he asked for but... well, if there were a woman involved, he'd have the decency not to expect me to fund the liaison.'

Flynn wasn't sure about Ronnie's grasp of decency but let this pass.

'When did you last see your husband?'

'On the morning of Friday the eighteenth of November. We breakfasted here together, then he went off to parliament. He knew I was returning to Biddenden House that morning and taking the staff with me.'

Goodspeed began noting what she said in his pocketbook. 'When did you expect to see him next?'

'That night or over the weekend. It wasn't unusual for him to stay in London without me. If it was just for a night or two, he'd go to one of his clubs.'

Flynn tried to phrase his next question as delicately as he could. Goodspeed had already checked with Brooks's and the Reform Club, and Lord Carstairs hadn't visited either since his disappearance.

'Do you think your husband planned to meet with someone that weekend? A close female friend, perhaps?'

'If he did, I don't know who it was, and neither do his pals. When he didn't turn up the following week, I came up to town and started asking around to see if anyone knew where he might have gone. But no one had seen him.' She gave Flynn a nervous look that told him she was about to confess something. 'I went to the National Portrait Gallery to see if I could find out where he was.'

This took Flynn by surprise. 'Why there?'

'Because during that last breakfast I'd had with Ronnie, he mentioned that something was going to happen at the gallery, though he didn't say exactly what or when. He told me it would be a complete hoot and that I'd enjoy it. He said the suffragettes were planning to have a good laugh at Churchill's expense.' She took a sip of gin. 'He and Winston never really got on.'

'So you went there first thing on the morning of Monday the fifth of December?' Flynn could barely contain his frustration. Was there anyone in London who hadn't been aware of this bloody suffragette prank?

She nodded. 'I'd been the Monday before, too. Ronnie said that was the day they were likely to strike, as it was the quietest time. After the fire, I started to think that perhaps he hadn't gone abroad and went along to see if it gave me any clues as to what he was up to.' She took a large gulp of gin. 'It's a shame he didn't get to see that portrait. He would have roared with laughter.'

Tears began to roll down her cheeks, and Flynn decided it would be prudent to leave Lady Carstairs to her grief for the time being. Mr Treadaway might prove to be a more reliable source of information.

'Perhaps you would allow Mr Treadaway to show us Lord Carstairs' study and describe the missing items?'

Lady Carstairs nodded and picked up the bell. Mr Treadaway appeared with the same alacrity as last time and took them into Lord Carstairs' study at the front of the house.

'Lady Carstairs informs us that you believe some things are missing?'

Mr Treadaway nodded. 'That is correct. I became aware of it when we returned to the house the week after Lord Carstairs disappeared. I thought we should inform the police.' He gave a slight cough. 'However, Lady Carstairs thought otherwise.'

'I understand.' Flynn gazed around the room. Along one wall was an impressive teak bookcase. On another, were dozens of colourful paintings, mostly landscapes from Middle Eastern countries, many of Morrocco. A large teak desk dominated the room, a green-leather-upholstered captain's chair behind it. Goodspeed went over to it and began to search the drawers.

Flynn turned to Mr Treadaway. 'Could you describe the items that are missing?'

The butler picked up a sheet of paper lying on the desk. 'I took the liberty of detailing the three objects in question, anticipating it would be needed.'

Flynn took it. 'Thank you, Mr Treadaway. That's most helpful.'

'As you can see, his lordship was fond of eastern artefacts.' Mr Treadaway pointed to the mantelpiece. 'On this side was an antique Persian vase with a colourful red mosaic pattern. On the other was a silver trinket box that I believe was valuable but of unknown provenance. His lordship thought it rather pretty. It was engraved with entwined fish. And in front of his desk was an antique Persian wool rug with a unique navy and red geometric design.'

'You think they could have been stolen?' Flynn had to consider the possibility that this could be a burglary gone wrong. Perhaps Carstairs had interrupted the thief. However, that wouldn't explain how he ended up at Riverside Lodge.

'As you can see, there are other valuable pieces in the room. I believe a thief would have taken those, too.' Mr Treadaway gave another of his delicate coughs. 'Lady Carstairs thought Lord Carstairs might have tired of the objects and decided to raise some cash by selling them. This house is to be sold, and his lordship might have decided these ornaments wouldn't fit with the décor he had planned for his new study at Riverside Lodge.'

'What did you think?' Flynn had a feeling the butler was more attuned to some of his master's foibles than Lady Carstairs.

'His lordship was particularly fond of the three items. I thought it unlikely he would part with them. However...' Mr Treadaway cleared his throat. 'His lordship could be volatile, and if he suddenly decided he needed some additional money, it was possible he could have sold them.'

Flynn nodded, his eyes travelling around the room. 'Is anything else out of place?'

'No,' Mr Treadaway replied. 'I've been through the whole house, and everything else is as it should be. I've checked his lordship's bedroom, and it's as I left it. It doesn't appear as if Lord Carstairs has slept here.'

'Nothing of interest in his desk,' Goodspeed remarked.

'When you left here on the morning of the eighteenth of November, were those items still here?' Flynn wondered if Carstairs had returned to the house after his day in parliament.

'I believe so. I feel certain I would have noticed if they'd been missing, particularly the rug.'

Mr Treadaway seemed the observant type, so Flynn thought he was probably right. 'Could you give me the names of the occupants of the houses on either side?'

'Mrs Hopkins, a widowed lady, lives at number twenty-one. And there isn't a house on the other side.'

Goodspeed frowned. 'There clearly is.'

Mr Treadaway's craggy face broke into a smile – not an expression Flynn had seen on him before. 'Numbers twenty-three and twenty-four are false fronts. There are no houses behind them.'

Flynn caught on. 'I've read about this. When the railway company built the underground line linking Paddington and Bayswater, they demolished the houses and rather than rebuilding them, they created false fronts.'

'That is correct. It amused Lord and Lady Carstairs to live next door to the false houses. It made quite a talking point at dinner parties. Guests would go outside to examine the frontages for themselves.'

Flynn thanked Mr Treadaway, and he and Goodspeed went outside to do exactly that.

'Well, I'm blowed.' Goodspeed stared up at the elegant facades of the five-storey townhouses that looked identical to their neighbours. Their porches had projecting ionic columns on either side, topped with balustraded balconies that matched the other houses in the terrace.

Flynn examined them closely, eager to find tell-tale signs that they weren't what they seemed. He noticed that the windows were painted a pale grey, and there were no letterboxes on the doors.

'Why?' Goodspeed asked.

'To begin with, the railway company needed the space when they first started work on the line in the 1860s. Once it was complete, it had to have an open-air section to release the build-up of smoke and steam from the locomotives. What you're looking at is a five-foot thick wall with nothing behind, except air vents.'

Goodspeed scratched his head. 'Incredible.'

Flynn walked over to their carriage. 'I need to go to St Mary's Hospital to speak to Bernard Spilsbury. He's the pathologist working on Carstairs' body. Can you call on Mrs Hopkins at number twenty-one and see what she has to say? Then when you get back to the yard, ask Jack to come here and call on all the other houses at this end of the street.'

'Will do, sir.'

* * *

It was nearly seven o'clock that evening before he and Goodspeed sat down in Flynn's office to compare findings.

Goodspeed took out his pocketbook. 'Mrs Hopkins, the widowed lady next door at number twenty-one, saw a chauffeur-driven car pick up Lady Carstairs and Mr Treadaway on the morning of Friday the eighteenth at nine-thirty. Her drawing room is at the front of the house. She didn't see Lord Carstairs leave that morning, but she did see him return that evening. He got out of a hackney carriage at around seven-thirty and went into the house. He was on his own.

About three-quarters of an hour later, she saw a car draw up outside, and a man got out and went inside. She didn't see when he left, as she went into the dining room shortly after. The maid closed the curtains at that point and confirms seeing the same car parked outside.'

'Interesting. So we know Carstairs left parliament and returned to Leinster Gardens.' Flynn tapped his pen on his desk. 'Get someone in Kent to talk to the staff at Biddenden House – discreetly. I don't want Lady Carstairs to find out. I just need to know what time she and Mr Treadaway arrived there on the eighteenth of November.'

Goodspeed looked surprised. 'You suspect her?'

'I want to rule her out. *But...* she knew her husband had been unfaithful on at least one occasion with Sylvie Blanchet. And she's recently come into money. Perhaps she decided life would be better without him. However, I'm more interested in this man who visited Carstairs that night. Did Mrs Hopkins give you a description of him?'

'She didn't see clearly as it was dark. He was of medium height, wearing a dark suit and derby hat.' Goodspeed grinned. 'Yes, I know, that could be most of the men in London. She briefly saw his face when he walked under the street lamp, which is directly outside her house, and believes she would recognise him if she saw him again.'

'What about his car?'

'She knows it was a landaulette but wasn't sure of the make. She described it, and again, she could have been describing half the cars in London. Black, shiny and with four doors.' He closed his notebook. 'What did the pathologist have to say?'

'After he examined Lord Carstairs' body at Riverside Lodge and in the mortuary, he agreed with Sergeant Donaldson that the body was tipped into the coal bunker, probably some hours after death.'

'Carstairs could have been killed anywhere.'

'I think it's most likely to have been Leinster Gardens. Spilsbury found red and navy woollen fibres on Carstairs' clothing. I told him about the missing Persian wool rug that Mr Treadaway described, navy and red with a geometric design. He thinks Lord Carstairs' body may have been wrapped in it.'

Goodspeed whistled. 'Someone kills Carstairs in his study and moves his body to Riverside Lodge?'

'I feel certain that's what happened.'

'Do you think it could be the same person who killed Marian Dean?'

'There's no evidence to suggest it,' Flynn replied. But his instincts told him it was the same killer.

28

Coral was sitting in Victoria Embankment Gardens when she saw Flynn come through the gates. She'd been on her way to Scotland Yard to talk to him but had stopped halfway, questioning why she was still acting as the go-between. She felt like walking away from the whole mess. Why should she spend her Friday night sitting in that bloody interview room again?

But then there was Marian. She had to carry on for her sake and for the promise she'd made Florence Dean. And, although she was angry with Penny and the Pankhursts for the arson attack on Riverside Lodge, she didn't like the underhand way they were being forced into submission. Someone was trying to frighten and discredit the union by implicating them in Ronald Carstairs' death.

Flynn strode with purpose, his jaw set and his mind clearly preoccupied. Was he on his way to her home? If she stayed still, he might walk straight through the gardens without noticing her. She was tired and part of her wanted to postpone any conversations, or arrests, until the next day. But she was also curious.

'Flynn,' she called, and he turned sharply at the sound of his name.

Was it her imagination, or did his expression soften when he saw it was her?

'Coral. What are you doing here?'

The first time he'd called her by her first name was when he'd returned her wedding ring. It still sounded strange to hear him say it.

'Getting cold.' She rose from the bench. 'I wanted somewhere to think. You look tired. Have you just come from Scotland Yard?'

He nodded. 'It's been a long week. I need to talk to you about what's happened. Have you had dinner? Would you like me to take you somewhere to eat?'

To her surprise, he held out his arm to her. She could image Penny's outrage if she took it. So, she smiled and did just that.

'There's a small restaurant on Savoy Street that I used to go to with Ernest. Queenie's Kitchen. It's quiet, and the food is simple but good.' Coral's fingers twitched as she mentioned Ernest. She knew Flynn shouldn't have returned her wedding ring until the case was over. And with the discovery of Ronald Carstairs' body, she had a feeling he'd be wanting it back. Had he come to ask her for it?

They walked along Victoria Embankment, chatting about the boats on the river and how many times Flynn had sketched the view of the Houses of Parliament from Westminster Bridge. She'd expected to feel awkward walking arm in arm with him, like he was escorting her to a prison cell. But, to her surprise, it felt natural to have Flynn by her side.

'Your pictures are selling well. I'll miss seeing the one of parliament and Big Ben, though I think I would have bought the one of the river with the glistening lights.'

'At weekends, my wife and I used to go on riverside walks. She'd decide which view she liked the best and then I'd sketch it.'

'Where did you learn to paint?' Coral had recently found herself wondering about his background. How had he come to be a policeman when he'd obviously studied art?

'At the Slade School of Fine Art. Oscar talked me into it. We'd been studying history and politics at the University College. Or failing to study, I should say. We both decided to apply to Slade. I was accepted; Oscar wasn't.'

'Then why did you become a policeman?'

Flynn smiled. 'The life of an impoverished artist is fine for a single man. But then I met Julia and within weeks, I'd asked her to marry me. We both wanted children, so it was time to pack away my paintbrushes and find a proper occupation. I wasn't qualified enough to follow my father into teaching, so I decided to become a constable with the Metropolitan Police.'

'You were a bobby on the beat?' Coral tried and failed to imagine a young Flynn in uniform.

'Oh yes, I had to work my way up. Julia and I lived in a tiny flat, struggling to make ends meet. Then my uncle died and left me his house on Bedford Square. He was an artist and had been disappointed when I gave up painting. I think he hoped his bequest would allow me to fulfil my artistic ambitions. And it did in a way. I started to paint again in his attic studio. But by that time, I was a detective sergeant and content in my job at Scotland Yard.'

'Have you always lived in London?'

'Yes. I don't think I could live anywhere else.'

'Me neither. Ernest and I once joined a touring company. It was a huge adventure to begin with: travelling around the country, performing on different stages every night. But we were both relieved to get home to London. It's where I was born and probably where I'll die.' And in the not-too-distant future, she reflected, if she continued her life as a suffragette. She was sure the smell she'd noticed in Penny's garage had been gunpowder.

'Do you miss acting?' Flynn asked.

'I still keep my hand in. Lavender tells me her producer has me lined up for a part in a new show he's planning.' This was a slight exaggeration, though Lavender had said he'd consider her. She wondered what Flynn thought about this. Being an actress wasn't exactly considered a reputable profession. But then he knew she posed nude for artists and was a suffragette, so she supposed she couldn't sink much lower in his eyes. Yet here he was, with his arm linked through hers.

When they reached Queenie's Kitchen, he held open the door for her, and she couldn't help but enjoy the feeling of being escorted to dinner by a handsome man. The restaurant was the same as Coral remembered, intimate and cosy with the aroma of meaty stews and melting candlewax. A waiter escorted them to a table by the window and handed them each a menu. She noticed the selection hadn't changed much since she'd last visited, which was some time ago.

'Ernest and I always used to have steak and kidney pudding and red wine. He claimed it was the most restorative meal after a performance.' Coral wondered why she couldn't seem to stop reminiscing about her husband, even though every time she mentioned his name, it brought up the spectre of her wedding ring.

'That sounds delicious.' Flynn closed his menu. 'My daughter hates kidneys, so it's not something we have at home.'

'How is Teresa?'

'Confusing. One minute, she's still my little girl, and the next, she's telling me off as if she's my mother.'

Coral laughed, and they chatted easily about Teresa, food, and art, seeming to have made an unspoken decision not to talk about murder until they'd finished their meal.

Coral found she liked seeing Flynn eat. He enjoyed food as much as she did, which made him a pleasure to dine with. Ernest had always had a good appetite until those final weeks. It had been painful to watch him waste away, unable to find anything that could tempt him. She'd sat by his bedside, spooning soup into his mouth until he'd turn away.

'What are you thinking?' Flynn gently touched her hand. 'You look sad.'

'I was remembering my husband. How much he used to enjoy his food. Before his illness.' Coral moved her hand to brush away a tear, feeling embarrassed by the sudden intimacy.

He nodded. 'It's hard when there's little you can do to relieve the suffering. Nothing you can offer that gives a moment's respite or enjoyment. Julia got so thin...' His voice trailed off, and his eyes drifted to stare out of the window into the darkness.

'I'm sorry. I didn't think. Of course, it must have been painful for you, too.'

Flynn turned back to her and smiled. 'In some ways, we have much in common. Yet in others...' He held up his hands in a bewildered gesture.

Coral let out a gurgle of laughter. 'We couldn't be more different. If it wasn't for your paintings, I doubt we'd ever have met. Well, unless you happened to arrest me.'

He chuckled. 'Please try to avoid doing anything that would lead to that.'

Coral was about to say that she intended to when the waiter came over and asked if they'd like a dessert. To her delight, Flynn ordered the chocolate pudding.

'I'll have the same, please.'

'I like this place,' Flynn declared when the waiter returned shortly after with two steaming bowls of chocolate pudding covered in custard.

'Divine.' Coral sighed after taking a mouthful.

Only when their bowls had been removed and coffee cups put in their place did Coral ask, 'I presume it was Ronald Carstairs' body at Riverside Lodge?'

Flynn nodded. 'I'm afraid so. I need to ask you about the night of the twenty-fifth. You and I both know that Penelope Bright and Irene Grayson were the ones to start the fire at Riverside Lodge.'

She was about to protest, but he held up his hand to stop her. 'I'm not going to arrest them. Their friends have given them alibis, which I don't believe for a second. All I want is for you to tell me, unofficially, what happened that night.'

Coral played with her wedding ring. He'd taken a risk by giving it back to her. She had to repay that kindness.

She took a sip of coffee, then recounted the events of that night in Fulham. 'Penny and Irene swear they didn't go inside the villa. They poured petrol into two bottles, stuffed them with rags, lit the ends of the rags, then threw them in through the windows.'

Flynn nodded. 'That was the fire chief's assessment of the situation.'

'They had no idea a body was inside. And I can assure you Ronald Carstairs' corpse was not in our car that night.' The thought made Coral feel nauseous.

'It's more likely he was killed earlier, probably on Black Friday, and his body moved to Riverside Lodge shortly afterwards.'

'Where do you think he was killed?' she asked.

'At his townhouse in Leinster Gardens. Ronald Carstairs went back there after leaving parliament that Friday. I've arranged for the pathologist who examined his body to visit the house to see if he can find any clues as to where he might have been killed.'

'I don't understand why Lady Carstairs didn't report him missing.'

'It seems Ronald Carstairs was quite a character,' Flynn said with a smile.

When he told her about the items missing from the study, she couldn't help asking if it might have been a burglary.

'Doubtful. There were other valuable pieces that were left behind, and a thief wouldn't bother moving the body.'

'So who would?'

'Someone who wanted to destroy the evidence, which leads us back to your friends, Penelope Bright and Irene Grayson.'

'They think we're being set up.' Coral told him about the anonymous letters Penny had received.

Flynn eyes narrowed as he listened. 'I have a feeling someone in parliament was enjoying settling scores with his colleagues. First Churchill and Lloyd George, then Jennings.'

'But it must have been working both ways. How else did Nathan Jennings know we were planning a protest at the National Portrait Gallery?'

'Not just Jennings. The reason Lady Carstairs was there that morning was because Lord Carstairs had mentioned something was planned. She hoped it would give her some clue as to her husband's whereabouts.'

Coral felt a chill when she thought back to that morning at the gallery. How ignorant they'd been, waltzing in and assuming they'd take everyone by surprise with their hilarious prank. Yet the joke had been on them.

'Could Ronald Carstairs have been telling tales on his fellow politicians?'

Flynn sipped his coffee. 'The more I find out about him, the more I think it would appeal to his sense of humour.'

'But who told him what we had planned and where does Marian come into all this?'

Flynn looked thoughtful. 'Could you go and see Marian Dean's grandmother again? See what you can find out about the meeting between Marian and Lord Carstairs. I think she'd feel more comfortable chatting informally to you than being questioned by me and Goodspeed.'

Coral was absurdly pleased that he trusted her with such a task.

'I'm going to talk to Charles Dean and Nathan Jennings again,' he continued. 'Now Carstairs' body has been found, they might be more willing to tell me where they got their information from. And why Jennings was so keen to know who painted the Churchill portrait.'

'Could he be the killer? It seems a bit pathetic, but if he suspected Carstairs was the reason he got pelted with eggs, he might have wanted revenge? He was with him in parliament on Black Friday and at the gallery when Marian was stabbed.'

'It's possible, though I don't see why he would kill Marian.' Flynn paused. 'You said she was becoming increasingly committed to the cause and infatuated with Christabel Pankhurst. Could she have found out about the villa from her brother or Nathan Jennings and decided to kill Ronald Carstairs to try to prove herself to the Pankhursts? And been killed in revenge?'

'Had you asked me that a week ago, I would have said no, of course not.' Coral recalled Marian's zeal and commitment. 'But here we are, and I have no idea what to think. If Marian did murder Ronald Carstairs, who would want to kill her? Lady Carstairs?'

Flynn shrugged. 'Like you, I've no idea what to think. And until I know for sure, I'm not ruling out any possibilities.'

Coral saw his eyes flit to her wedding ring, and with a pounding heart, she slid it from her finger. 'I suppose Ronald Carstairs' murder changes everything?'

He looked startled when he saw what she was doing. 'It does. I shouldn't have returned it to you until the case is over. It's evidence, and I will be asked where it is.'

'I know.' She held the ring between her fingers and then moved her hand across the table towards him. 'I'm grateful to you for returning it. However, I don't want to get you into trouble. I want you to solve Marian's murder.'

29

When they left the restaurant, Flynn had to resist the urge to pat his breast pocket to check the ring was still there. He was still reeling from the trust Coral had placed in him and imagined he could feel the weight of it against his chest. Of course, what he was feeling was the weight of expectation.

He had to solve this case to prove he deserved her trust. And that meant asking uncomfortable questions.

'I'm not making accusations,' Flynn began, as he took her arm, 'but I do need to know where you all were on the night of Black Friday. Penelope Bright, Irene Grayson, Marian Dean and...'

'And me,' she finished. 'I took Marian to her grandmother's. She'd had a rough time that afternoon. Then I went home and didn't go out again. Lavender was at work, so I have no witnesses to that. Penny was at a meeting at Clement's Inn until midnight, so there are plenty of witnesses. Genuine ones,' Coral added with wink.

He smiled. 'And Irene Grayson?'

'Did you hear what happened at the Reform Club that night?'

Flynn frowned, trying to remember; then it came to him. 'A man delivering the evening newspapers went through the various lounges distributing *Votes for Women* pamphlets.' He stopped, realising who it must have been. 'Not a deliveryman, a delivery woman? Irene Grayson?'

Coral nodded.

If he recalled correctly, the incident had been at about seven o'clock that evening, when the place was full of politicians straight from parliament. Mrs Hopkins had told Goodspeed she'd seen a man arriving at Leinster Gardens at eight-fifteen that night. Could that man have been Irene Grayson in disguise? He decided not to mention this suspicion to Coral.

Instead, he asked, 'Do you really believe someone would commit murder to discredit the suffragettes?'

'I don't think Ronald Carstairs was killed for that reason. It seems more likely that whoever did it had a personal motivation for wanting him dead. Being able to blame the deed on the suffragettes was probably a happy coincidence for the killer.'

Flynn had a feeling she was right. He wanted to discuss it further, but they'd already reached Adelphi Terrace. Coral had removed her arm from his and was fumbling in her purse for her door key.

'How about a brandy to finish the night off?' she asked without looking up.

'That would be lovely,' he replied before he could talk himself out of it. What was the harm in having a drink on a Friday night when it was his weekend off? That evening, he'd experienced a barrage of emotions that he was still trying to untangle, yet he didn't want it to end.

Earlier, when they'd chatted about his paintings and she'd said how much she liked the one with the lights glistening on the river, he'd wanted to rush home and start sketching a new picture just for her.

And before that, he'd taken himself by surprise when he'd asked her to dine with him. He wondered if he'd be brave enough to ask her out again, once the case was over.

The feeling that embarrassed him most was the pride he'd felt at escorting such an attractive woman into a restaurant. This was closely followed by guilt. In his life, the ladies on his arm had always been family members. His mother, his wife, and his daughter. There was something almost illicit in what he felt at being alone with Coral.

In the hallway, he removed his hat and coat and was about to follow her into the drawing room, when she stopped and sniffed the air like a hunting dog.

'Someone's smoking,' Coral whispered. 'Lavender doesn't allow smoking in the house.'

He sniffed. Someone was definitely smoking. He pushed past Coral and swung open the door of the drawing room – and came face to face with Goodspeed.

Flynn was sure the embarrassment on his sergeant's face was reflected on his own. Goodspeed was seated in the armchair Flynn had occupied on his first visit to the house, a glass of brandy in his hand.

'Sir.' Goodspeed scrambled to his feet, placing the glass on the mantelpiece. 'I just walked Miss Lacey home.'

'Good evening, Detective Inspector Flynn.' Lavender was lounging in the other armchair, her glossy dark hair spilling over her shoulders. She smiled as her eyes flitted between him and Coral. 'Have you two been anywhere nice?'

'Dinner at Queenie's Kitchen,' Coral murmured.

'Divine. I bet you had chocolate pudding. Sit down, and I'll get you both a drink.'

'No.' Flynn barked the word rather more harshly than intended. In a softer voice, he said, 'Thank you, I must be getting home.'

Goodspeed, who was still standing, moved towards the door. 'Me too. Er, thank you for the drink, Miss Lacey.'

'My pleasure, darling.' Lavender rose from the armchair, the draped sleeves of her silver dress shimmering as she blew him a kiss. 'Goodnight, Evan.'

Goodspeed bolted from the room, and Flynn wasn't far behind after mumbling goodbye to Coral.

'Sorry about that, sir.' Goodspeed lit a cigarette as they walked up to the Strand to find a taxi.

'You've nothing to apologise for.' Flynn smiled, seeing the absurdity of the situation. He was Goodspeed's senior officer, not his mother, for goodness' sake. If his sergeant chose to walk an actress home from the theatre, that was his business.

Goodspeed gave him a sideways glance. 'Did you and Mrs Fairbanks have a nice dinner?'

Flynn ignored the question. 'I'll be glad when this bloody case is over.'

But Goodspeed wasn't deterred. 'Why? So you don't have to see Coral Fairbanks again? Or because then you can see her without worrying she's a murderer?'

Flynn tried to give his sergeant an admonishing look, though his heart wasn't in it.

'I know she's not a murderer; otherwise, I wouldn't have had dinner with her,' he replied, still feeling the weight of Coral's wedding band in his breast pocket. This was getting far too complicated.

* * *

On Monday morning, Flynn found himself back in the bowels of Whitehall, in Nathan Jennings' office.

'Was it Ronald Carstairs who told you something was going to happen at the National Portrait Gallery?'

Jennings glared at him from behind his wide oak desk. Apart from a blotter, an inkstand, and a lamp, the desk was bare. Didn't the man do any work? Flynn's own desk was covered in folders and papers.

'How do you know that?' Jennings demanded.

'Because he also told his wife, Lady Carstairs. What made him tell you?'

Jennings sighed, his face relaxing as if the game was up. 'I'd suspected Ronnie of being the spy for some time. When I had the proof, I confronted him with it.'

This intrigued Flynn. 'What proof?'

Jennings stroked his moustache, looking rather pleased with himself. 'I set a trap. He was the only person who knew I was going to Ascot that day. I didn't tell anyone, not even Charles. I gave Ronnie the exact time of when I'd be arriving, and lo and behold, as soon as I stepped out of my car, I was pelted with eggs.'

'What made you suspect Lord Carstairs?'

'It was Ronnie's sense of humour. Politics was a game to him, and the only side Ronnie was ever on was his own. I used to drink with him at Brooks's, and whenever there was an incident, I saw his glee at what had befallen one of his colleagues. It was then I realised these things tended to happen to politicians Ronnie had recently had run-ins with. So, I made a comment that I knew would upset him, and he took the bait.'

'What happened when you confronted Lord Carstairs with your evidence?'

Jennings smirked. 'He didn't bother to deny it. In fact, I think he was pleased to have someone to boast to. He apologised to me for the Ascot incident and said I was jolly clever to have set him up. We ended up having a laugh about it.'

Flynn wondered if Winston Churchill would be quite so forgiving if he knew who was behind the horse whip incident. And Lloyd George would be fuming if he found out one of his own parliamentary colleagues had divulged the address of his mistress. However, Carstairs was no longer around to deal with the repercussions of his actions. Maybe his death itself had been a repercussion of what he'd done.

Perhaps sensing Flynn's thoughts, Jennings adopted a serious expression. 'Of course, I told Ronnie it had to stop. And he agreed. Then, on Bla... On Friday the eighteenth of November, when we were sitting in the Commons and all hell was breaking loose outside, he whispered to me that the suffragettes would have the last laugh on Winston.'

'You were aware of the home secretary's orders to use violence against the WSPU delegation?' Flynn couldn't stop himself from asking the question.

Jennings flushed, realising he'd said too much. 'We'd heard rumours. I knew Winston thought he had to crack down hard. The prime minister gave in to him... and, well, you saw the result.'

'I did indeed. Did you ask Lord Carstairs what he meant by the comment?'

'I tried to and he just said there would be a special exhibition taking place at the National Portrait Gallery. I didn't know what he meant by that, and I never got the chance to ask.'

'The incident with the Churchill portrait took place over two weeks later. Why did you wait that long to visit the gallery to warn Mr Scott?'

'Because I didn't know what was going to happen or when. I'd intended to talk to Ronnie about it again and try to put a stop to any more of his tricks.' Jennings held up his hands in a hopeless gesture. 'But he disappeared. I was at a loss to know what to do. When I mentioned it to Charles, he suggested we have a quiet word with Mr Scott. I thought it was a sensible suggestion, so that's what we did.'

Flynn was interested to hear it had been Charles Dean's suggestion to visit the National Portrait Gallery. Had he been keeping an eye out for sister while he was there?

'Why did you ask Mrs Fairbanks who painted the Churchill portrait?'

Jennings didn't seem surprised that he knew this. 'Ronnie was friends with lots of artists. I thought if I found out who it was, it would give me some clue as to where he was getting his information from. And who he was giving information to.'

'Did he ever mention the name Penelope Bright?'

Jennings shook his head. 'Who's Penelope Bright?'

Flynn explained about the anonymous notes.

'Strange. I thought Ronnie had a... well, I thought he might have had a mistress in the organisation.'

Flynn had also considered that possibility. Instead, it seemed that Lord Carstairs had resorted to the old-fashioned method of sending anonymous letters.

'Why do you think Lord Carstairs told you about the "special exhibition" as he called it?'

'Because he took great delight in engineering these things. It's probably why he mentioned it to his wife. He thought it a great hoot.'

'If you were concerned about Lord Carstairs' behaviour, why didn't you inform the prime minister?'

'In hindsight, I should have. But Ronnie was an old friend. He's helped me over the years, and it felt disloyal to tell tales on him.'

Flynn didn't believe this for a second. Jennings had his own reasons for not reporting Lord Carstairs, and he didn't think loyalty was one of them. It was more likely he was giving his old friend enough rope to hang himself with.

'What about Riverside Lodge?' Flynn saw Jennings' expression become more guarded. 'Have you ever been there?'

'Not to the villa, no. They'd only just finished building it. I know the area, though. I'm a member of the Hurlingham Club. Charles and I often play polo there.'

Flynn wondered if the polo field had recovered from Coral's efforts with a metal stake. Why did he suddenly feel an odd sort of pride in her? He pushed that feeling aside to be examined later.

'I'd hoped to speak to Mr Dean this morning.' Flynn got the impression Jennings relied heavily on his private secretary. 'Is he here today?'

'He's still on leave. I'm expecting him back this week.' Jennings' eyes drifted across his empty desk. 'We have lots to catch up on, I'm sure.'

'It's curious someone gave the suffragettes details of Riverside Lodge.' Flynn watched Jennings' face closely. 'The anonymous letter encouraged them to set fire to it. Lord Carstairs would hardly do that and we suspect his body was already concealed in the coal bunker by that stage.'

'I think it's obvious what happened. Mrs Pankhurst ordered Ronnie's assassination.' Jennings must have seen his sceptical expression because he continued more forcefully. 'Those women were angry that day. I have some sympathy – the situation was badly handled; I don't deny it. They decided to take revenge on a politician, found poor old Ronnie on his own that evening and killed him. Then they took his body to Riverside Lodge and tried to burn the place down to hide the evidence.'

Flynn wondered how Jennings knew that Lord Carstairs had been alone at Leinster Gardens on the night of Friday the eighteenth of November.

30

On Monday afternoon, Coral finished her shift at the Stanmore Gallery, then took a hackney carriage to Porchester Terrace to visit Marian's grandmother.

All weekend, she'd tried to put Flynn out of her mind, but her thoughts kept drifting back to their dinner together. And wondering how their evening might have ended if they hadn't returned to find Goodspeed in her drawing room.

Lavender told her that when he'd turned up at the theatre that night, she'd decided to try to help Coral by quizzing him for information about the case. Coral wondered if this was strictly true. She had a feeling Lavender liked Goodspeed more than she was letting on – or even admitting to herself.

The butler opened the door of Florence Dean's Georgian townhouse, and she was once again shown into the drawing room.

'Mrs Fairbanks. How lovely to see you.' Florence held out her hands to Coral. 'Do you have news?'

'I'm afraid not.' Coral sat beside her on the sofa. 'I came to ask you some questions regarding the time Marian met Ronald Carstairs.'

Florence blinked. 'I've read about his death. Surely there can't be a connection with what happened to Marian?'

'Probably not, but Detective Inspector Flynn is following up every lead.'

'You've spoken to him?'

'Yes. I mentioned to him that Marian once told me she'd met Lord Carstairs. I wondered if you could tell me more about that.'

'It was when Charles was seconded to Lord Carstairs' office and worked as his private secretary for a short while. Lady Carstairs asked him about his family, and when she found out we lived just a few roads away from Leinster Gardens, she invited Charles, Marian, and me to call on them for afternoon tea.'

'When was that?'

'It must have been around six months ago. Marian had only just moved down from Yorkshire. It was a rather jolly afternoon, as I remember. We looked at the false-fronted houses next door, and Marian was fascinated by them. Lord Carstairs took quite a shine to her. He was a rogue of a man – I could see that. But he seemed harmless enough. I didn't get the impression he had designs on her.'

'What did you talk about?'

'Parliament. Charles' job. Lord Carstairs mainly discussed art and his collection of Middle Eastern artefacts. I remember he took Charles and Marian into his study to show them some of his prize possessions.'

'Did he make any reference to the suffragettes?'

Florence smiled. 'Charles had warned Marian not to mention the subject. Of course, much to his annoyance, she told them she was a member of the WSPU. Lady Carstairs said something like "good for you", and Lord Carstairs just laughed. I think Marian assumed he was going to be a stuffy old man who dominated his wife. Nothing could have been further from the truth. Lady Carstairs was as lively as her husband.'

This reflected what Flynn had told her about his meeting with Lady Carstairs. It seemed to Coral that Lord and Lady Carstairs may have had an unconventional marriage, but it hadn't been a loveless one.

Florence touched her arm. 'At Marian's funeral, I placed a bouquet of flowers on her grave tied in purple, green and white ribbons to recognise her contribution to the suffragettes. It's hard sometimes to balance the love you have for your family with your personal beliefs, but I believe it's what Marian would have wanted.'

Tears sprang to Coral's eyes. 'She won't be forgotten by her friends – I promise you that.'

As Florence couldn't recall much else about the tea party at Leinster Gardens, they moved on to reminisce over Marian, and Coral left Porchester Terrace with nothing new to tell Flynn. Seeing Florence made her feel guilty that she was no nearer to discovering who'd killed Marian. If it was the same person who'd murdered Ronald Carstairs, she was blowed if she could see the connection.

As she walked along Bayswater Road, she couldn't resist turning left onto Leinster Gardens, curious to see the Carstairs residence and the false-fronted houses for herself.

But the road was longer than expected, and as she trudged along the pavement, the light started to fade. As it did, the temperature dropped, and she pulled her woollen coat tighter around her. The noise of traffic began to fade until the only sound was the tapping of her heels on the paving slabs.

Then she heard another sound. Someone else's footsteps, though more muffled than her own. Perhaps the tread of a man's flatter shoes?

Coral quickened her pace, looking over her shoulder. The gas lamps hadn't yet been lit, and she couldn't see far, but she thought she glimpsed a shadow some distance behind her.

She kept walking, noting the door numbers on the houses as she went. When the footsteps got closer, she regretted leaving behind the comforting bustle of the main road. She'd never been to Leinster Gardens before and had no idea the street was so long and so quiet. No motor cars or carriages passed, and the houses all seemed to be in darkness.

Panic began to rise. Had her preoccupation with finding a link to Ronald Carstairs allowed her to ignore her initial suspicion that someone was simply targeting suffragettes?

'Mrs Fairbanks.'

Coral jumped at the sound of someone calling her name and swung around to see Charles Dean hurrying toward her. She didn't know whether to be afraid or not. She remembered his comment as he left the Stanmore Gallery... *I wouldn't want it to happen to anyone else.*

'I'm sorry, I didn't mean to scare you. I thought I'd be able to catch up with you on Bayswater Road, and then I saw you turn up here.' He was flushed and out of breath.

She glanced around. If he did produce a weapon, she would have little chance of outrunning him.

'What do you want?' She tried to sound calm but could hear the shrillness in her voice.

'To tell you something. Something I want you to tell Detective Inspector Flynn. My grandmother said you're in contact with him. Is that correct?'

Coral nodded, her breathing beginning to steady.

'I went into work this afternoon and Nathan Jennings informed me of his meeting with Detective Inspector Flynn. He told Flynn that Lord Carstairs was leaking information to the suffragettes. That's true. What he didn't say was that he'd tried to blackmail Lord Carstairs over it.'

'Nathan Jennings wanted money?' Although she'd been suspicious of Jennings, she hadn't considered that his motivation.

'No, nothing like that. I overheard them talking, and Nathan was threatening to tell the prime minister what Lord Carstairs had been doing unless he resigned from his cabinet post. Nathan's wanted the job of Secretary of State for the Colonies for some time now, but Carstairs stood in his way.'

Coral took a moment to digest this. 'Do you think he could have murdered Lord Carstairs?'

'I don't know what to think. All I know is that Nathan is saying the suffragettes killed Carstairs. I'm not so sure.' Charles stared at her as if she might have the answer, and she guessed he was beginning to speculate on Jennings' possible involvement with his sister's death. He looked young and confused – as if he was no longer certain of the things he'd once believed.

Coral nodded. 'I'll tell Flynn what you've told me.'

'Thank you.' Charles turned to go, then said, 'Where are you heading? Would you like me to walk with you or fetch you a taxi?'

'No. Thank you. I'll be fine.'

He hesitated. 'If you're sure.'

Coral breathed heavily as he walked away. Was she sure? Would it have been wiser to have gone with him? Or could he have been trying to lure her somewhere?

She glanced at the nearest house. She'd reached number fifteen, so she might as well keep going.

As she got closer to number twenty-two, she saw a police carriage and a car waiting outside. When she saw Flynn coming out of the front door, she would have been tempted to run into his arms if he'd been on his own.

But there was a gentleman with him, and it wasn't Goodspeed. He carried a black bag, and Coral suspected he was a medical man. She watched as he got into the waiting car before hurrying over to Flynn.

He looked at her in surprise. 'Coral. What are you doing here?'

'I've been to see Marian's grandmother. She told me she and Marian once had tea here with Lord and Lady Carstairs. After what you told me about this place—' she gestured to the false-fronted houses '—I wanted to see for myself.'

'Come inside. I'd like to show you something.'

Coral was only too happy to get out of the cold.

In the hallway, Flynn ushered her through the first door into a room at the front of the house that overlooked the road.

'Is anyone at home?' she whispered.

'Mr Treadaway, the butler, is upstairs, packing Lord Carstairs' belongings. Lady Carstairs is at Riverside Lodge with the builders.' Flynn walked over to a large teak desk. 'This is Lord Carstairs' study. And the man you just saw leaving was Bernard Spilsbury, a pathologist.'

Coral knew the name from the newspapers. 'The one who gave evidence at the Dr Crippen trial?'

Flynn nodded. 'He examined Ronald Carstairs' body and confirmed he hadn't been killed at Riverside Lodge. He'd been stabbed some hours before his body was dumped there. He's just examined this room and found traces of blood on the underside of the desk.' He pointed to a stain in the teak. 'He believes Ronald Carstairs was stabbed right there, which is where the Persian rug would have been.'

Coral shivered as she looked at the desk and then the carpet, noticing a darker area where the fabric had been protected from fading by the rug. She gazed around the room, with its colourful paintings and teak furniture, and thought it appeared oddly familiar, although she was sure she'd never been here before.

'Does he think Lord Carstairs was killed on the night of Black Friday?'

'It seems most likely, given that he wasn't seen again after that day.'

Coral knew what this meant. 'Charles Dean told me that Nathan Jennings believes suffragettes killed Lord Carstairs. Do you believe that?'

His hesitation before replying told her he hadn't dismissed the idea.

'Retaliation for what happened that day could be a possible motive,' he admitted. 'The WSPU had been betrayed. The prime minister had lied to them and they'd been viciously treated when they tried to protest.'

His use of the word *they* seemed to indicate a conspiracy. Coral thought it was more likely to be a rogue suffragette acting alone – and the two most zealous members of their group were Penny and Marian.

Coral told him about her meeting with Florence Dean. 'Marian and Charles came into the study when they visited here.'

Flynn's eyes narrowed. 'You said Marian had been attacked on Black Friday and you walked her back to her grandmother's. Do you think she could have come here later that night?'

Coral didn't want to believe that so she didn't reply. Instead, she described her encounter with Charles Dean.

'I knew it.' There was a hint of triumph in Flynn's voice. 'I had a feeling there was more to Jennings' ploy to prove Carstairs was the spy. He'd only bother going to those lengths if he thought he could get something out of it.'

'You said a man visited Lord Carstairs that night. Perhaps it was Nathan Jennings,' Coral suggested.

'I haven't discounted that,' Flynn replied.

Coral guessed he also hadn't discounted Irene Grayson, who'd been dressed as a deliveryman that night to get into the Reform Club.

'Do you still think the same person is responsible for both killings? Because if you're right, and it was a suffragette, why would they kill Marian at the National Portrait Gallery, with all the risk that entails? Any one of us could have easily lured Marian to a quiet spot somewhere. We have dozens of secret meeting places across London.' Coral wasn't about to name any of them. 'We could have arranged to meet her there and done the deed in safety.'

Flynn nodded slowly. 'I take your point. What made it so urgent that she had to die there and then?'

Coral didn't have an answer to this. They left the study, and while Flynn spoke to Mr Treadaway, Coral went outside to wait for him. When he came out, they stared up at the false-fronted houses.

'How very London.' Coral knew Flynn would understand what she meant by this.

He smiled. 'It is, isn't it? Always something new and eccentric to discover.'

Coral imagined spending a day with Flynn, walking around the city. She could tell him stories about the theatres she'd worked in, and the many ghosts that were supposed to haunt them, and he could tell her tales of grisly crimes committed in dark alleys.

These daydreams were interrupted by the sound of a woman calling. 'Hello. Hello, there.'

Coral turned to see a lady of about sixty with grey hair rushing over to them. In her hand was a newspaper.

'Are you a policeman? I saw you here with Detective Sergeant Goodspeed the other day.'

'I'm Detective Inspector Flynn. It's Mrs Hopkins, isn't it?'

'That's right. Your sergeant called on me to ask when I'd last seen Lord Carstairs, and if I'd noticed anyone visiting him. I told him about a gentleman I'd seen calling here on the night of Friday the eighteenth of November.' Mrs Hopkins held up the *Evening Standard* and pointed to a photograph on the front cover. 'This is the man. Nathan Jennings. He's just been appointed Secretary of State for the Colonies.'

31

'Mr Jennings, you told me the last time you saw Lord Carstairs was in parliament on the afternoon of Friday the eighteenth of November, before you left at five o'clock. Yet an eyewitness saw you calling at Lord Carstairs' home on Leinster Gardens that night at a quarter past eight.' Flynn watched Nathan Jennings shift in his seat. He'd hoped for panic or even fear, but the politician just looked uncomfortable.

'I apologise. I'd forgotten about that.' Jennings interlocked his fingers, placing his hands on his desk in what appeared to be a contrite gesture.

'And when we found Lord Carstairs' body, you didn't remember?' Flynn stared at him with raised eyebrows.

Jennings unlocked his fingers and began to fiddle with the buttons of his morning suit. 'I realise I should have come to you sooner, but it was a delicate matter.'

'What was a delicate matter? His murder?'

'I hope you're not accusing me...' Jennings' attempt at indignation failed, and it was clear he wasn't going to put up much of a fight. That morning, Bally had warned Flynn not to be too heavy-handed – and he had a feeling he wouldn't need to be.

'You were blackmailing Lord Carstairs,' Flynn stated. 'Is that why you went to see him that night? To make sure he gave you what you wanted?'

'I was not blackmailing him,' Jennings mumbled.

'You didn't threaten to inform the prime minister of his anonymous tip-offs to the suffragettes?'

Jennings flushed, seeming about to crumble. 'That was my duty.'

'Have you carried out your duty and told the prime minister? Perhaps you mentioned it when he was appointing you Secretary of State for the Colonies?'

'I wouldn't call it blackmail.' Jennings held up his hands in a gesture of surrender. 'I was giving Ronnie the chance to do the decent thing. Resign or I'd tell the prime minster what I knew.'

'And he refused?'

'At first. Ronnie never liked being told what to do. He thought he could ride it out, but that night, well, he realised he had to go. He told me he'd arrange to see the prime minister the following day.'

'Were you angry with him?'

'No. I was glad he'd seen sense. We had a drink together and discussed what had happened in Parliament Square. I'll be honest, I don't think he was resigning because of my threats. Knowing Ronnie, he would have tried to call my bluff. I think he'd had enough because of what happened that afternoon. He blamed Winston, saying it was ridiculous for him to have brought in police from Whitechapel to rough up the suffragettes. It was obvious it would back-fire.' Jennings stroked his oily moustache, his ridiculous vanilla pomade beginning to offend Flynn's nostrils. 'That was when he said the suffragettes would be holding a special exhibition at the National Portrait Gallery. He didn't say what was going to happen, but I could see that it amused him. He and Winston have had their spats over the years, and Ronnie made some comment about this being his parting gift.'

'Whereabouts in the house did you have this drink?'

'In Ronnie's study. He answered the door himself, the staff had all gone with Violet to Biddenden House, and he poured us both a whisky and soda.'

'You knew he was alone in the house?'

'Yes. He told me he was going to stay at the Reform Club that night, try to see the prime minister the following morning, then go down to Kent.'

'What time did you leave Lord Carstairs?'

'I was only there for around half an hour. I suppose I left at about a quarter to nine. I had my car and asked him if he'd like me to run him over to the Reform Club. He said he had some business to attend to first and would get a hackney there later.'

'How did Lord Carstairs seem when you left him?'

Jennings shrugged. 'Same old Ronnie. Nothing much bothered him. I hoped we could still be friends, though I knew he'd try to get back at me at some stage. He was like that. But I'd be looking out for him.'

Flynn couldn't help reflecting that these men, who behaved like children, had the gall to deny women the right to vote, saying they weren't mentally capable of using it responsibly.

'Did you see any other vehicles on Leinster Gardens that night?'

'No. It was quiet—' Jennings suddenly stopped, finger resting on the Cupid's bow of his moustache. 'Now I think about it, there was a motor car parked on the road.'

How convenient, Flynn thought as he asked, 'Whereabouts?'

'Next door. Outside the false-fronted houses – you know the ones I mean?'

Flynn nodded. Mrs Hopkins hadn't mentioned another car, though if it was parked outside numbers twenty-three and twenty-four, she would only have seen it if she'd been standing right by the window. However, her maid might have noticed it when she was drawing the curtains.

'It was there when I arrived and when I left.'

'What sort of car?'

'I didn't take much notice. Usual landaulette type, I think. Not as smart as mine but quite large.'

Flynn digested this information, considering his options. Jennings could be lying about another vehicle to disguise the fact that he'd killed Carstairs that night and taken the body in his own car to Riverside Lodge. He was familiar enough with the area, having played polo at the Hurlingham Club. It was the anonymous letter to Penelope Bright that bothered him. Before, when Flynn had mentioned her name to Jennings, he genuinely hadn't seemed to have known who she was.

'Is that all, Detective Inspector? I have a busy day.' Jennings made a motion towards his desk as if it were covered in paperwork, then seeming to realise it was bare, folded his arms across his chest.

Flynn rose from his chair. 'That's all for the time being, but I will need to speak to you again.'

As much as he'd like to arrest Jennings and lock him in the interview room with Penelope Bright, he doubted Bally would allow it. He needed more evidence if he was to charge him with anything – and perhaps with what he now knew, Lady Carstairs might be able to provide it.

* * *

Flynn stood outside 22 Leinster Gardens while Goodspeed went to interview Mrs Hopkins' maid. He didn't have to wait long before his sergeant reappeared, shrugging.

'She says that now she thinks about it, there could have been another car parked by the false-fronted houses when she drew the curtains that night. But she's not certain.'

Flynn groaned. Just the type of witness he hated. 'What about the other neighbours? Did Jack find out anything?'

'No one remembers seeing anything out of the ordinary. Or having visitors themselves that might account for any cars. The lad called on practically the whole street.'

This didn't surprise Flynn. Jack was still desperate to redeem himself.

'He also went to Kent to talk to the local police near Biddenden House,' Goodspeed continued. 'Lady Carstairs and Mr Treadaway arrived there near lunchtime on the eighteenth of November and didn't come back up to town again until the following week.'

Flynn nodded. 'I thought it was unlikely they were here, but you just never know. Come on, let's see what her ladyship has to say about Jennings' attempt to blackmail her husband.'

Mr Treadaway showed them into the drawing room where he'd set out a pot of coffee and cups in anticipation of their arrival. Lady Carstairs was forgoing gin that afternoon in favour of cakes and seemed to be working her way through a plate of petit fours.

Flynn got straight to the point and gave her a brief account of his meeting with Nathan Jennings.

'Conniving little runt,' was her response.

Goodspeed snorted with laughter at this, earning himself an approving look from Lady Carstairs. Even Flynn couldn't help smiling at her assessment of Jennings.

'I suppose it was Ronnie's fault for being so naughty.' Lady Carstairs dabbed at her mouth with a napkin. 'Do have a cake, Detective Sergeant Goodspeed.'

Flynn contented himself with a cup of coffee, breathing in the strong aroma with appreciation, while Goodspeed devoured a petit four in one mouthful.

'You didn't know your husband was writing these anonymous letters to Miss Penelope Bright?' Flynn asked.

'Never heard of her. But it strikes me as the type of prank Ronnie would play.'

In Flynn's view, instigating attacks on fellow politicians amounted to more than a prank, though he kept this view to himself.

'I have some news for you.' Lady Carstairs reached over and plucked a set of keys from a side table. 'These are the keys to Riverside Lodge.'

Flynn nodded. 'Yes. I was told you had a set as well as the local agent.'

'No, you don't understand.' She waved the keys at him, causing them to jangle. 'I didn't know we had a set. I thought I was going to collect them from the agent when I went to inspect the property. Of course, the fire happened, and I never ended up going. Yesterday, when I went to Riverside Lodge, the foreman, Mr Arthurs, told me he'd delivered these keys here on the Friday after they'd finished work on the property.'

'So they've been here all along?' Flynn asked, unsure of the point she was making.

'No. That's just it. Mr Arthurs found these in the yard by the back door to the scullery of Riverside Lodge. He knows they're the same ones he delivered here because of this little blue tag with RL on it.' Lady Carstairs held up the tiny piece of card threaded to the keys.

Goodspeed reached for his pocketbook. 'You're saying he delivered them here on Friday the eighteenth of November?'

'That's right. This chap, Mr Arthurs, locked up Riverside Lodge himself. All the doors had been fitted by then, and he took a set of keys to the agent, then drove over here and posted a set through the letterbox. They were in a brown envelope with "Keys to Riverside Lodge" written on the outside.'

'What time was this?' Flynn was keen to slot this new piece of information into the chronology of events of the night of Black Friday.

'He said it would have been around a quarter past six that evening. He knocked on the door but as there was no reply, he put the envelope through the letterbox.'

'Your husband was seen arriving back here at seven-thirty that evening. On finding the envelope on the doormat, where do you think he would have put it?' Flynn asked.

'He'd have tossed it onto his desk. He would take his hat and coat off and go straight into his study. Treadaway would leave any post for him on his desk, and Ronnie usually had a quick shuffle through before coming in here to fix us both a drink.' Tears formed in Lady Carstairs' eyes. 'I'll miss that. Ronnie coming in and sitting with me. We used to have gin and tell each other what sort of day we'd had.'

Flynn left it to Goodspeed to comfort her while he ruminated over what she'd just told them. Ronald Carstairs had taken Jennings into his study, poured him a drink, and the two had chatted for about half an hour. It was likely Jennings had seen the brown envelope on the desk. But had there been another visitor who'd also seen it?

After killing Ronald Carstairs, had the keys made Riverside Lodge seem the obvious place to take the body?

32

Coral stood on Trafalgar Square, staring across at the entrance to the National Portrait Gallery.

'I have a feeling you're here for the same reason I am,' said a suave voice she recognised.

She turned to find Oscar Lambourne watching her. He was dressed in a long black coat with a red silk muffler. A black top hat sat on glossy dark hair, and he raised it from his head as he bent to kiss her cheek.

Coral smiled. 'What reason is that?'

'You think by going inside and looking around, you'll be able to solve the mystery,' he replied.

'I thought by coming back and doing what Marian did, I might remember something.'

'But now you're here, you're reluctant to enter the place where she was killed?'

Coral nodded. 'I can't bear to think of her lying there in the cloakroom.'

Oscar held out his arm. 'Why don't we take a tour of the galleries together? Two minds might be better than one.'

Coral accepted the offer with gratitude. She hadn't seen Oscar for a while, but having known each other for so many years, they were always easy in each other's company. Oscar had adored Ernest and loved to reminisce about the shows they'd worked on together – and Coral loved to listen, even though she'd heard the stories many times before.

Oscar was famous in the business, having managed to become both rich and well respected through his productions – if you were employed on one of his shows, you knew it was going to be a cut above the rest in terms of wages and working conditions. In recent years, he'd faded into the background a little, only occasionally dabbling in plays by new writers who interested him. But socially, he was still very much part of the theatre and art world.

'Have you seen Guy recently?' he asked as they made their way up the steps into the foyer.

It took a moment for Coral to realise he was talking about Flynn. It had never occurred to her to call him by his first name, though he now used hers when they were alone together.

'I saw him yesterday. At Ronald Carstairs' home.'

Oscar's eyebrows shot up. 'Really? Then there is a connection. Tell me all about it.'

Coral supposed it was alright to talk to him as Flynn had already involved him in the case by showing him the Churchill portrait. It seemed Oscar was still intent on buying it, as after she'd given him a potted account of events, he asked her to pass on an offer to Irene.

They stood in the foyer chatting for some minutes, waiting for the lunch hour visitors to return to work, before Oscar asked, 'Where should we begin?'

'I want to follow the route Marian took,' she replied.

Oscar nodded, and they strolled along the corridor, first passing the doors to the Contemporary Gallery, then the Royal Gallery and finally the Westminster Gallery.

Coral saw Oscar's amusement when she pulled her wide-brimmed hat a little lower over her face in case Mr Norris was on duty. When an attendant in a black serge uniform walked by, she was relieved to see it wasn't him.

She and Oscar took a turn around the room, as Marian and Penny had done, coming to a halt at the spot where they'd hung the Churchill portrait. The hole had probably been filled in; however, it was obvious the patch of torn silk wall covering couldn't be repaired. Instead, the portrait of Ronald Carstairs had been shifted slightly to the left to hide the damage.

'The man himself,' Oscar murmured.

With a jolt, Coral realised she was staring at the room she'd visited the previous day. The scene of Ronald Carstairs' murder. That's why it had seemed familiar.

Should she examine the painting for clues? After all, that was how Flynn had discovered the wedding ring he'd found at the Hurlingham Club was hers – by scrutinising *Dawn Beauty*. She still couldn't help wondering if he'd liked what he'd seen. Is that why he'd taken a second look? Or had it been because he'd suspected the ring might be hers and decided to check if she was wearing it in the picture?

Coral pushed Flynn from her mind and tried to concentrate on the portrait before her. In it, Ronald Carstairs looked every inch the country gentleman in a brown three-piece tweed suit, a pipe in his hand.

The objects surrounding him showed his love of art and the Middle East. There were the same colourful paintings on the walls that she'd seen the day before, and she spotted a couple of the items Flynn said had been stolen. On the mantelpiece was the mosaic-patterned antique Persian vase, and Lord Carstairs was standing on a thick rug with a navy and red geometric design.

Were there clues to be found in these items? For a start, why did Carstairs' murderer take them and not the other treasures in the room? But if there was some significance, Coral failed to see it. The colourful geometric design of the Persian rug looked familiar, though she thought it might be because she'd seen a similar one in the countess's apartment. It was a style Minerva would like.

Someone tutted behind her, and she realised she'd been standing in front of the portrait for too long. She supposed there would be a macabre interest in it since Ronald Carstairs' murder. The lady behind her clearly wanted Coral to move out of the way so she could get a closer look.

'What were you hoping to see?' Oscar led her towards a lacklustre painting of William Gladstone that no one was taking much interest in.

'I'm not entirely sure.' She explained how Flynn had discovered the wedding ring he'd found was hers after spotting it in *Dawn Beauty*.

Oscar chuckled. 'Knowing Guy, he returned it to you, even though he shouldn't have.'

She nodded. 'But after they found Lord Carstairs' body, I gave it back. I knew he'd get in trouble otherwise.' Coral interlaced her gloved fingers, feeling its absence. 'He promised to return it to me once he's solved the case.'

'My, my, you two have been having quite the time of it.' Oscar's eyes twinkled as he gave her arm a squeeze. 'Don't worry. I've known Guy Flynn for over twenty years. You'll get your wedding ring back.'

Coral hoped he was right. Her instinct had been to trust Flynn – but what if he didn't solve the case?

'Where to now?' Oscar asked.

'That's the mystery.' Coral walked to the door of the Westminster Gallery. 'Marian left while Penny and Irene were still hanging the portrait. She went out of this door and should have turned right and gone down the corridor, through the foyer and out the main entrance. Only she didn't.'

They turned left and walked a little further along the corridor, gold lettering on the doors indicating the library, the secretary's room and the trustees' cloakroom.

Taking a long breath, Coral pushed open the door of the cloakroom. It held no shocking surprises, and all she felt was sadness that Marian should have died in this drab little room. It was spotlessly clean, with no indication that anything evil had taken place there.

Oscar examined the tiny window. 'Could Marian have stolen the Blanchet painting and passed it out to someone?'

'Flynn's measured it and says it would have fitted,' Coral replied. But she just couldn't picture Marian as a thief.

They left the cloakroom and stood in the corridor.

'Nathan Jennings and Charles Dean were in here.' Coral pointed to the trustees' boardroom. 'Shortly after they arrived, Mr Scott – the director of the gallery – went into the back room to bring them some coffee. While he did this, Nathan Jennings went into the cloakroom, and Charles Dean stayed in the boardroom.'

'Let's toy with a few scenarios.' Oscar's eyes darted between the doors. 'Nathan Jennings comes out of the boardroom. Maybe he'd spotted Marian a few minutes earlier as he'd walked past the Westminster Gallery. If she was leaving at that moment, Jennings could have dragged her into the cloakroom and stabbed her.'

'But why?'

'That I don't know. The other scenario is that her brother spotted her and killed her, though I don't see how he could have contrived to do that, as he was only alone for a short time, and Nathan Jennings was in the cloakroom where the murder took place. Unless they were in it together.'

Coral shook her head. She didn't believe that, not after having witnessed Charles Dean's grief.

'Then, I'm afraid, my dear, that only leaves your two friends, Penny Bright and Irene Grayson.'

Coral nodded, knowing it would come to this. 'Why would they, though?'

'Say one of them stole the Blanchet painting.' Oscar took her arm, and they walked down the corridor and into the Contemporary Gallery.

'I suppose one of them could have come in here and removed the picture while we were all in the Westminster Gallery. It was on the same wall as the door, over here.' Coral led him to the spot. 'So they wouldn't have been seen by anyone walking by.'

'Yet Marian saw something and...' Oscar raised his hands in frustration. 'But she left before them, so why go into the cloakroom? It still doesn't make sense, does it?'

Coral shook her head. 'The doorman saw Irene leave with the trolley and nothing was on it. And a newspaper vendor saw Penny, me and Lady Carstairs leave through the front entrance, and none of us were carrying anything.'

Feeling defeated, Coral took Oscar's arm, and they strolled back to the foyer and out onto the steps.

'I think I'll leave the detective work to Guy.' Oscar bent to kiss Coral's cheek. 'I'm sorry that didn't resolve anything. Would you like me to escort you somewhere?'

Coral shook her head. 'I'm going back to the Stanmore Gallery to see the countess before she goes away.'

'Ah yes, Christmas in Nice. Wish her bon voyage.' Oscar raised his top hat, and Coral watched him stroll away, his dark figure disappearing into the crowds heading to theatre land.

He was right; they hadn't resolved anything. But Coral was sure something she'd seen that afternoon was relevant – only she couldn't place what it was. The more she thought about it, the more elusive it became, and eventually she had to admit defeat.

It was only five days to Christmas and she should be thinking about what gifts to buy for her mother, sister and brother-in-law. She and Lavender would spend the day being disapproved of by their respective families before returning home to compare notes on their ordeal. Lavender had already acquired a bottle of vintage port and a wheel of stilton for their Christmas day supper.

Coral began to walk across Trafalgar Square, then stopped by one of the bronze lions guarding Nelson's Column as a memory suddenly dropped into place. It was the Persian rug from Ronald Carstairs' study. She had seen it before, and it wasn't in the countess's apartment.

To the surprise of the attendant at the reception desk, Coral burst back through the doors of the National Portrait Gallery and hurried down the corridor.

In the Westminster Gallery, she was relieved to see the lady who'd tutted at her had gone, and no one was presently standing by Ronald Carstairs' portrait. Aware of the attendant watching her, Coral leaned in to examine the lower section of the painting.

Shock and sadness collided with dismay as she realised the repercussions of what she was looking at. Coral was certain Marian had seen the same thing. And had been murdered because of it.

33

When Lady Carstairs insisted Goodspeed have another cup of coffee and just one more tiny cake, Flynn gave him a barely discernible nod to accept. His sergeant rolled his eyes, knowing his job was to charm her into possibly revealing more than she intended about her marriage and Lord Carstairs' indiscretions.

Flynn excused himself, saying he needed to have a word with Mr Treadaway, and found the butler sorting through boxes in the study.

'Mr Treadaway, during the course of packing Lord Carstairs' belongings, have you found anything that you might consider unusual or out of place?'

'No. Everything was as normal,' Mr Treadaway replied, yet Flynn noticed he had the appearance of a man undergoing an internal battle.

'Please tell me if you think of anything that might help us piece together what happened that night. No matter how trivial,' Flynn prompted.

Mr Treadaway faltered, then walked over to Lord Carstairs' desk and picked up a framed painting that was lying on top of it. He handed it to Flynn.

'I should like to seek your advice on what to do with this.'

Flynn held up the oil painting and stared into the laughing blue eyes of the late Lord Carstairs. It was an intimate portrait, showing just the face, nothing else. Although it somewhat flattered its subject, making him look younger than the newspaper photographs Flynn had seen of Carstairs, the artist had certainly captured the essence of the man.

'It's good likeness. Did Lord Carstairs commission it?'

'That is the problem. Its provenance is unknown. His lordship kept it hidden in his bedroom.' Mr Treadaway gave one of his delicate coughs. 'He and Lady Carstairs have separate bedrooms. I believe the painting was given to him by a friend. Perhaps a lady friend.'

'A mistress?' Flynn suggested.

'That is an assumption.' Mr Treadaway didn't make it entirely clear if he meant it was an assumption he made or Flynn.

'You think a lady friend had the portrait painted to give to Lord Carstairs as a gift?' Flynn asked for clarification.

Mr Treadaway nodded. 'It crossed my mind.'

Flynn was beginning to see the butler's predicament. 'When did you first become aware of this picture?'

'About a year ago. I was helping his lordship dress for dinner, and it was propped up on his dressing table.'

'Did he say who painted it?' Flynn examined the picture, but there was no signature and no markings on the back.

'He did not. He made a comment, something like "rather good, isn't it?" and I replied that it was indeed. That is the only conversation we ever had about it.'

'Had Lord Carstairs been out somewhere that day?' Flynn asked.

'I don't know. I'd just arrived from Biddenden House that evening with Lady Carstairs. Lord Carstairs had stayed in town that weekend. We had presumed he'd stayed at one his clubs for a couple of nights, but I noticed his bed had been slept in.'

'So Lord Carstairs would have had the house to himself over the weekend. Did this happen often?'

'Fairly frequently. Lady Carstairs prefers to stay at Biddenden House and all the permanent staff live there. A few of us accompany her ladyship when she comes up to town for any period of time.'

'If Lord Carstairs had been entertaining a lady here the night before, would you have any idea who she might be?' Flynn asked. 'Did you ever see him with anyone?'

'His lordship was kind enough to ensure that I was never put in that predicament.'

Flynn was sure that kindness had nothing to do with it. Carstairs had known servants always talk, no matter how loyal they might be.

'Thank you, Mr Treadaway. I appreciate your frankness. Would it be possible for me to take this picture with me?'

'Please do, Detective Inspector.' The butler appeared relieved that the burden was being taken out of his hands. No doubt, he'd anticipated an uncomfortable conversation with Lady Carstairs over its origins.

In the carriage, Flynn held the painting up to show Goodspeed. 'Do you notice any similarities?'

His sergeant looked confused. 'Similarities to what?'

'The Churchill portrait, of course. The skin tone and the brushwork.'

Goodspeed examined the picture and seemed to be making a valiant attempt to find some likeness. In the end, he just shrugged. 'Not really my area of expertise, sir.'

'Fair enough, Sergeant.' Flynn began to doubt the similarities himself. Why would Irene Grayson paint a portrait of Lord Carstairs? Unless someone had commissioned her to paint it, though she wasn't that well known for her portraiture.

However, she had met Lord Carstairs and was familiar enough with Lady Carstairs to have recognised her in the gallery on the day of the murder. And whoever commissioned the portrait would have needed to be discreet if she were Lord Carstairs' mistress. She couldn't have risked asking a famous artist.

Perhaps making a study of a politician had given Irene the idea for the Churchill portrait, although that had been painted with malice. Whoever had painted this portrait of Carstairs clearly had affection for the man.

And that was what puzzled Flynn. He could see no reason why Irene Grayson should have any affection for Lord Carstairs.

34

Coral let herself into the Stanmore Gallery, then went upstairs to the countess's apartment to find the front door open and luggage lined up in the hall.

In the lounge, Minerva was attempting to say goodbye to Sultan and Seraphine, who were more interested in attacking the fur stole draped over her shoulders. The countess was dressed in a long black travelling cape and a tall fur-trimmed hat that gave her the appearance of a Russian general.

Harriet was seated by the glass table, pointing to a map and giving Irene instructions on the best route to take to Dover.

The countess gave up trying to hug the cats and turned to Coral. 'Where have you been? You look frozen. Beryl, pour Mrs Fairbanks a cup of tea.'

'The National Portrait Gallery with Oscar Lambourne. He wished you bon voyage.' Coral gratefully took the tea from the maid and wrapped her hands around the warm cup.

'Dear Oscar, such a darling.'

Harriet glanced up from her map. 'Have you seen Flynn? Any developments?'

Coral shook her head. 'Not that he's told me.'

The countess tutted. 'I hoped this business would be cleared up before we left. Perhaps by the time we return, it will be. You have our address in Nice. Write with any news.'

Coral nodded, sinking into one of the soft armchairs. She wanted to know what Irene was doing there, but waited until the countess and Harriet went into the hall to organise their luggage before asking.

'They're paying me to drive them to Dover and bring the car back,' Irene explained, reaching for the silver cigarette box. 'You know the countess, she never travels light, and it's easier than trying to get all their luggage into a taxi.' Her hand shook as she lit a cigarette. 'Why were you at the National Portrait Gallery? I don't think I could face going into that place again.'

'It wasn't pleasant,' Coral admitted. 'I thought by going back something might occur to me that would help solve the mystery. I don't think I could have done it if Oscar hadn't offered to go with me. He still wants to buy your Churchill portrait.'

Irene waved a dismissive hand. 'I don't care what happens to the bloody thing. I wish I'd never painted it.'

Coral wished that too. 'Do you remember when you wheeled it into the gallery, it was wrapped in brown paper and carpet. Was it you who put the wrapping around it?'

Irene let out a stream of smoke and wrinkled her nose as she tried to recall.

'I wrapped it in brown paper and took it over to Penny a couple of weeks beforehand.' She gave a short laugh. 'I didn't want to risk my neighbours seeing it. The countess was hatching her plan to hang it in the National Portrait Gallery and asked Penny to bring it here to show you and Marian. It was wrapped in turquoise cloth then. But when I went to the garage that Monday to change into my deliveryman uniform, Penny had put everything into the car and added some padding.'

'She wrapped the picture in carpet?' Coral took a sip of tea, her throat tight as she tried to swallow.

Irene nodded. 'You know Penny, always thorough. I think she decided to give it an extra layer, partly to protect the painting while it was being moved and partly to make it more difficult for anyone to try to take a look at it.'

It's what Coral had anticipated. 'Do you know where Penny got the carpet from?'

Irene shrugged. 'Not a clue. Where does half the stuff in that garage of hers come from? Why do you want to know?'

Coral decided not to confide in Irene until she was certain of her theory. 'Probably nothing. Just an idea I had. I'll go and ask Penny if she remembers.'

Irene looked like she was about to say more but was summoned by an imperious command from the hallway.

Under the countess's direction, Coral helped Irene and Beryl lug all the cases down the stairs and out to St James's Square, where the Rolls-Royce was parked. After the car was finally loaded to the countess's satisfaction, Coral waved them off and then walked around to Pall Mall, contemplating her next move. Should she go and speak to Penny, or would it be more sensible to visit Scotland Yard and try to talk to Flynn first?

Coral did neither of these things. The shout of '*Evening Standard*' brought something Flynn had said to mind. Jack Hall had spoken to a newspaper vendor with a stand close to the National Portrait Gallery. The man had seen three women leaving the gallery between nine and half past on the morning of Marian's death.

Coral hurried across Trafalgar Square, sending pigeons flying into the air, in her haste to find the man. On the corner of Charing Cross Road, she spotted a newspaper vendor bellowing 'Latest news' to attract passing trade.

She walked over to him and picked up a newspaper, handing him a couple of coins.

'Could I ask you a question about the morning the body was found in the National Portrait Gallery? Were you here then?'

He nodded, glancing at her with suspicion. 'You don't look like a policeman to me.'

She smiled. 'I'm not. I was at the gallery that morning. I was one of the three ladies you told the police you saw leaving.'

He scanned her up and down, then said, 'Yeah, I think you were. I started to pay attention because of those two gents who went in. I guessed they were from the press. One of them had a camera, and I'd seen the other one before. The big fella. I wanted to know who they'd come to photograph. Hoped it might be someone famous. After you came out, there were two others, an older and a younger lady both with reddish sort of hair.'

'Two ladies came out after me?' Coral said sharply.

He bit on a grubby thumbnail and thought about this. 'I think so. You came first. Then, a moment or so later, an older lady came out, and a few minutes after that, maybe five, there was a young woman with a bad leg. She had on one of those dresses with a bustle at the back. You don't see the younger ladies wearing 'em so much nowadays.'

'A bad leg?' Coral's grip tightened around the folded newspaper.

'Well, she walked slowly. Perhaps with a bit of a limp, like she'd hurt her leg.'

'Are you sure we left in that order?'

The man blinked as if doubting himself, then nodded. 'Yeah, that's the way it happened, I'm sure.'

'Thank you. You've been most helpful.' Coral thrust another few coins into his hand, then hurried away, this time certain of her destination.

She didn't stop until she reached Scotland Yard, imagining Flynn rushing down the stairs to see her, perhaps with Goodspeed in tow. They'd take her into the drab interview room and once they'd listened to her story, the burden would be lifted from her shoulders, and they'd decide what to do next.

But when she got there, the desk sergeant told her that Detective Inspector Flynn and Detective Sergeant Goodspeed had been out for most of the after-noon and he had no idea if they'd be returning that day. Coral left a message for Flynn, saying she needed to speak to him urgently, with little faith that the bored-looking sergeant would pass it on.

She reluctantly left the building, wondering if she should wait. But it was cold, and Flynn might not come back that day. He said he lived on Bedford Square, though she could hardly go knocking on doors trying to find out which house was his.

Ignoring the voice telling her to go home and wait for Flynn, she kept walking until she reached Penny's garage. It was dark when she arrived, the corner of Long Acre and Endell Street illuminated by the soft glow of a single street lamp. Coral thought she could also discern a faint light seeping from below the wooden doors of the garage.

She stood for some minutes, weighing up the risks of tackling Penny alone. Her desperate need to know the truth persuaded her she could handle any situation that arose – particularly if she could find the toolbox and arm herself with a hammer without Penny seeing.

Before she could talk herself out of it, she knocked five times in quick succession on the double doors. A moment or two passed, then Penny peered out of the side door, looking breathless.

'Coral. You scared me. I wasn't expecting anyone at this time.'

'Can I come in?'

Penny hesitated, then stood back to allow her to enter. Coral immediately started to prowl around the garage, smelling the same sulphuric odour she'd noticed on her last visit.

'Why don't you come and sit down?' Penny wiped her flushed face and indicated the rickety chairs.

Coral ignored her, spying a toolbox with a wrench sticking out of it.

'Are you trying to make a bomb?' She bent down and made a grab for the wrench. 'I can smell gunpowder.'

'Just a small device. Enough to knock a few walls down.' Penny picked up a length of iron pipe from the workbench and began to move closer. 'And despatch a few more politicians into a coal bunker.'

35

When they reached Scotland Yard, Goodspeed jumped down from the carriage and Flynn followed more cautiously, still cradling Ronald Carstairs' portrait in his arms.

'Guy.'

Flynn swung around at the sound of his name and saw Oscar Lambourne walking towards him.

'Perfect. You're just the person I wanted to see. Come up to my office, I need your help with something.'

'With pleasure. First, could I have a word in private?' Oscar glanced at Goodspeed who was holding open the door.

'Go up to my office – we'll join you shortly,' Flynn called to his sergeant.

Goodspeed went inside, and Flynn turned to Oscar. 'What's troubling you?'

'Coral Fairbanks. I saw her this afternoon at the National Portrait Gallery. We attempted a little sleuthing with no success. She told me about her wedding ring.'

'I have it safe.' Flynn was thankful his friend had the sense not to mention the matter in front of Goodspeed.

'I'm glad to hear it. Because it's very precious to Coral, and I could see how upset she was by its absence.'

'I do appreciate how much it means to her.' Flynn was irritated that his friend felt the need to point this out. 'I have got to know Coral a little over these last few weeks.'

'That's what I thought.' Oscar gave him one of his enigmatic looks. 'If you want to get to know her better, you need to return that ring.'

'Help me solve this case, and I will. Until then, it's evidence.' Flynn pushed open the door with more force than was necessary. 'Come with me.'

To his relief, Oscar gave a brief nod, then followed.

Goodspeed was waiting for them in Flynn's office. He seemed a little aggrieved by Oscar's presence.

Flynn laid the portrait of Ronald Carstairs on his desk, then unlocked the cupboard and took out the Churchill portrait. He placed the two paintings side by side and invited Oscar to study them.

'Do you see any similarities?'

Oscar took his time, moving from picture to picture, peering to examine details more closely.

'Yes,' he said slowly. 'On both, flecks are picked out in white paint, and there's liberal use of vermilion and Prussian blue. Both have fairly thick surfaces, as though several layers have been applied. This artist tends to over-paint rather than scrape away, giving this raised appearance here and here.' Oscar pointed. 'I'd say they were both by the same artist.'

Goodspeed grunted. 'They don't look anything like each other to me.'

Oscar smiled. 'You're right, the intention is different. Churchill is a caricature, not a real person to the painter. But Ronald Carstairs is very real. I'd say the artist has spent time with him. This wasn't done from a photograph.'

Goodspeed gave a low whistle. 'Irene Grayson and Ronald Carstairs?'

'What do you know about Irene Grayson?' Flynn asked.

'Only what I told you before.' Oscar ran a gloved finger over the Carstairs portrait. 'There is one thing, although I'm not sure whether it concerns Irene. Her father, Sir Leonard Grayson, had some sort of falling-out with Carstairs. No one knows what about. The assumption was that Carstairs was sailing too close to the wind with one of his derogatory comments about a certain politician, and Grayson refused to represent him in a libel case – essentially because the accusation was true.'

'Has that ever stopped Leonard Grayson before?'

Oscar sniggered. 'No. He's not known for his integrity. He prides himself on winning, whatever the truth of the matter.'

'Say that wasn't the reason for their falling-out. Perhaps it had something to do with his daughter and Ronald Carstairs?' Flynn turned to Goodspeed. 'Let's get over to Camden Town. I want to speak to Irene Grayson and have another look at those paintings of hers.'

It was gone five by the time Flynn and Goodspeed arrived at Irene Grayson's basement flat – only to find it in darkness.

Goodspeed rapped the knocker several times, but there was no answer. Flynn tried the handle, and to his surprise, found the door was unlocked.

Inside, the scene was much as it had been on their previous visit, the aroma of French cigarettes and turpentine lingering in the air. The seascape Irene had been working on was still on the easel and looked finished to Flynn's eyes. Irene had a remarkable skill for depicting nature. You could sense the strength of the wind as it churned up the waves and battered the desolate cliff face. He took some time to admire it, then studied her other paintings while Goodspeed began to poke around the flat.

'Can't see anything out of the ordinary, although it's difficult to tell in a place like this,' Goodspeed called from the bedroom.

Flynn tore himself away from the paintings and went over to the bedroom door to peer inside. He understood what Goodspeed meant. Irene's unconventional flat was like a tiny curiosity shop, full of strange objects and ornaments, odd articles of clothing hanging on pegs and, of course, her wonderful works of art.

Flynn's gaze travelled around the small bedroom. It was in slight disarray, but that was in keeping with the rest of the flat. He didn't get the impression she'd run away, rather that she'd just popped out and would be home soon.

'There's no point in hanging around here all night waiting for her to come back. Let's pay her a visit first thing tomorrow...' Flynn stopped, a flash of red catching his eye.

Goodspeed looked up from the drawer he was rifling through. 'What is it?'

There was a small coal fire in the bedroom, and Flynn pointed to its black iron surround. On the mantelpiece was a vase glazed with a red mosaic pattern. Beside it was a silver trinket box engraved with entwined fish.

36

Coral turned on Penny in fury. 'Haven't you learned your lesson? As if the fire wasn't bad enough, you're now planning to blow people up.'

'I was only joking. I'm not Guy Fawkes. I just meant that if I could create an explosion outside parliament, I'd have MPs running to hide in the cellars.' Penny looked shocked by Coral's outburst. 'I admit it was in poor taste, given what happened to Ronald Carstairs, but—'

'What did happen to him?' Coral demanded.

'How would I know?' Penny stared at her in confusion. 'You can't believe what they're writing about us in the newspapers. We had no idea his body was there when we started the fire.'

'Didn't you? It seems to me you think you can do what the hell you like in the name of the cause.'

'That's not true.' Penny's face grew redder. 'I would never hurt anyone – you know that.'

'What's that in your hand then?' Coral pointed with the wrench she was still gripping.

Penny glanced down at the iron pipe as if she'd forgotten it was there.

'You fill it with gunpowder and light a length of string, and then...' She trailed off, seeing Coral's expression. 'It only causes a small explosion,' she muttered, placing the pipe back on the workbench. 'It's to damage property, nothing else. I'm not a murderer.'

'You stole the painting, though, didn't you? The Sylvie Blanchet self-portrait.' Coral began to examine the assortment of garments hanging on the clothes rail. She stopped when she came to an elaborately structured petticoat, designed to fit under a bustled skirt.

Coral held it up, pulling at the pliable wires dangling from the fabric.

Penny didn't try to deny it. In fact, she leaned against the workbench, looking quite pleased with herself. 'How did you guess?'

'A newspaper vendor saw you leaving some minutes after me and Lady Carstairs. I presume you went straight from the Westminster Gallery to the Contemporary Gallery and removed the picture from the wall while everyone else was gawping at the Churchill portrait. Then you left with it hidden under your bustled skirt, hooked to your petticoats.'

Penny nodded. 'Rather clever, I thought.'

'Except you walked with a limp.'

'It kept banging against me. My legs were covered in bruises just walking around the corner to the car. Apart from that, the whole thing went to plan.' Penny looked stricken when she realised what she'd said. 'I didn't mean Marian...'

Coral ignored her. 'Where's the painting now?' Her eyes scoured the garage. 'Did Irene know what you were doing?'

'Of course not,' Penny said with scorn. 'The countess and Harriet trusted me to do it on my own. And there's no point in looking for it. The countess is going to give it to Rosalind Blanchet when she's in Paris, before they go on to Nice.'

Coral groaned. She should have known. This had all the hallmarks of one of Minerva's stunts. And she doubted the countess had done this purely from the goodness of her heart either. Money would have changed hands.

Did it matter, though? The theft of the Blanchet picture meant nothing to Coral. It was Marian who dominated her thoughts, and she began to prowl around the garage again, her eyes now more acclimatised to the dim light.

'I told you, it's not here. The countess has it.' Penny moved closer, her voice rising in anger. 'I'll admit I stole the painting but I did not kill Marian.'

'I'm not looking for the painting.' Coral backed away from Penny, walking into the toolbox. As she steadied herself, she saw what she'd been searching for. A piece of rug was sticking out from underneath the car.

She gestured to it with the wrench. 'Where did that rug come from?'

'Coral, stop waving that thing around. You don't think I'd—'

'Just tell me where you got it,' Coral yelled.

Cautiously, Penny took a step forward and peered down at it. 'It's only an old rug. It had a stain on it, so I cut it in half and put that bit under the car to soak up oil leaks.'

'Where's the other half?'

'It's with the trolley.' Penny motioned towards it. 'I use it to hold things in place when they're being wheeled around.'

Coral darted over to where the trolley was standing by the wall. She pulled it out, and curved against the spine and prongs was a length of rug. 'Where did it come from?'

'Irene stole it from Charing Cross station. You remember that time she dressed as a railway porter—'

'No!' Coral shouted in exasperation. 'Not the trolley. This rug.' She picked it up and laid it on the ground to examine the distinctive pattern. Flynn had described it as an antique Persian wool rug with a unique navy and red geometric design. It was unmistakably the same rug she'd seen in the portrait of Ronald Carstairs.

Still clutching the wrench, she moved the toolbox and grabbed the other half of the rug from under the car and laid both pieces side by side. She peered at them closely, noticing small, round dark stains, almost indistinguishable on the vivid background of dark blue and red. On the half that had been under the car there was a larger patch, almost hidden by oil stains.

'Where did you get it?' Coral asked again.

Penny looked from her to the rug. 'I can't remember. Why?'

'Because it belonged to Ronald Carstairs. And I think these—' Coral pointed to the marks '—are droplets of his blood.'

Coral braced herself for Penny's reaction. Would she try to escape? And more, pertinently, would she try to destroy the rug, and perhaps Coral, before she did?

But Penny just walked over to the rickety chairs and sank into one, staring at her in bewilderment. For a few moments, neither one of them spoke.

Then Penny's eyes widened. 'The rug was in the back of the car when Irene brought over the Churchill portrait.'

'When was that?'

'The night of Black Friday. Or early the next morning. I got here at around half past ten on Saturday morning, and the car had been returned. Irene had taken it the evening before to drive to the Reform Club. When I opened the doors, the trolley was lying across the back seats and the Churchill portrait was on top of it. The rug had been wrapped around the picture to stop it from moving.' Penny gazed at Coral in horror. 'I don't understand. Why would Irene have Lord Carstairs' rug?'

Coral didn't reply. She'd assumed Penny had gone to Leinster Gardens in fury after the events of that afternoon. Finding Ronald Carstairs alone, she'd killed him and then organised the fire at Riverside Lodge to destroy his body. From Penny's reaction, she'd got it all wrong.

Had Irene left the Reform Club and driven to Leinster Gardens to attack Lord Carstairs? It seemed so out of character.

'Marian?' Penny muttered that single word, and Coral knew what she meant.

She dropped the wrench back into the toolbox and then walked over to Penny, sinking into the chair beside her.

'The portrait of Ronald Carstairs in the Westminster Gallery shows him in his study, with that rug at his feet. Lord Carstairs made a point of showing it to Marian and her brother when they visited him because it's unique – there isn't another one like it. That morning, at the gallery, Marian stood in front of that portrait.' Coral closed her eyes for a moment to picture the scene. 'You told us that while you and Irene were hammering the nail into the wall, Marian was unwrapping the Churchill portrait. She must have recognised the rug and known it had something to do with Ronald Carstairs' disappearance. She'd heard the rumours about suffragettes kidnapping him.'

'Irene killed her because of it?' Penny breathed the words, then her tone hardened. 'But you thought it was me?'

'I was trying to piece together what happened.' Coral didn't bother to defend her actions. After all, Penny had lied to her.

'But Irene...' Penny shook her head. 'I don't believe it. She wouldn't go to a politician's house and kill them. She just wouldn't.'

'Irene knew Lord and Lady Carstairs. They were friends with her parents. That's how she recognised Lady Carstairs when she saw her at the gallery.' Coral frowned at the bloodstained rug. 'But you're right. There has to be more to it.'

Penny nodded, staring unseeingly into the distance. 'I remember being at Irene's flat once and we started talking about our families. We'd been drinking wine and saying how becoming suffragettes had changed our lives. I asked if she ever thought about giving it all up so she could see her family again. Even though they didn't get on, I knew it was hard on her being cast out completely.'

'What did she say?' Coral asked.

'Something like, "if only that were all there was to it". I asked what she meant by that, and she told me that her father had once caught her with a man. And by that, I think she meant in some sort of compromising position. This man was older than her. A friend of her father's, and she'd been in love with him.'

Coral was silent as she tried to piece together what she knew of Irene's life. She remembered Irene telling her she'd left home at the age of nineteen after joining the suffragettes. That had been over two years ago. Is that when the relationship had begun? But Ronald Carstairs was fifty years old; nearly thirty years her senior.

Penny made a strange groaning sound. 'Irene had a knife.'

'What?' Coral turned sharply to look at her.

'At the gallery. She had a knife. To cut the string tying the carpet around the Churchill portrait.' Penny's face was ashen. 'She had the same knife when she went to the Reform Club to cut the string we used to tie up the bundle of newspapers. It was a sort of utility knife with a serrated edge. She kept it in the inside breast pocket of the uniform.'

It took Coral a while to digest this and organise her thoughts. Then she stood up, contemplating the collection of strange objects, some of them dangerous, that filled the garage.

'I've left a message for Flynn at Scotland Yard to contact me. When he does, I'm going to tell him what we suspect. And where to find the evidence.'

Penny followed her gaze and almost sobbed. 'Not my garage?'

'Clear out anything illegal.' She gave Penny a hard look. 'Like gunpowder. But don't touch the trolley or the pieces of rug – just leave them where they are. And the deliveryman uniform.'

All she could do was provide Flynn with what they had. But she couldn't give him Irene. She was on her way to Dover, and Coral guessed she had no intention of returning.

37

It was six o'clock by the time Flynn arrived back at Scotland Yard. He'd sent Goodspeed home when his sergeant had sheepishly told him Lavender Lacey had given him tickets to *The Chocolate Soldier*.

There was nothing more they could do until Irene Grayson reappeared. Two constables were waiting close to her flat with orders to arrest her when she returned.

'Sir,' the desk sergeant called as Flynn mounted the stairs. 'I forgot to tell you earlier. Mrs Fairbanks came to see you. She said she'd found out something and needed to speak to you about it urgently.'

Flynn turned to him in alarm. 'Where is she? Did she say where she'd be?'

'I assumed she was going home—'

Flynn shot him a withering glance as he bolted back out of the door. He began to run along Victoria Embankment, gripped by fear that Coral might be with Irene Grayson. Ignoring curious looks, he carried on running until he reached number five Adelphi Terrace.

He hammered on the door, bent double with exertion, and when Coral opened it, he let out a long breath of relief.

'Is Irene Grayson here?'

'She's on her way to Dover. I came to tell you—'

'Dover?'

'Countess Stanmore and her companion are going to Nice for Christmas. The countess paid Irene to drive them to Dover and bring the car back. I think Irene might try to board the ship. Do you have a car? The boat doesn't sail until ten o'clock. We could get there by then.'

He stared at her. 'You know it's her. How?'

'I'll tell you on the way.' Coral was already pulling on her coat and reaching for her hat. 'We need a car to catch up with them. Don't you have a police vehicle?'

He shook his head. 'Only Bally's official car. It's parked behind Scotland Yard.'

'Aren't you allowed to drive it?'

'In an emergency.' The answer to her question was actually no, he wasn't authorised to take Chief Superintendent Ballantyne-Smythe's car under any circumstances. It was used purely for official functions, not catching criminals. Flynn decided it was about time he made an exception to that rule.

He dashed back through the gardens and onto Victoria Embankment, this time with Coral running beside him. His instinct had been to stop her from coming with him but he recognised that Irene Grayson was more likely to cooperate if Coral spoke to her.

When they reached Scotland Yard, Flynn asked her to wait outside. After a little forceful persuasion, he finally got the desk sergeant to hand over the keys to Bally's dark green Wolseley motor car.

Coral followed him around to the rear of the building where it was parked, and with some difficulty, he managed to unlock it and hold open the passenger door for her. With trepidation, he then settled himself into the driver's seat, trying to look as if he knew what he was doing. He wasn't an experienced driver and wondered if he'd be better off paying the exorbitant fees of one of the taxi cabs. However, few would be willing to leave London and drive to Dover at that time of night in winter.

Flynn started the car after a couple of attempts, trying not to feel too alarmed by the strong smell of petrol emanating from the engine. He began to feel more confident behind the wheel once he'd manoeuvred the car out of the busy streets of London and was sure he was on the right road to Dover.

He glanced at Coral, huddled in the passenger seat. She'd wrapped herself in a thick blanket she'd found folded up in the footwell.

'How did you know it was Irene?' Although they'd left the noise of the city behind and were on the quieter roads heading south, he had to raise his voice above the wind that buffeted the car. He craned to hear as she explained about the portrait of Ronald Carstairs hanging in the National Portrait Gallery.

Flynn was impressed by her observational skills, though felt a little uncomfortable when she said, 'You discovered the ring you'd found was mine by examining Algie's painting of me. I thought I'd try the same process.'

'And you think Marian recognised the rug?'

Coral nodded. 'When she visited Leinster Gardens, Lord Carstairs took her and Charles Dean into his study to show them his Middle Eastern artefacts, including his unique Persian rug. And there was the same rug in front of her, both in the painting and wrapped around the Churchill portrait. She was the one to unwrap the picture while Irene and Penny hammered the nail into the wall.'

'You think she confronted Irene about it?'

'That was my first thought. Now I wonder if she made the same mistake I did and assumed Penny was somehow involved in Ronald Carstairs' disappearance. I think Marian must have waited for Irene to leave the gallery with the trolley and rug so she could ask her about it.' Coral turned to look at him. 'How did you know it was Irene?'

He described the portrait of Ronald Carstairs that Mr Treadaway had given him and the vase and silver trinket box they'd found in Irene's flat.

When he mentioned Oscar's comments about the enmity between Leonard Grayson and Lord Carstairs, Coral confirmed his suspicions by telling him how Irene had been caught by her father in a compromising situation with a man.

'Her portrait of Ronald Carstairs would certainly indicate she was in love with him,' Flynn mused. 'It reminded me of his relationship with Sylvie Blanchet, only she gave him a self-portrait.'

'Look how that turned out.' Coral shuddered – whether it was through cold or dread, he wasn't sure. 'I wonder why Irene took the other items from his study. And kept them.'

He'd been pondering this. 'My guess is she just wanted some keepsakes of him. We found them in her bedroom. I don't think she could bear to get rid of them, though it does make me wonder what made her turn on him.'

'Black Friday, I suppose. Tempers were running high. I think she went to the Reform Club to see if he was there, before going on to Leinster Gardens.

Perhaps she wanted to confront him over what happened that day and ended up killing him.'

Flynn listened as she told him about the serrated utility knife Irene kept in the breast pocket of the deliveryman uniform.

'Could she have managed to move his body on her own?' Flynn asked. 'The pathologist said it had been manhandled. It was tipped through a small shaft into the coal bunker. Then the keys left outside by the back door to the scullery.'

'I think so, with the help of the trolley. She's disguised herself as a railway porter in the past and moved luggage around. By wrapping the body in the rug, she was probably able to manoeuvre it from the study at the front of the house to the car parked outside.'

Flynn stretched his gloved hands, trying to ease their stiffness. 'She knew to leave the car outside the false-fronted houses to avoid being seen. Perhaps she'd parked there before. It seems she was in the habit of visiting him when Lady Carstairs was out of town.' Flynn suddenly hit the steering wheel. 'I've just thought of something. If Irene saw the envelope with the keys to Riverside Lodge on Carstairs' desk, it might have led to their argument. Once the Leinster Gardens house was sold, he wouldn't have the same opportunities to see Irene. Perhaps he decided it was time to end their relationship.'

Coral shivered. 'I can't help feeling sorry for her. She would only have been nineteen when the relationship started. Life has been hard for her since then. She gave up everything. All she has in the world is in that flat, and she's been shunned by her family. To be turned away by him as well was perhaps too much for her.'

Flynn thought of the tale Oscar had told him about Sylvie Blanchet. How his abandonment of her had led to suicide. In this case, had it led to Carstairs' own death?

He glanced at Coral. 'But who stole the Sylvie Blanchet painting? I don't see how Irene could have taken it. She couldn't have killed Marian and then gone to the Contemporary Gallery and removed it from the wall. There wouldn't have been time. Besides, the doorman says there was nothing on the trolley except brown paper and the piece of rug.'

Coral seemed to hesitate before replying. 'It must have been an opportunistic theft. Someone taking advantage of the chaos.'

Flynn didn't agree but stayed silent. That painting hadn't been chosen at random. Someone had stolen it for a reason – and his money was on Penelope Bright. Somehow, she'd managed to get it out of the gallery, and he reckoned it was hidden in the garage on Long Acre that Coral had mentioned.

His priority tonight was to catch a murderer. But the following day, he and Goodspeed would search every inch of that garage – and it wouldn't just be the two halves of the rug they were looking for.

38

As Flynn drove down the hill to the port, Coral saw the landscape picked out in lights. There was even a tall Christmas tree on the harbour wall.

A passenger ship was in the dock, and she exchanged a look with Flynn. Was it possible Irene had found her way on board?

'I'm not sure I can stop it from sailing,' he said, as if reading her thoughts.

She nodded, finding it strange how in tune they were. A few weeks ago, she wouldn't have believed they could become as close as they had – not with the barriers that divided them.

But then Flynn asked an unexpected question. One that brought it home to her just how different their lives were.

'Do you want us to find Irene?' His matter-of-fact tone made the question even more startling.

'Of course. Why else—'

'If we do, I'll arrest her. The case will go to court, and if she's found guilty, she'll be hanged for murder.'

Coral stared at his impassive face, suddenly aware of what his job meant. She'd been so caught up in solving the mystery and catching the culprit, she hadn't paused to consider the repercussions. What they were doing would result in Irene's death.

She didn't want that. No matter what Irene had done, she didn't want her to die.

It took Coral a while to find her voice, then she asked, 'What will happen if she gets to France?'

'It will be easy for her to hide and difficult for us to pursue her. Unless she comes back to England, it's likely she'll get away with it.'

Coral thought about Florence Dean. She wanted justice for the Dean family. But at what cost?

Flynn brought the Wolseley to a halt in the motor enclosure. 'What type of car does the countess have?'

'A Rolls-Royce Silver Ghost landaulette.'

'Not the most inconspicuous car to run away in.' Flynn turned off the engine and opened the door, edging stiffly out of the driver's seat.

Coral reluctantly shrugged off the blanket and got out of the Wolseley, numb with cold.

'I can't see it.' Flynn was gazing at the rows of cars. 'I'm going to the port office to find out how many sailings there are tonight and check with the boarding officials to see if Irene Grayson appears on any of the passenger lists. See if you can find Countess Stanmore and Miss Walker.' He put his hand on her shoulder. 'If you see Irene, come and tell me. Do not approach her.'

Flynn strode off in the direction of the port office while Coral began to work her way through the throngs of people gathered by the dock. She heard the countess before she saw her, giving instructions to a porter on which order to store her luggage. Coral pushed through the crowds until she spotted the tall fur-trimmed hat.

Harriet gaped when she saw her stumbling towards them. Even the countess momentarily lost her usual poise, her mouth dropping open.

Harriet regained her wits first. 'Coral, what is it? Has something happened?'

'I need to speak to Irene. Where is she?'

The countess took her arm. 'On her way back to London. She left us a short while ago. Why?'

Coral became aware of the attention they were attracting. 'I can't tell you here.'

Minerva dismissed the porter with a wave of her gloved hand, then gestured to Coral and Harriet to follow her into the waiting room. She chose a quiet corner and motioned them to sit.

'Has something happened?' the countess whispered. 'Do you know who killed Marian?'

Coral took a few breaths, hating to say the words out loud. 'Irene murdered Marian. And Ronald Carstairs.'

Harriet shook her head in disbelief. 'No. That can't be right. Not Irene.'

'Is that what Flynn told you?' The countess reached into her purse for her cigarette case. 'He must be mistaken.'

Stumbling over her words, Coral told them what she and Flynn had discovered. She expected them to question her, or even argue, but they just stared in stunned silence.

After a while, Coral asked, 'Did Irene have any luggage with her?'

The countess shook her head. 'There was barely enough room in the car for our cases. Irene only had a small bag.'

'Where did she park the car?'

'In the motor enclosure.' Harriet took Minerva's shaking hand in hers. 'She fetched a porter and helped him unload our luggage, then she drove off. I saw the car going back up the hill.'

Coral stood up. 'I need to tell Flynn.'

'He's here?' The countess's eyes darted to the door.

Coral understood the reason for her alarm. 'Don't worry, I haven't told him about the Blanchet painting that's hidden in your luggage. I'm guessing that when Irene showed you the Churchill portrait, it gave you the idea of how to steal Sylvie Blanchet's picture for her daughter?'

The countess offered a reluctant smile. 'You know me too well. It all seemed to come together as if it were meant to be. Rosalind desperately wanted the only self-portrait her mother painted, and I believed she should have it.'

Coral knew it was never that simple with the countess. 'For a fee?' she enquired.

Minerva inclined her head. 'The WSPU needs funds more than ever, and this was a way of keeping the union going. We can't continue the fight without money. Rosalind Blanchet is a rich young woman, who supports the cause. She was willing to pay us to take the risk to steal the picture for her.'

'Us?' Coral cocked her head to one side. 'It was Penny who took all the risks.'

The countess breathed out a plume of smoke. 'I explained my plan, and she was willing to help. The painting goes to its rightful owner, and we get the money. A happy outcome for everyone.'

Coral wasn't sure the National Portrait Gallery would see it that way, but she decided not to argue. She didn't care about the picture. If it meant so much to Rosalind Blanchet, then why shouldn't she have it? She was more concerned about Irene. When Coral had asked her where the rug had come from, Irene must have realised she would soon be found out.

Coral peered out of the window and saw the passengers were beginning to board.

The countess followed her gaze. 'When we get to Calais, we're taking the night train to Paris. We'll stay there for a couple of days to see Rosalind before travelling on to Nice.' She exchanged a glance with Harriet. 'If you want us to remain here, we will.'

Harriet nodded. 'Do you want us to talk to Flynn?'

Coral hesitated, then shook her head. Flynn didn't suspect the countess's involvement with the suffragettes. And now wasn't the best time to tell him.

'You might as well go. There's nothing you can do here.'

The countess stood and bent to kiss Coral's cheek. 'Write to us if you need anything. And please let us know about Irene. If she needs help...' Minerva's eyes mirrored Coral's own confusion. 'I can't turn my back on her.'

Coral nodded and watched as Harriet took the countess's arm and led her from the waiting room to join the other passengers. Through the long windows, she could see the moving lights of the cars making their way up the winding road that led away from the docks.

Why had Irene come all this way, only to drive off again? There was nothing in Dover except the port. And the white cliffs.

Cold dread suddenly made her feel nauseous. Coral rushed to the door, then ran across the concourse to the port offices. She found Flynn talking to the telegram operator.

He turned to her. 'There's only one sailing tonight, and Irene Grayson isn't listed as a passenger. She could have sneaked onto the ship—'

'She hasn't. She never intended to go abroad.'

'Then where is she?'

'I think she's up there.' Coral pointed into the darkness.

'The cliffs...' Flynn stopped as he realised what she was saying.

39

'We have to find her.' Coral took Flynn's hand and began to drag him from the port office.

'Send that message,' Flynn ordered the man behind the counter as he let Coral pull him away. 'I've reported Irene Grayson as a fugitive.'

They ran back to the motor enclosure, and – with some difficulty – Flynn managed to restart the Wolseley. Coral watched with impatience, fearing they were already too late.

Flynn put his foot on the accelerator, and after a few faltering jerks, they started speeding up the hill. When they reached the top, he turned right and drove more slowly along the cliff road.

Coral's eyes flickered between the cliff edge and the road ahead, looking for either the car or Irene. The landscape was desolate, and she remembered Irene's painting of Cornish cliffs. What had she said about yearning for wild coastlines and endless sea? *Sometimes my work tells me what I want.* Is this what she was running to?

They'd only gone a short way when Coral spotted the Rolls-Royce parked at an angle on a rough patch of grass by a fork in the road.

'There.' She reached out to grip Flynn's arm. 'That's the countess's car.'

Flynn slowed and came to a halt behind it, leaving the headlamps on. Before he could try to stop her, Coral scrambled out of the Wolseley and began to run towards the cliff edge.

'Coral. Stay here. Let me go...'

She heard him stumbling after her but kept going. Ahead, she could see the lights of the harbour in the distance and something else. A faint light hovering nearby.

More cautiously, she moved forward, taking tiny steps, until she saw what looked like a figure huddled on an outcrop below.

'Irene,' she called, feeling her voice disappear into the stinging salt air that tore at her face.

Coral thought she heard someone say her name, but the force of the wind made it difficult to tell. Then she heard it again.

'Coral.' It was nothing more than a whisper.

She took a few steps closer to the cliff edge and saw Irene wrapped in a shawl, holding a small electric torch. She was staring into the darkness.

'You look cold, Irene. I've got a blanket in the car. Why don't you come and get warm?'

'Is that you, Coral?' Irene didn't turn in her direction. Instead, she just gazed out at the black ocean as if the voice was a figment of her imagination.

'I'm here,' Coral called. 'I want to help you.'

Slowly, Irene shifted to peer up at her, wobbling slightly as she did. Coral's chest tightened when she saw how precariously she was seated.

'I wish you could help me.' Irene pulled the shawl tighter. 'I wish I'd told you everything a long time ago when it would have made a difference. It's too late now.'

'It's not. I can still help you.' Coral wished she had a torch so the girl could see her more clearly in the darkness.

Irene shook her head. 'I killed Marian. Nothing can put that right. Tell her family how sorry I am.'

'Irene. Please come away from the edge. I know you didn't mean to do it. Any of it.'

Irene shook her head, more vigorously this time. 'I'm not sorry about Ronnie. He ruined my life and it meant nothing to him. I'm glad he can't do it to anyone else.'

Coral took a tiny step towards her. 'You must have loved him very much.'

'I did. For a long time. He was the first man to ever talk to me. I mean properly talk to me. We'd discuss art and politics, and he treated me as an equal. He even encouraged me to join the suffragettes.' Irene sniffed and wiped her nose with a shaking hand. 'Perhaps he was just using me. He enjoyed playing those tricks. I was the one to write those letters to Penny. I knew she wouldn't be able to resist.'

'You sent the letter telling her about Riverside Lodge?'

Irene nodded. 'I wanted it to burn down and take him with it. I knew his wife was having it built. What he didn't tell me was that they were selling the house on Leinster Gardens. It's where Ronnie and I used to meet when Violet was in Kent. He said it would have to stop.'

'I'm sorry. That must have been upsetting for you.' The wind was whipping at Coral's coat, causing her to tremble with cold. She wanted to move closer, but it was hard to see how near to the edge she was or how firm the rocks were beneath her feet. If she tried to reach for Irene, she could end up sending them both over the cliff.

Suddenly, she felt Flynn's arms around her.

'Don't go any closer,' he whispered. 'It's too dangerous.'

'Who's there?' Irene called, and Flynn backed away.

'It's just me, Irene. Why don't you come over to me? You can tell me all about Ronnie.'

Irene didn't move. But she carried on talking.

'I'd suspected for a while he wasn't being honest with me. Then...' She gave a small sob. 'I was upset after Black Friday and wanted to speak to him. We hadn't arranged to meet, so I went to the Reform Club to see if he was there. Then I went to Leinster Gardens, but Nathan Jennings turned up. Ronnie told me to hide in the other room while they were in the study, but I listened at the door. When Jennings tried to force him to resign, Ronnie said he was happy to go after what had happened that day. He said it had been a disgrace, and Asquith was a fool for trusting Churchill. I was proud of him for that.' She sobbed again, more loudly this time. 'Then he told Jennings that after he resigned, he planned to go travelling with Violet for six months before they moved into Riverside Lodge. He once promised me we'd go abroad together – make a tour of Italy or Greece. He said it would be good for my art. All lies.'

'That was cruel of him.' Coral felt Flynn's presence behind her and hoped Irene hadn't seen him.

'After Jennings left, I told Ronnie I'd been listening. He didn't bother to make excuses; he just said we'd had a good innings, and it was over. I suppose I always knew it would come to an end, but it was as if I'd never existed. It tarnished everything that had gone before. He'd always been so kind, so loving. Now he didn't seem to care what happened to me. I'd given up everything for him. I had no family, no money. Without Ronnie, there was nothing.'

'You have your friends. We'll help you.'

'No, you won't. Not after Marian. And I don't blame you. I wish I'd had the sense to kill myself instead of her. But she took me by surprise. She was hiding in the cloakroom, and when I came by, she called to me. I went in, thinking she was hiding from her brother. Then she pointed to the rug and said she'd seen it before. She said she was sure it had come from Lord Carstairs' study and was afraid Penny had kidnapped him. I told her not to be so silly but she wouldn't listen.' Irene made a choking noise.

'It's alright,' Coral said soothingly. 'I know you didn't mean to hurt her.'

'She picked up the rug and said she was going to show it to her brother. I couldn't let her take it. I lashed out with the knife, only this time it was panic not anger that made me do it. After the fire hadn't taken hold, I knew it wouldn't be long before they found Ronnie's body. And Penny would remember where the rug came from because I'd used it to wrap Ronnie's present.'

'His present?' Coral turned to exchange a startled glance with Flynn.

'The Churchill portrait. Ronnie was so proud of me for painting it. He'd roared with laughter when I told him we planned to display it in the National Portrait Gallery. So, I wrapped it in the rug and took it to Penny's garage that night. My final gift to him.'

'Was that after you'd taken his body to Riverside Lodge?' Coral was beginning to realise the strength of the hold Ronald Carstairs had exerted over Irene.

'I had to wrap him in the rug to move his body onto the trolley. When I got to Riverside Lodge, I managed to tip him into the coal bunker, then I took it home with me. I was going to keep it, because I knew he loved it, but I still had the vase and the trinket box.'

'Why did you take those things from his study?' Coral tried to edge forward, but Flynn reached for her hand.

'To remember him by, I suppose. He loved them so much. More than he loved me.' The whimpering sound that came from Irene was like an animal in distress. 'I've made so many mistakes.'

'I can help you put them—' Coral was interrupted by the noise of a prolonged blast from a horn and looked down at the lights of the harbour. The ship was starting to move away from the dock.

Irene turned to gaze at it. 'I thought of stowing myself on board. Running away and beginning my life again. No more Irene Grayson. I could be whoever I wanted to be.'

'You could still do that. I'll help you.' Coral was aware that Flynn might have other ideas, but all she cared about was getting Irene to safety.

'It wouldn't be fair. Not after what I did to Marian. Tell them I'm sorry.'

'No!'

For a brief moment, the wind dropped and a feeling of calm descended on the weather-beaten cliff top.

'Goodbye, Coral...' The whispered words floated in the air, then Irene and the flickering torchlight were gone.

'Irene!' Coral screamed into the darkness. She tried to run to where Irene had been, but the arms around her were too strong.

Coral pushed at Flynn's chest as he pulled her closer, murmuring something into her ear. Unable to move, all she could do was stare at the spot where Irene had been, willing her to reappear.

40

'Isn't it too marvellous?'

The lump in Coral's throat prevented her from speaking, so she squeezed Lavender's hand in response. They stood in the shadow of Big Ben, watching suffrage societies from around the world gather in Parliament Square, preparing to march from Westminster to Hyde Park.

Policemen lined the roads but made no attempt to impede or halt the procession. Unlike Black Friday, the mood was joyous with a sense of serenity. Crowds clapped and cheered as the ladies marched by, holding pennants embroidered with the name of their society. Some were attired in their national dress while others wore historical costumes. One young lady came on horseback as Joan of Arc.

The air was filled with music and singing, and stretching as far as the eye could see was a stream of purple, white and green banners – the colours that had come to represent the cause.

'This is more like it.' Sid Watson kissed her cheek before dashing after Luke, who seemed to be wandering in a world of his own.

Coral watched as Luke stopped suddenly on Parliament Street, gazed around, then nodded. Sid knew his cue and quickly cleared a gap in the crowd so they could set up the camera. Coral guessed Luke had chosen the perfect vantage point for capturing each group as they passed. She'd go in search of them later and ask if she could have prints of some of the photographs.

Lavender nudged her. 'Look who's come to see us.'

Coral turned to find Flynn walking towards them, Goodspeed on one side and his daughter, Teresa, on the other.

Coral hadn't seen much of Flynn since that terrible night in Dover nearly three months ago. But one evening, she'd returned from work to find a parcel in the hallway.

'Your favourite detective inspector delivered it himself,' Lavender had told her with a wink.

Coral had peeled off the brown paper to reveal one of Flynn's paintings, simply signed GF. It was so beautiful, it had taken her breath away. Only later, when she was examining it for the hundredth time, had she realised what he'd done. He'd painted a view of the river from her home. Or the view that you would have seen from Adelphi Terrace before the Victoria Embankment had been built.

She'd written him a thank-you letter, and he'd called at the Stanmore Gallery a few times after that. However, their conversations were usually stilted as they were too afraid to stray from safe topics such as his paintings or how Teresa was getting on with her studies. Coral often found herself longing to sit across a table from him, sharing a meal as they'd done when they were investigating the case together. But she guessed that would never happen again.

'Mrs Fairbanks.' Flynn raised his hat. 'Teresa would like to join the march. I wonder if I could entrust her to your care?'

'Of course. Please join us.' Coral reached out and took Teresa's hand.

'Thank you, Mrs Fairbanks.' Teresa smiled, but her eyes were fixed on Lavender, as were Goodspeed's.

'Evan, darling. How lovely to see you.' Lavender blew him a kiss, then turned to Teresa. 'Pleased to meet you, I'm Lavender Lacey.'

'I know,' Teresa breathed. 'I've seen you on stage. You have a beautiful voice.'

'Thank you, darling. Today I'll be singing with gusto. Do you know "The March of the Women"?'

Flynn's smile faltered as Lavender began to teach Teresa the words to a song that had become the anthem of the Women's Social and Political Union.

'I'll meet you in Hyde Park,' he called, but Teresa was too captivated by Lavender to hear.

'I'll look after her,' Coral promised, smiling at his resigned expression. She was about to say more when she was distracted by the sight of Marian's grandmother, Florence Dean, coming towards her, carrying a lilac pennant embroidered with a single white rose.

'The white rose of Yorkshire.' Florence held it aloft. 'It was Marian's favourite flower.'

'It's beautiful. I'll be thinking of her as we march.' Coral held out her arm to Florence, craning to see Flynn, but he and Goodspeed had disappeared into the crowd.

'So will I.' Florence took Coral's arm and thrust her pennant high into the air.

'Time to go, ladies,' Lavender announced. 'Good strong harmonies now.'

With linked arms, Coral, Florence, Lavender and Teresa took their place in the procession, raising their voices to sing:

> *'Shout, shout up with your song!*
> *Cry with the wind for the dawn is breaking.*
> *March, march, swing you along,*
> *Wide blows our banner and hope is waking.'*

Coral thought how much Penny would have loved to have been walking with them.

They'd both made statements regarding their part in the Hurlingham Club vandalism, the Riverside Lodge fire, and the events at the National Portrait Gallery.

Coral's ring had been returned to her with a warning not to engage in further acts of civil disobedience. Just thinking about her wedding ring made Coral reach for her left hand to ensure it was safely in place beneath her white glove.

Penny had been convicted of arson but given a lesser sentence as she'd confessed and surrendered to the police. She was currently serving a short sentence in Holloway Prison, where she'd gone on hunger strike to protest at being treated as a common criminal rather than a political prisoner. She was due to be released soon, and Coral would be at the gates waiting for her. She'd heard Penny was in a poor state and needed nursing back to health.

Flynn had searched the garage on Long Acre and found what Penny had left for him to find. The deliveryman uniform, the porter's trolley, the pieces of rug – and not much else.

And this is where the problem between her and Flynn lay. He wasn't happy at having failed to solve the mystery of the Blanchet painting. He'd guessed at Penny's involvement, although he didn't seem to have any suspicions of the countess. As for Coral, well, she knew he was wary of getting too close to her.

Yet when she turned to gaze at the crowds, it was Flynn's eyes that met hers. He and Goodspeed were walking beside them, clapping and cheering along with the other policemen lining the route.

'New beginnings,' he mouthed, giving her a searching look.

Coral smiled, then nodded. 'New beginnings,' she mouthed back.

* * *

MORE FROM MICHELLE SALTER

Death at Big Ben, the next instalment in this page-turning cosy mystery series from Michelle Salter, is available to order now here:

https://mybook.to/DeathBigBenBackAd

AUTHOR'S NOTE

This book begins on 18 November 1910. Black Friday.

On this day, a delegation – led by Emmeline Pankhurst, founder of the Women's Social and Political Union (the suffragettes); Dr Elizabeth Garrett Anderson, the first woman in Britain to qualify as a physician and surgeon; and Princess Sophia Duleep Singh, the Indian goddaughter of Queen Victoria – tried to deliver a petition to the prime minister, Herbert Asquith.

They were accompanied by over 300 women, who marched on parliament after Asquith reneged on his repeated promises to introduce a Conciliation Bill to allow some women the right to vote. The bill would have given the vote to about a million women, mostly wealthy property owners. Although it was a compromise, it was enough for Mrs Pankhurst to suspend militant action in anticipation of the bill passing into law.

The women were greeted in Parliament Square by lines of policemen and crowds of bystanders who attacked them for the next six hours. Officers had been brought in from areas like Whitechapel and were unfamiliar in dealing with suffragette protests.

The women were beaten by police and thrown into the hostile crowd, where they were subjected to more violence. Hundreds of female protesters reported having their breasts grabbed and their long skirts lifted up to their waists.

The suffragettes claimed plain-clothes policemen had gone amongst the bystanders and were deliberately inciting the violence. In all, 115 women were arrested – but only 4 men. All of them were released the following day without charge on the orders of Winston Churchill, who was Home Secretary at the time.

There has been quite a lot of debate over Churchill's role in Black Friday. Some suggest that what took place was a deliberate ploy and he'd encouraged police brutality. Others say that he knew the police had overstepped the mark, which is why he ordered the release of all those arrested. Whatever the truth of the matter, he ignored all calls for an inquiry into Black Friday.

As well as Black Friday, many other events, people, and locations mentioned in this book are real, including the false-fronted houses that can still be found on Leinster Gardens.

ACKNOWLEDGEMENTS

Thanks to the brilliant Boldwood team, especially my editor, Emily Yau; Marcela Torres in marketing; Rose Fox my eagle-eyed proof editor; and Rachel Lawston for the fabulous cover design.

As ever, I'm indebted to the numerous people, books, libraries, museums and archives that contributed to my knowledge of this period. A book that was especially useful was *Rise Up Women! The Remarkable Lives of the Suffragettes* by Diane Atkinson.

I'd also like to thank friends for their support: Jeanette Quay for videos, Barbara Daniel for advice and encouragement, Vicki Jull for film star names, and Moon, my oldest friend (length of time we've known each other rather than age!), for wine.

Thanks to my parents, Ken and Barbara Salter, for always supporting and encouraging me (special thanks to Dad for being my research assistant).

ABOUT THE AUTHOR

Michelle Salter writes historical cosy crime set in Hampshire, where she lives, and inspired by real-life events in 1920s Britain. Her Iris Woodmore series draws on an interest in the aftermath of the Great War and the suffragette movement.

Sign up to Michelle Salter's mailing list for news, competitions and updates on future books.

Visit Michelle's Website: www.michellesalter.com

Follow Michelle on social media:

ALSO BY MICHELLE SALTER

The Iris Woodmore Mysteries

Death at Crookham Hall

Murder at Waldenmere Lake

The Body at Carnival Bridge

A Killing at Smugglers Cove

A Corpse in Christmas Close

Murder at Mill Ponds House

The Fairbanks and Flynn Mysteries

Murder in Trafalgar Square

Standalone Novels

Murder at Merewood Hospital

Boldwood

Boldwood Books is an award-winning fiction publishing company seeking out the best stories from around the world.

Find out more at www.boldwoodbooks.com

Join our reader community for brilliant books, competitions and offers!

Follow us
@BoldwoodBooks
@TheBoldBookClub

Sign up to our weekly deals newsletter

https://bit.ly/BoldwoodBNewsletter